A Love & Lyrics Novel

USA TODAY BESTSELLING AUTHOR

NIKKI ASH

No matter what, we're forever.

Silent Chaos

Cover Design and Formatting: Jersey Girl Designs
Photo: Wander Aguiar Photography
Editor: Jenny Sims with Editing 4 Indies

Author's Note

Like real life, the characters are far from perfect, make morally gray decisions, and deal with subjects that may be sensitive for some readers. If you are looking for a safe romance, this series is not for you. Trigger warnings (which contain spoilers) can be found on my website: Love & lyrics Trigger Warnings

Playlist

"Villain"- Lily Rose
"Black"- Dierks Bentley
"Alone"- I Prevail
"Worship You"- Kane Brown
"Break Up in a Small Town"- Sam Hunt
"Like I Loved You"- Brett Young
"Rubberband"- Tate McRae
"You Broke Me First"- Tate McRae
"Heartless"- Kanye West
"Apologize"- Timbaland (feat. OneRepublic)
"Loyal"- Chris Brown (feat. Lil Wayne & Tyga)
"Used to Love You Sober"- Kane Brown
"Love the Way You Lie"- Eminem (feat. Rihanna)
"So Sick"- Ne-Yo
"I Hate Everything About You"- Three Days Grace
"Me & U"- Cassie
"Problem"- Natalia Kills
"History"- Olivia Holt

Your gray eyes

Your sweet smile

You fucked me over

And now I wanna forget

- Braxton Lutz, *Raging Chaos*

One

Braxton

THE PRESENT: HIGH SCHOOL PRE-GRADUATION PARTY

"TELL ME THIS ISN'T REAL. TELL ME YOU DIDN'T JUST FUCK THE CAPTAIN OF THE goddamn football team in his bedroom... in his fucking bed."

I step toward my girlfriend, my body vibrating with a mixture of pain and anger and confusion. When I received several texts from different people telling me what happened, I thought it was a sick joke, a misunderstanding, until I got on Instagram and found the post myself.

A picture of Kaylee in her bra and underwear lying on the bed. A selfie of the two of them—him not wearing a shirt and her still in her bra. And the last one... the one that hurt the most—them kissing. His goddamn lips on hers. Touching what's supposed to be mine. The caption read: **No better way to end high school than scoring with the cheer captain. #touchdown**

"Tell me!" I bark, making her jump. Fresh tears well in her

lids and fall over, coursing down her cheeks as if she's the one who's been hurt and betrayed. As if she isn't the one who just destroyed everything. "Tell me the pictures are a joke." I step toward the only girl I've ever loved, the only girl I've ever given my heart to, and palm the side of her face, needing to feel her soft skin for what I know will be the last time. Because I can forgive a lot of things, but I can't forgive cheating.

"Kaylee," I choke out. "Please, baby," I beg, not wanting any of this to be real. Wanting to go back to my house, go to sleep, and wake up with all of this being nothing more than a fucking nightmare. "Tell me what I saw isn't true."

As I stare into the red-rimmed gray eyes of the girl I've spent the past ten months giving my heart to, I can't help but wonder where the hell it all went wrong.

Two

Braxton

SUMMER BEFORE SENIOR YEAR

"IT'S SO FUCKING HOT OUT," GAGE SAYS, DROPPING INTO A SEAT OUTSIDE THE COFFEE shop where Declan and I are already sitting and drinking our iced coffees. We have a bunch of papers strewn everywhere—lyrics, songs, sheets of music. The three of us, along with Camden—who's out of town for the summer with his pop star sister who's on tour—are in a band. I know, I know... Who hasn't been in a band? Well, unlike most teenage bands, we're actually damn good, and thanks to Camden's family, who owns Blackwood Records, one of the largest record labels in the country, we'll be getting signed after we graduate in June.

"It's too damn hot," Declan agrees. "I think I saw it's going to be in the hundreds today." He lifts the paper and reads over the most recent song I wrote. It's called "Cheater" and is an ode to my piece-of-shit mother who cheated on my father, saying she wasn't meant to be a mother or a wife, then walked out the door, never looking back.

"Fuck, it's too hot to work on music." Declan drops the paper and takes a sip of his coffee.

"It's too hot to move," Gage bitches. "Who in the hell can even think in this heat?"

We live in New York, and there's a heatwave coming through. When most think of New York, they think of the frigid as hell winters, but if you live here, you know firsthand that the summers are a bitch. The humidity can shed ten pounds off you just by walking outside.

"You know what we should do?" Declan says, turning his phone around and showing us his screen—a picture of a bunch of kids from our school at the beach.

"I'm in," Gage says.

"You don't even like any of those assholes," I say with a laugh. Gage is literally the least social person I know—unless it's with someone in our very small circle.

"I don't need to like them to get in the water and cool down." Gage stands. "It's too hot to even smoke. Fuck it, let's go."

Declan chuckles, and I glance at him, raising a brow in question. "He saw Tori in the picture. He's been eyeing that cheerleader for months."

"Tori?" I say with a laugh. "Actually, I can totally see it. She's all cheerleader meets emo with her short skirts, black lipstick, and fishnet stockings. She's like the least peppy cheerleader on the squad. It's the perfect match made in hell."

Declan nods, and Gage punches me in the arm. "Fuck you, asshole. Let's go."

A couple of hours later, we're walking onto the beach wearing our board shorts with towels tucked under our arms. I immediately spot Layla, one of our good friends, lying out with her two best friends, Tori and Kaylee, and they're surrounded by a bunch of jocks. When Layla glances up, her lips pursed together in obvious annoyance, she nudges Kaylee, who then looks our way, her gray eyes meeting mine.

This gets Tori's attention, whose gaze seems to go straight to Gage. Something is said among the girls, and then a second later, the three of them saunter our way. I assume they're coming over to say hi, so I'm confused as shit when they head directly toward each of us individually.

"Quick, pretend you're in love with me and kiss me," Kaylee murmurs. Before I have a chance to ask what the hell she's talking about, her arms wrap around my neck and her mouth encloses over mine. Her lips are soft and supple, and when her tongue slips into my mouth, she tastes like the sweetest goddamn strawberries I've ever tasted.

Without thinking, I deepen the kiss, reaching down and lifting her off the ground. Her legs go around my torso, and her fingers drag through my hair, gently tugging on the ends. Our tongues collide with each other, stroking, caressing. I've kissed countless girls. It's one of the perks of being in a band in high school. Girls flock to you. They want a taste of the bad boy. I don't know what it is about the sight of a guy with a guitar in his hands, but they want it—want me. But never have I felt like this when kissing a girl. My heart thumps against my rib cage, my body's on fire, and my dick is as hard as a rock.

And then she ends the kiss. Her hypnotic gray eyes meet

mine, and I force myself to suck in a harsh breath, having to remind myself how to breathe.

"Thank you," she says with a soft smile on her face and a hint of blush on her cheeks. "The football players were begging us to go out with them tonight, and Layla said we already had plans. They were asking who with, and then you guys walked up, and..." She shrugs, dragging her teeth across her bottom lip until it pops out, making me want to capture it with my own mouth. "I owe you one."

We stay like this for a couple of beats—Kaylee in my arms, her thighs pressed into my sides—and then I do something that shocks the hell out of us both. My mouth ascends, and my lips capture hers again. When her tongue finds its way back into my mouth, I suck on it, tasting her sweetness, getting lost in everything Kaylee Thomas. I grind her center against my dick, and she moans into my mouth. I have no clue what's happening, but I never want it to stop. I was just giving Gage shit about having eyes for a cheerleader, and now here I am, standing in the middle of the beach, making out with the head fucking cheerleader.

"Wow," Kaylee breathes when the kiss ends. "That was incredible. I don't think anyone will be asking me out now." It takes me a second, but then I remember that's why we were kissing in the first place.

"Go out with me," I blurt out, aware of the irony in my request. She throws her head back in a laugh, thinking I'm fucking with her. "I'm serious. Go out with me."

Her gorgeous eyes lock with mine. "You're serious?"

"Yeah, tonight... tomorrow... go out on a date with me."

"Okay."

"Yeah?" I didn't think it would be that easy. She was just complaining about guys bugging her, so I kind of assumed she'd turn me down. Layla, Tori, and Kaylee have been on a self-imposed anti-boyfriend kick all year—since Layla caught her boyfriend cheating, and it broke her heart.

"Yeah."

"Well, damn," Declan says once I put Kaylee down, and we walk over to join everyone. The jocks are all gone now, and only Gage, Tori, Declan, and Layla are sitting where the girls' stuff is. "How come you didn't kiss me like that, Layla, huh? I want a do-over."

Layla laughs and shoves his chest playfully. "Funny."

I notice Gage is staring at Tori like he wants to eat her alive, so I wonder how their kiss went. If it was as amazing as the one I just experienced with Kaylee.

"Have you guys heard from Camden?" Layla asks, pulling out her phone to I'm sure text him. "I think he's in Nashville." Camden and Layla met right before our sophomore year when she moved in next door. Camden's been in love with her ever since, but she has no clue. We've all told him to tell her how he feels, but he's too damn chicken.

"I'm going in the water," Tori says, standing and shaking the sand off her body. She glances at Gage. "Wanna join me?"

Gage shrugs, playing it cool. "Sure."

"I wanna go too," Layla adds, shoving her phone in her bag.

Declan stands to join them as well, leaving Kaylee and me.

"You guys coming?" Layla asks.

"Nah, you go," Kaylee says, her gaze darting over to me.

"Braxton and I have to discuss where he's taking me out tonight."

Layla's eyes go wide. "What? When did that happen? While you were kissing?" Kaylee laughs. "What happened to our anti-boyfriend pact?" Layla pouts.

"It's officially summer," Kaylee says, "which means it's over."

Fuck yes.

Layla side-eyes her. "Whatever." She steps off the beach blanket. "Oh, shit! The sand is hot!"

"Jump on," Declan drawls, and Layla does so, laughing as he runs toward the water with her on his back, not stopping until they're completely submerged. Gage and Tori follow, stopping before they get to the water.

"Now, about that date," Kaylee says once we're alone. "What time are you picking me up?"

Three

Braxton

OCTOBER: SENIOR YEAR

"THIS IS CRAZY!" KAYLEE YELLS, HOLDING ME TIGHTLY AS WE DRIVE DOWN THE ROAD toward The Hamptons. It's our four-month anniversary, and to celebrate, I stole my dad's motorcycle and asked Camden for the keys to his parents' beach house since nobody's there this weekend. I texted Kaylee to pack a bag and to tell her mom she's spending the weekend with Layla.

With the cool breeze whirring around us, Kaylee snuggles up to me, her head resting against my back. Her hands find their way under my shirt, and she presses her cold fingers against my hot stomach. We've been taking it slow for the past few months. Going on dates, hanging out. Kaylee's a virgin, so I didn't want to rush her. But when she told me she was ready, I wanted it to be perfect. We might be young, but that doesn't mean I have to fuck her in the back seat of a car. I want tonight to be memorable for us both.

Two hours later, we step into the beach house. We've been here before for barbecues and shit, so we both know our way around. Camden's dad's one rule is no one is allowed in the master bedroom, so we go straight to the guest room that houses a queen-size bed and an en suite bathroom, and set our bags down.

"I'm going to take a shower," Kaylee says, suddenly sounding nervous.

"You hungry? I was thinking we could go out to dinner."

"Okay, that sounds good."

While I wait for her to get ready, I look up restaurants in the area and make reservations at one that looks good. I'm checking out the menu when Kaylee walks out in nothing but a towel wrapped around her. Her face is clean from all the makeup she was wearing earlier, and her blond hair is wet. She's never looked so beautiful.

She stops in front of me, nervously sucking her bottom lip into her mouth. I open my legs, and she steps between them, dragging her fingers through my hair. She tugs on the strands, and I glance up at her. Our mouths collide, and she moans as she climbs onto my lap, straddling me. I planned to make tonight special by lighting some candles and shit, but the moment she undoes her towel, dropping it to the floor, nothing matters but being with her.

Every man's wet dream, Kaylee has an athlete's body, lithe and toned, tits that fit perfectly in the palm of my hands, and an ass that's just thick enough to grab handfuls of. Every man can look all they want, but she's mine... all fucking mine. And I'm the only one allowed to touch her, kiss her, caress her.

We kiss for several minutes as I work her body to get her off. We've done this part several times, and at this point, I know her body as well as, if not better, than she does. Once she's orgasmed, screaming my name as her body trembles in pleasure, I lay her in the center of the bed. We've talked about it, so I know she's on birth control, and we're both clean. I kiss my way along her neck while she strokes my dick. It doesn't need any help getting hard, but I love the way she touches me and loves to explore my body.

After ensuring she's wet enough, I push slowly into her tightness. Her face scrunches up in pain, and I kiss her softly, gently, wishing I could take it away. Once I'm all the way in, I stop, giving her a second to breathe. I've had sex a couple of times before Kaylee, but none of the girls were virgins, so I looked it up online to be prepared and make it as good as it could be for her.

"I'm good," she breathes after a few seconds. "I'm okay."

With our eyes open and locked on each other, I slowly pull out and then push back in. She's tight and warm and so fucking perfect. I don't stand a chance at lasting, so before I blow my load, I find her clit and massage the already sensitive nub to get her off again. When she climaxes, her entire body shakes, and her pussy chokes the hell out of my dick, sending me straight over that cliff with her.

As we both take a moment to slow our breathing, I look down at her. Her eyes are slightly glassy, looking sated, her cheeks are flush, and her lips are swollen from our kissing. She's gorgeous, so goddamn perfect, and I don't care how young we are because I know she's the one for me. I've felt it from the moment she kissed me that day at the beach, and every day we spend together only strengthens my feelings toward her.

"I love you," I tell her, pressing my lips to hers. When our mouths connect, it's as if the entire world disappears, leaving just the two of us in our own little bubble.

"I love you too," she says when the kiss ends, palming my cheek. "And I totally think we should do that again before we go to dinner."

While Kaylee rinses off and then gets ready, I find my way out to the back patio. It's a cool night out, so I light up the outdoor firepit and have a seat in one of the Adirondack chairs, getting lost in my words. Being with Kaylee brings out so many emotions in me that I find myself constantly writing lyrics. Most of them never amount to much, but some end up as songs.

"Whatcha got there?" Kaylee asks, plopping onto my lap.

"A possible song." I hand her the paper, not caring that every word on it is about her.

"Gray eyes, smile as bright as the sunrise. Her love is better than the best high." She turns and kisses me gently on the corner of my mouth. "I love when you write about our love. It makes it feel so… concrete. Permanent."

"It is." If I have it my way, we'll be together for the rest of our lives.

"That's what my mom thought about my dad too," she says sadly. "Before his accident."

She never talks about her dad, so I simply nod and wait for her to continue.

"He used to work for Empire," she resumes. "It's a marketing and advertising company. Every night when I was little, he would come home and work. I craved his attention, so I would bring my toys into his office and play while he worked. One day, he was struggling with a marketing pitch and asked my opinion. We spent hours working on it together. His pitch went over so well he was promoted, and that night, he brought home dinner and a cake, saying I was his good luck charm."

Kaylee's smile turns watery. "Every night after that, he would let me help him. It became our thing. Until his accident. He was stepping onto the street to grab a taxi when he was hit and dragged several yards. They had to perform surgery on his back, and while it was successful, he was left in permanent pain."

She swallows thickly, and I have a bad feeling where this is going. "They warned him the drugs could be addicting, but he said he had it under control." She shakes her head. "He didn't. One minute, he was my dad sitting with me in his office working, and the next, he was an addict, alcoholic stranger who would take his anger and pain out on my mom. It got so bad that he almost beat her to death. Thankfully, she left him."

"Where is he now?" I ask.

"I'm not sure. He lost his job and disappeared after she left him." A single tear slides down her cheek, and I catch it with my thumb, hating to see her sad. "I miss him... the *him* before the accident. I miss sitting in his office and working with him."

She's mentioned before that she plans to major in marketing and advertising, and now that makes sense. She wants that piece of her dad back.

"That won't be us," I tell her, cupping her face. "We're concrete, permanent, and nothing can change that."

Four

Braxton

DECEMBER-SENIOR YEAR

"MERRY CHRISTMAS!" KAYLEE SAYS, JUMPING INTO MY ARMS AND PEPPERING KISSES all over my face.

"Merry Christmas, Crazy," I murmur, using the nickname I've dubbed for her as I walk us through her apartment. Being with Kaylee is as easy as breathing. She's carefree, always happy, and never gets mad. But she's also crazy as fuck. It's like riding the most exhilarating roller coaster. You know you're safe, but your heart still races with every dip and turn. It's both exciting and scary.

I try to set her down, but she clings to me like a koala bear, so with a laugh, I sit on the couch with her legs wrapped around my waist.

"I got you something," I tell her between kisses.

"Oh, a present?" Her eyes light up in excitement.

If you didn't know her, you'd think she's materialistic, but the truth is, I could give her a hand-written note, and she'd be just as excited. Kaylee just simply loves being thought about. I think it stems from her childhood. Her dad was—well, still is—a druggy alcoholic, who always puts his addiction before everyone and everything else.

Her mom was a victim, and once she was out of the shitty situation, she put herself first, needing to make herself happy again. She serial dated until she found herself a new husband, and they started a new family.

Meanwhile, Kaylee was ignored and left to her own devices. She told me once that her parents have forgotten countless holidays and birthdays, including her recent one when she turned eighteen. Layla and I threw her a huge party. So when she's given attention, she soaks it up like sunrays on a cold day.

I pull a small box out of my pocket and hand it to her. Her forehead wrinkles in confusion, and when she opens it, displaying a small white gold ring with two infinity symbols interwoven, she looks up at me in shock.

"It's a promise ring," I tell her, taking it out of the cushion it's nestled in. It's not big or flashy, but I played my guitar for hours on the street corner by the coffee shop, singing the songs I've written that Camden usually sings to earn enough money to buy it.

"I want you to know that you're the one for me. I love you and want to spend my life with you. I know it's kind of small, but—"

"Stop," she rasps, tears filling her eyes. "It's perfect. I love it. I love you." She lets me slide it on the finger that I hope will one day house an engagement and wedding ring and beams down at it like it's a million-dollar ring.

"It's probably cliché as fuck," I say, "but it's two infinity symbols, symbolizing you and me never ending."

She smiles a watery smile and nods. "I love that."

"One day, when the band takes off, I'll replace this with something better, more expensive," I vow.

"I don't want anything else," she says, tears sliding down her cheeks. "I want this ring forever." She palms my face. "I want *you* forever."

Five

Braxton

MARCH-SENIOR YEAR

Kaylee: Come pick me up. I have the best idea!

Me: Where are you?

Kaylee: I just got home from cheer camp. Come over!

"GOTTA GO," I TELL THE GUYS, WHO ARE DISCUSSING A SONG CAMDEN RECENTLY WROTE. It's spring break, and we're hanging out at Camden's house since he's got a state-of-the-art studio in the basement of his house. Before his dad became the president of Blackwood Records, he was a huge musician—hell, his songs are still popular all these years later.

"Where are you going?" Declan asks.

"Girls are back from camp."

That has Gage standing. "I'm out."

"Damn, c'mon," Camden whines. "We've almost got this song on lock."

"Later," I say as Gage and I climb the stairs.

I faintly hear Camden muttering that we're pussy whipped, but I ignore it because he isn't wrong. One day, if he actually gets the balls to tell Layla how he feels and they finally get together, he'll get it. But until then, he'll continue to watch Layla from afar while she dates David the douche.

Since Tori lives in the opposite direction of Kaylee, Gage and I bump fists, then go our separate ways. I jump on the train and get off at her stop a few minutes later, practically sprinting to her place. It's been seven days since I've seen her, and I'm dying to kiss her, touch her, taste her.

I've barely knocked on her door when it swings open, and Kaylee pulls me inside by the front of my shirt, kissing the hell out of me. I'm assuming by the way she's attacking me in her foyer that we're alone, so I lift her into my arms and walk us to her bedroom, where I can properly welcome her home.

Our clothes are quickly shed, and I'm on top of her, kissing my way down her body until I get to her pussy. Spreading her legs, I devour her, licking and sucking on her clit until she's writhing under me and coming apart.

"God, I've missed you," I murmur as I crawl back up her body. My mouth crashes against hers, and she moans, loving her taste on my lips. I enter her in one fluid motion, and she groans. I would love nothing more than to fuck her for a long-ass time since being inside her is my favorite place in the world, but it's been a damn week, so all too soon, I'm coming deep inside her.

"I missed you," she says, kissing the corner of my mouth.

Her legs are wrapped tightly around me, and even though I'm now semi-soft, I can feel her walls tightening around my dick from her orgasm.

"I missed the hell out of you," I tell her. "Now, tell me about this *best idea*."

When her face lights up, I know she's about to say something crazy, but I'll go along with it because like Camden said, I'm pussy whipped and completely okay with it.

"You still have your fake ID, right?"

"Yeah..." Since my birthday isn't until June, I'm younger than everyone, still seventeen.

"I was thinking," she says slowly, "we should go get tattoos."

"What?" I say through a laugh. Don't get me wrong. I'm down for it. I plan to get plenty once I'm old enough, but Kaylee has never mentioned wanting to get anything more than the sexy naval ring she got when she turned eighteen a couple of months ago.

"Something to commemorate our time together," she says with a soft smile. "I know you gave me this promise ring, but you don't have anything like that. I was thinking we could get matching tattoos, so when you're in LA and I'm here, every time you look at it, you can think of me."

My heart drops at her words. "I won't need anything to think about you because I'll be with you." We've talked about this, and we're in this together. I'm not going anywhere without her. She knows this.

Her smile turns sad. "I didn't get into U of C. I was waitlisted."

"But there's still a chance, right?"

She shakes her head. "I talked to my mom, and even if I were to get in, she doesn't have the money to help me with college, and any assistance from my dad is out of the question. I applied for financial aid, but because my mom is married to Peter, they count his income, and he makes too much, so I didn't qualify."

"Then we can take out a loan," I point out, refusing to give up.

"And graduate hundreds of thousands of dollars in debt?"

"We'll figure it out." I meant what I said. I'm not going anywhere without her.

She nods but doesn't look convinced. "Regardless, I thought getting matching tattoos would be the perfect way to link ourselves to each other forever."

I want to tell her the perfect way is for us to get married in June when I turn eighteen, but instead, since I'll give her whatever she wants, I agree. "What tattoo are you thinking of?"

"The same symbol as my ring. Two infinity symbols woven together.... never ending." She pulls my face down to hers. "Because no matter what, we're forever."

Six

Braxton

JUST BEFORE THE PRE-GRADUATION PARTY

"YOU'RE MAKING A MISTAKE!" DAD BARKS, FOLLOWING ME THROUGH OUR HOUSE AS I get ready to head to the pre-graduation party. "Why the hell can't you see that?"

I groan, sick of this same argument we've had countless times over the past several weeks since I mentioned I might not be going to LA with the guys after graduation. It's not that I don't want to be part of the band... I do. But Kaylee can't afford to go to college in LA, and even if she could, she didn't get in. If I leave, we'll be living over three thousand miles apart, and while she's told me we can make it work over the distance, I don't see how, when neither of us can even afford a plane ticket to visit each other.

"I don't care what you think," I say. "Kaylee isn't Mom, and I'm not you. We're forever, and I'm not about to put the band before her." Everyone who has ever supposedly loved her has put her last, and I'm not going to do that to her. She deserves to be put first.

Dad backs up as if he's been punched in the face, and I feel bad about what I said. "I'm sorry," I say. I didn't mean to hurt him, but I know that's what he's thinking. He followed my mom to LA, giving up a huge opportunity, and in the end, she left him—*left us.* So I get why he's cynical, but Kaylee and I aren't them.

"I don't want to see you make the same mistakes I made," he says. "You're young. You don't get it, but there'll be a million girls like her."

"I disagree." I grab my phone from the nightstand and check to see if Kaylee has messaged me back. We were supposed to go to the party together, but she hasn't responded. "I'll be back later," I tell my dad as I walk out the door.

When I get to Kaylee's place, her mom—Ginny—opens the door, with Kaylee's three-year-old brother peeking out from behind her leg. "Hey, Braxton," she says. "Kaylee isn't here."

Damn, where the hell is she? "All right, thanks," I tell her. "If you see her, can you tell her I'm looking for her, please?"

"Of course, and have a safe trip to LA."

I freeze in my place at her words. "I'm not going to LA," I correct her. "I'm staying here, in New York." My phone goes off in my pocket, but I ignore it to focus on our conversation.

Ginny frowns. "Oh, I must've misunderstood. Well, New York isn't too far from Boston."

"What's in Boston?" My phone continues to vibrate, but I ignore it.

Her frown deepens. "Where Kaylee is going to school. She didn't tell you? She got into the same college as Layla and received a scholarship for her grades. They're going to be sharing a dorm."

Dread clogs my throat. "It must've slipped her mind," I say, my blood running cold.

My phone vibrates for what feels like the millionth time, and I pull it out as I quickly say bye to her mom. I have several missed calls and texts and some notifications from Instagram.

I open my messages and find some from Declan saying we need to talk, it's important, and to call him, a couple from Camden saying the same thing, and a few from some random people.

Confused as hell, I pull up the texts from the random people.

Kaylee is such a bitch. If you need a rebound fuck, call me.

Fuck that ho.

I can't believe she fucked Jack.

What the hell is going on? One of the messages includes a link, so I click on it. It takes me to a post on Jack's page and what I see damn near brings me to my knees.

No. No. No... Fuck, no. She wouldn't do this. She wouldn't cheat on me. I glance down at the tattoo of the infinity symbols on the outside of my hand. No, this can't be right. We're forever.

Seven

Braxton

THE PRESENT: HIGH SCHOOL PRE-GRADUATION PARTY

"BRAX..." KAYLEE CHOKES OUT, AND THAT ONE WORD, THE WAY SHE SAYS IT, TELLS ME everything I need to know. It's not a mistake or a sick joke. She cheated on me with the goddamn quarterback. She gave him what she swore was mine, what she promised would be mine forever.

She reaches out for me but then quickly stops herself, pulling her hand back as a fresh round of tears fills her lids. I hate to see her cry, and any other time, I'd be pulling her into my arms and promising her anything in my power to make the tears stop. Only right now, there's nothing that can fix her tears. Because they're self-inflicted. She did this to us. I don't know why, but she did.

My phone buzzes like crazy in my pocket, so I pull it out to tell whoever is calling that now isn't a good time. But when I answer Declan's call, his words silence me. "Tori's dead. Gage is at the hospital. You need to meet us at Camden's place as soon as possible."

We hang up, and I look at Kaylee. "Something happened to Tori." Her brow furrows in confusion, telling me she has no clue. Of course she doesn't because she was too busy fucking that jock in his bed while destroying my damn heart. "She's dead."

The next few days that follow are a blur...

Layla gets engaged to David—Camden never did tell her how he felt.

We bury Tori—Gage checks the fuck out.

Camden's dad suggests we leave for LA immediately—we all agree.

And just like that, we step onto the private plane and never look back... At least not for several years, that is.

Eight

Kaylee

SIX YEARS LATER

"C'MON, BABY... YOU'VE BEEN TEASING THE HELL OUT OF ME WITH THOSE SEXY OUTFITS all damn tour. Just give me one taste."

I glare at Sam York, my first client since I graduated from NYU with my public relations and marketing/advertising degree and got hired by Evolution PR, and scoff. "Sexy outfits?" I glance down at my professional dress pants and button-down blouse that shows zero cleavage. I couldn't be dressed any less sexy if I tried. "You're drunk and delusional." The guy has been hitting on me since the tour began, but I've carefully managed to steer clear of him, counting down the days until the tour ends.

I didn't even want this job. I want to do marketing and advertising for the PR company, but they insist their employees get hands-on experience to learn about the people and brand they're marketing. I imagine not all employees are stuck going on tour with a musician, but my graduation lined up with his tour, and the fact that the original publicist backed out at the last second led to me being on tour with one of the most popular—and asinine—pop stars. My hope is once this tour is done, I'll be able to get into a position of my choice. Of course he'd pull this shit the day before it's time to go home.

Sam steps toward me, backing me up against the wall of the tour bus, and I extend my hand, refusing to allow him any closer. "You need to go sleep it off," I warn. "Sexual assault is a real thing, even for a pop star like yourself."

"Baby," he slurs, pushing past my hand and getting all up in my personal space. "Stop playing hard to get." He reaches for a breast and squeezes it hard, and I lose my cool.

"I'm not playing!" I wind my hand back and slap him in the face.

Because he's wasted, he stumbles back. "Bitch," he murmurs, coming at me hard. He pushes me against the wall and cups the area between my legs. "Stop being a fucking cock tease."

My fight-or-flight instincts kick in, and I lift my knee into his groin, making him stagger back in pain. "You're going to regret that." Without waiting for him to make his next move, I run off the bus and over to the other bus, where my bunk bed is. Once I'm safely there, I release a harsh breath, thankful I go home tomorrow. Fucking loser probably won't even remember the way he acted tonight. Assholes like him, who think they're above everyone else, always get away with shit like this. Not this time. Tomorrow morning, I'm going to tell my boss what he did. I'm not letting him get away with it.

"KAYLEE, YOU NEED TO WAKE UP," IRIS, THE TOUR MANAGER, SAYS. I OPEN MY EYES AND find the bus is filled with light. It must be morning.

"Are we back in LA?"

"Yeah," she says, her lips pursed. "Pack up your things quickly. There's a car waiting to take you to the airport."

The ride to the airport is quick, and a few hours later, I arrive back in New York. Another car waits to take me to Evolution. When I enter the lobby, Evelyn is waiting for me, her face devoid of all emotion.

"Please have a seat," she says once we're in her office with the door closed.

I've been preparing what I'm going to say and how I'm going to word the way Sam behaved, but before I can begin, she speaks first.

"It's been brought to our attention by Sam York's team that you behaved inappropriately during the tour. He said last night you went as far as to sexually assault him, and when he refused your advances, you got physical—"

"He said what?" I hiss. "*He* was inappropriate. *He* tried to—"

Evelyn raises her hand, silencing me. "It doesn't matter. It's your word versus his. You never should've been on his bus alone with him. He's upset and making threats."

"What an asshole," I breathe. "So what do we do?"

"*We* don't do anything," she says. "In exchange for him not running my company into the ground, I agreed to let you go."

"You're firing me?" This is insane. "What do I do now?" My

heart is racing in my chest. I busted my ass for this degree. I worked hard on that tour and didn't do anything wrong.

"I suggest you find a new career. Once it gets out how you behaved..." I open my mouth to correct her, but she shakes her head. "Whether it's true or not, you'll be blacklisted from this industry." She stands, making it clear this conversation is over. "Your last paycheck will be direct deposited. I wish you the best, and I'm sorry it didn't work out."

Nine

Braxton

"THAT'S IT, BABY. TAKE MY ENTIRE COCK DOWN YOUR THROAT." I PAT THE WOMAN'S head and continue reading through the group messages. I don't remember bringing this chick home with me last night, but when I woke up to her slurping on my dick, I wasn't about to stop her. It's the perfect parting gift—meaning as soon as I come down her throat, we'll be parting ways.

Camden: You're late to the meeting.

Me: Take notes for me.

Camden: We need a new publicist since you and Gage tag-teamed the last one... Nobody wants to work with us.

Gage: <shrugs>

Me: Such a waste... she wasn't even good in or out of bed. We have Jill...

I glance down at the woman still sucking my cock like a champ. She's been doing it for a while now, so I imagine her mouth is sore, but she still hasn't given up. "You're doing good," I praise her. "Maybe take me a little deeper."

She does as I suggest, gagging when my head hits the back of her throat. She's not the best dick sucker, but I'd give her an A for effort.

Camden: Jill is the tour manager. She has enough going on. She doesn't have time to babysit you guys. We need a new publicist before we go on tour. I need you here so we can discuss it.

Declan: Speak for yourself. I don't need a babysitter. That would be the other two dumbasses.

Gage: <shrugs>

The heavy breathing of the woman sucking my cock has me looking down. She's going to town on it, licking and sucking it like a lollipop, but it's doing nothing for me. She's not the first woman who hasn't been able to bring me to a release... not since... Fuck, I'm not going there.

Me: I don't care what you decide. I'm in the middle of something important.

Gage: I'm good with whatever you decide.

Declan: I'm almost there. I'm not getting stuck with another airhead on this tour.

Camden: Brax, I think you should be here...

Me: If you're worried about me fucking her, send a pic

and I'll let you know.

Camden: GET THE FUCK DOWN HERE!

Me: No can do. Gotta go.

I chuck my phone onto the nightstand and focus on getting my dick sucked, refusing to believe that I'm broken. When the woman takes me deep again and nothing happens, I sigh in frustration. "Hey, babe, sorry to cut this short, but I gotta go."

She looks up, her mascara dripping down her cheeks. "But you haven't come yet." She pouts.

"It's not happening, but I appreciate the effort." I stand and tuck my dick back into my pants. "There's money in the bowl near the door for an Uber."

Once she's out the door, I head into the bathroom so I can shower, feeling dirty as fuck. I turn the hot water on to full blast and step under the spray. I squirt some body wash into my hands, lather it up, and clean my body. When my hand lands on my soft dick, I stroke it up and down, getting it hard, needing to prove that I'm not broken and just having a dry spell of sorts.

My eyes close, and I focus on getting harder and harder. I try to imagine the woman from earlier on her knees, sucking my dick, yet thoughts of someone else appear instead: blond hair, gray eyes, red lips, perfect tits, toned thighs, an ass I can grab on to, and—

I come hard all over the shower wall—proving that I'm okay and pissing me off at the same time. Because *she's* the last person I should be thinking about when I come, but ever since I ran into her a few months ago when we were having dinner with our friends, I can't get her out of my head. I hate her. I loathe her. But fuck if I don't still want her.

I tell myself it's because we're in the same city. I haven't seen her in years, so it's fucking with my head. She's all over the gossip sites for trying to fuck that pop musician. That's all it is. Seeing her face everywhere and hearing about her is messing with me. Once we're back on tour and I'm away from her, shit will go back to normal.

"IT FEELS LIKE WE WERE JUST ON TOUR," I WHINE AS I DRAG MY HUNGOVER ASS UP THE stairs and onto the plane.

"That's because we were," Declan agrees. "Less than a year ago."

"I think after this one, we should take a long break," I say, fully aware I sound like an ungrateful asshole, but my head is pounding, and I'm already dreading living the next two months on the tour bus, on planes, and in hotels.

"I'm down for that," Camden says. "I'd like to be home for a little while after the baby is born anyway." A small smile spreads across his face, and even though I think love is bullshit, I can't help but be happy for my friend. Because he finally got the woman he's loved and wanted for years. It might've taken them awhile to find their way to each other, but they're now married, expecting a baby, and fucking happy. I hope it works out for them better than it did for me.

"Is Layla here?" I ask Camden, referring to his wife. He'd mentioned that she and her five-year-old son, Felix, would be joining us for a few days since our first stop on the tour is LA.

"Yeah, she's laying Felix down for a nap in the bedroom," Camden says. "Listen, I need to talk to you real quick. I've been trying to tell you something but—"

Before he can finish his thought, a blur of blond catches my attention. I glance over at the door of the plane and what I see has my heart picking up speed, my palms sweating, and my already pounding head throbbing in pain. This can't be happening. I'm seeing shit, I have to be. There's no way she's here on this plane. I close my eyes and then reopen them, but she's still there, standing in the doorway.

"What the fuck are you doing here?" I ask as Kaylee steps onto the plane.

"She's our new publicist," Camden says, shocking the hell out of me. "I told your ass to come to the meeting."

I swing my glare over to him. "You didn't say it was *her*."

"Should've come down." He shrugs. "Nobody wanted to risk their career coming on tour with you and Gage. She was willing. We had to make a decision, so it was made."

"Look on the bright side," Declan says, humor in his tone. "You won't be sleeping with our publicist on tour."

His words hit me like a punch to the gut. I look over at Kaylee, who's still standing at the door of the plane, waiting to see how this all plays out. My thoughts go to our past, to how much I fucking loved her, to how much she hurt me, took my heart and put it through a shredder. Then I remember the shit I've heard about her online. The rumors running rampant about what happened between her and Sam York.

With a smirk I hope relays how much I hate her and how

much she disgusts me, I look her dead in the eyes. "Wouldn't put it past her to try. I heard she practically raped Sam York. Better keep my door locked just in case." Then I glance over at Camden, who's glaring daggers my way. "You sure Layla is okay with her going with us? She might try something on you."

Camden sighs, and Declan groans. Kaylee... She growls. Legitimately fucking growls.

"Fuck you!" she hisses. "I didn't touch him, and I sure as hell wouldn't touch you with a ten-foot pole."

I step over to her, ignoring her intoxicating scent—the same pink rose shit she used to wear when we were together, that I used to spend hours inhaling and getting lost in—and drag my gaze over the full length of her body. She's dressed professionally in a black button-down shirt and slacks, her heels low. Her shirt is on the tighter side, clinging to her breasts, which are perky and peeking out from the top where a few buttons are undone. The material of her pants molds to every perfect curve. She might be fully dressed and not showing a single inch of skin, but I've already seen her body, memorized every inch of it, so I can imagine what's underneath. What used to be mine... until she gave it to someone else.

Pain roils in my stomach at the thought, and it doesn't take much to muster up a look of disgust. "Pretty sure you already did, sweetheart."

"Yeah, before you became a manwhore. All those groupie sluts you've been sleeping with... you probably have a dozen STDs."

So it's going to be like that, huh? Okay... Game on.

"Let's not forget who the head slut is," I say, feigning

nonchalance like a pro when the truth is, my body is vibrating in anger. Because who the fuck does she think she is pointing fingers? "Who fucked another man while we were still together?" I say, making her flinch. "I might be a manwhore, but you're just a fucking whore."

"Enough!" Camden barks. "I'm not going to play referee this entire tour."

"Then you should've thought about that before you hired the woman who fucked me over."

"What's going on?" Layla steps out from where the bedroom is and sighs, her hand going to the bump she's sporting. She and Camden are expecting a baby in October. A little girl. "Felix is sleeping."

Her gaze goes to me, and while I don't want to stress her out, I have no doubt Kaylee being on tour with us was Layla's doing. They're best friends and have been since our sophomore year of high school. "We're screaming because someone thought it would be a good idea to hire *her*." I don't bother saying her name since we all know who I'm referring to. "I get she's your best friend, but..."

"Can I talk to you alone?" Layla says, giving me a look that I can't say no to. Like she and Kaylee, we've been friends since Layla moved here, and I love her like a damn sister.

I nod, and we head to a secluded area of the plane.

"I know this is hard," she says softly, "but I need you to be okay with this for me, please."

"Layla... you're asking a lot." She knows what went down all those years ago. She knows how much I loved Kaylee, how much it hurt to find out that she was all too willing to spread her legs for the asshole jock who was after her for years, who she told me she couldn't stand. We were supposed to be forever, yet she so easily discarded me like yesterday's trash.

"I know," Layla says. "But she worked so hard in college to get her degree. You know all she's ever wanted to do is marketing and advertising." I do know that, which is why I was shocked she was a publicist and not working in the marketing/advertising department.

"Why the hell is she working as a publicist?"

"She took a job with Evolution, and they said they wanted her to get hands-on experience first, so they sent her on tour with Sam York to learn about marketing during a tour. She didn't do what he accused her of, and now she's been blacklisted everywhere. Nobody wants someone who's been tainted working on their team. If she's able to be your publicist for an entire tour, she'll have a better shot of getting another job because everyone knows your publicists never make it." She looks at me with her damn puppy dog eyes. "Please, Brax. She needs a clean slate and a good recommendation, and you guys need a publicist for the tour."

"Fine," I relent. "But don't think I'm going to make it easy on her."

She nods solemnly. "I understand. Thank you."

We walk back out, and everyone—including Kaylee—has found their seats. Gage and Declan are sitting next to each other discussing the details of the tour Jill sent over—she's meeting us in LA since that's where she's located. Camden is sitting across from Kaylee, talking low. Layla goes over and sits next to her husband, snuggling into his side. He kisses the top of her head, and not for the first time, my heart squeezes in my rib cage.

It was easy to tuck my heart away for the past six years. None of us were interested in settling down. Our only focus has been on making music. But then Camden saw Layla again, and the dynamic changed. He's become a father and a husband, and watching them, mixed with seeing Kaylee again, has the hurt and resentment I felt all those years ago rising to the surface.

Kaylee glances over at me, realizing the only seat left is next to her, and smiles sadly, as if silently asking for a truce. Well, fuck that shit. She's not getting one. She wants to be on this tour to save her ass? Fine. But I meant what I said to Layla. I sure as shit won't make it easy on her.

Ten

Kaylee

THIS WAS A MISTAKE. A DESPERATE, STUPID MISTAKE. WHEN LAYLA SUGGESTED IT, I told her she was out of her mind. Me spending two months on the road with Braxton? She couldn't be serious. But she insisted it would also benefit the band because while they have Jill, they need a publicist to help with the promo of the tour as well as keep the guys organized and in line and make sure they're where they need to be. Jill can't do it all. Since Braxton and Gage apparently screwed the last woman who went on tour with them, Easton—Camden's dad, the band's manager, and the president of Blackwood Records—said it would help him out since the PR companies they use won't allow anyone to go on tour with the guys.

I suggested a male publicist, and Easton laughed humorlessly, saying the last guy they hired ended up all over social media after being recorded with strippers while they were in Vegas.

Apparently, no one is immune to their charms.

So like the masochist I apparently am, I agreed to go. The pay is damn good—although I have a feeling it's more than what they usually pay. It probably includes hazard pay for all that I'll be dealing with. I should've requested *that* when I took the job with Sam York, but at the time, I didn't know what I was getting myself into. Between his drug problem and constantly hitting on me, I should've known it would end with him fucking me over. But even working with him didn't prepare me for going on tour with Raging Chaos.

The first two concerts in LA were easy. I handled the radio giveaways, organizing the meet and greets for the winners, and it all went smoothly. Gage and Braxton both behaved. Camden and Declan were social and chatty. The guys took pictures and signed merchandise, and for a minute, I thought, *I can totally do this.* But I should've known there was a reason for the obedience: Layla and Felix. They were there with Camden—celebrating Felix's birthday—and that kept the guys in line. Then she and Felix got on a plane, and we got on the buses, and everything changed.

We've been in Vegas for less than eight hours, and as I stand in my doorway to my hotel room, watching as Gage and Braxton stumble down the hall with multiple women in tow—who look to be hookers or at least dressed like ones—I'm not sure I can do two months of this. I know I have no right to feel the way I do. If anything, I deserve it. But holy shit, my heart hurts watching Braxton, his lids slightly droopy from being drunk and maybe high, being draped by two women who are all over him like fleas on a stray dog.

When I heard the noise, knowing we were the only ones on this floor, I opened my door to make sure everything was okay. Big mistake. My door creaked loud enough to grab Braxton's attention. His gaze met mine—a mixture of anger and indifference—and I had no choice but to stand in place and watch them walk past me. The alternative would've been to quickly close my door, which would've shown Braxton I was affected. The last thing I need to do is lower my guard and risk him using it to fuck with me.

Gage and the women go in first, but Braxton stops just outside the doorway. His eyes meet mine, and I hold my breath, waiting for the blow to come. He stares at me, and my heart thumps in my chest, wondering what's going through his head. If he's thinking about how much I hurt him. It's been six years, and he still hates me so much. Not that I blame him, but I thought time healed all wounds and all that...

"Brax, c'mon!" a woman yells. "I'm naked and waiting!"

"Coming," he says, his eyes not leaving mine. "We're going to need some lube... and condoms. I prefer Trojan."

For a second, my brain doesn't comprehend what he's saying... *that he's saying it to me*. Until he adds, "Learned a while back that condoms are a must. Never know who else the person you're fucking has fucked." And then it hits me like a train going full speed without any working brakes—he wants *me* to go get him the lube and condoms. And he's referring to me being the person he was fucking and not knowing who else I was fucking. The accusation stings, but I refuse to let him see that.

"I'm not your errand girl. If you want that shit, go get it your damn self."

He releases a sharp laugh, then stalks toward me, stopping so close I can smell the liquor on his breath and the smoke from the casino. But beneath the liquor and smoke, there's another scent, one I would recognize anywhere. It's the cologne I bought him for Christmas—our one and only Christmas together. It smells fresh and masculine and brings back memories of every time he would wear it when we were together.

Images of me snuggling against him, inhaling his scent, and kissing his flesh surface, and before I can stop myself, I blurt out, "You're wearing the cologne I got you."

Braxton flinches but quickly composes himself, his glare intensifying. He reaches into his pocket and pulls out a hundred-dollar bill, reminding me of his request. When he extends his hand, trying to give it to me, and I don't take it, he steps closer, invading my space. "Condoms and lube... *now.*"

"I'm not your errand girl," I repeat, jutting my chin out in defiance.

His finger and thumb pinch my chin, lifting my face to look at him, and my breath hitches. It's been six years since we've been this close, since he's touched me, and I've missed it... *missed him...* every single day.

"If you ever want to get another job in this industry," he says, his mouth mere inches from mine, "you'll be whatever the fuck I want you to be." He reaches around and slides the bill into my back pocket. "Don't make this shit harder than it needs to be."

Without waiting for me to respond, he releases my chin and turns his back on me, sauntering back to his room while I stand, frozen in shock, wondering what the hell happened to the man I used to know. Was it the fame? The fortune? And then, I'm overtaken with a bout of guilt as a thought occurs to me. Was it me and what I did to him… *to us* that's caused him to be like this? Am I the reason he's now a cold, heartless, womanizing bastard?

Tears prick my lids. It's one thing for me to hurt—it's nothing less than I deserve—but the thought, that after six years, Braxton's still hurting because of me, because of my actions, is like liquid guilt being injected straight into my vein, spreading through my bloodstream like acid and burning me from the inside out.

I let a couple of tears fall before I inhale a deep breath and swipe them away. I don't deserve to cry, and doing so is a waste of time anyway. What's done is done, and there's no going back.

With my head held as high as I can manage, I head down to the hotel store and get the items he's requested and then take them up to him. Thankfully, he's not the one who opens the door. Gage is. He's clearly high and maybe drunk, but that doesn't stop him from giving me a look of sympathy before he thanks me and closes the door.

Instead of going back to my room, I make my way downstairs, needing to get some air. I'm not really dressed for the Strip, but it doesn't matter. Nobody will be paying attention to me anyway.

I step outside, and the pungent smell of smoke combined with the sound of loud music assaults my senses. I'm halfway down the sidewalk when I hear my name being called. I turn around and find Declan walking over to me.

"Hey, did you need something?"

He shakes his head. "Nah. I was having a drink at the bar and saw you. Thought I'd join you."

We walk alongside each other for a few minutes before he finally speaks. "He still loves you."

"He hates me."

We keep walking until we're in front of the famous Bellagio fountains. It's in the middle of a show, so we stop and watch it in silence.

"He hates what you did," Declan says softly but loud enough for me to hear over the show. "But he doesn't hate you. Maybe you can fix it. It's been six years. You made one bad choice, but you can make things right. I can see it in your eyes that you still love him."

I smile sadly at Declan. He's always been such a romantic. Every song he writes is sweet, filled with hearts and flowers. He doesn't discuss his home life often, but I know it's not a good one. Yet he still believes in love and happily ever afters.

"It's too late," I tell him truthfully. "I hurt him too badly."

"I don't believe that," Declan says, pulling me into his side and kissing my temple. "It's never too late for love."

MY ALARM SOUNDS PROMPTLY AT SEVEN O'CLOCK, AND I SERIOUSLY CONSIDER TURNING it off, covering my head with my blanket, and remaining in bed. But I can't do that because the guys have an interview this morning for a local radio station, then a soundcheck afterward, and a concert tonight, followed by a meet and greet the local radio station is hosting as a contest on their social media.

After taking a shower, blow-drying my blond hair straight,

and getting dressed in a pair of black dress slacks and a blouse that's just as black—because these days my life feels equivalent to attending my own funeral—dramatic, much? Maybe—I head over to the guys' room. I have a key card, but I knock first before I enter.

I'm expecting the place to look like a porn studio—no, I've never seen one, but I can imagine—with naked bodies strewn about, but the place is clean. Since the suite has several bedrooms, I go to the first door I see and knock. Camden opens the door—fully dressed. "Morning."

"Morning. We have to get going to the radio station."

"All right, thanks," he says with a slight frown marring his features.

"You okay?"

"Yeah, just missing the hell out of Layla and Felix."

My heart swells, loving that my best friend found such an amazing man. After everything she's been through, she deserves nothing less. "When are they meeting up with us again?"

"Back here, next week, for the Billboards, but only Layla. Felix is staying with her mom."

I forgot about the upcoming award show. While the guys and I will be coming back here for the award show, Jill and the rest of the team will be heading to San Jose. After the show, we'll be flying to meet up with them at the next tour stop. "Not too far off."

"We agreed we wouldn't go too long without seeing each other." He shrugs. "They're meeting us in Tampa after that. We're going to take Felix to the theme parks there and in Orlando."

"And that will lead up to the Fourth of July." The guys took the week off for the holiday. I have no idea what I'll be doing. Layla invited me to join them, but I'm not in the mood to play the third wheel to their love fest. The problem is, I'm kind of homeless until I find a place to live once we get back from the tour. Maybe I'll rent a cheap room somewhere and spend the week relaxing. It's been a while since I've done that.

"I can't wait," Camden says, a real smile stretching across his face. "The last leg of the trip will suck. Two weeks without seeing them, but then we'll be home."

"It'll fly by," I tell him, praying I'm right because we're only on day five of the tour, and it feels like it's going to last a lifetime.

"Morning," Declan says, coming out of the room he must've shared with Camden and kissing my cheek. "Did you give any thought to what we talked about last night?"

I actually did think about it for hours until I finally fell asleep. I considered what he said—that deep down through the hurt, Braxton still loves me and I, him—and I've decided I'm going to talk to him about it when we have time. I'm not expecting us to be together again. I'm not Declan with his rose-colored glasses, but I do think if we talk—something we never got a chance to do—maybe we can find common ground and be friends... or at least be friendly with one another.

"I did," I tell him, not giving him anything more since I'm still not sure how I want to handle it.

"Good. What time do we leave?"

I glance at the itinerary on my phone Jill sent me. "Twenty minutes, and we won't be back. We're leaving straight from the show to head to Sacramento."

Turning on my heel, I head straight for the other door,

knocking and opening it without waiting for someone to give me the okay. Big mistake. I was so lost in my thoughts, thanks to Declan, that I didn't consider what would be behind the other door.

I take in the scene in front of me, refusing to cry or throw up. Braxton is naked from the waist up, passed out on the queen-sized bed. With him are two very naked women. One is sprawled out across his stomach, and the other is lying across the foot of the bed. There are empty liquor bottles and the box of condoms and bottle of lube I brought him last night on the nightstand.

I step slowly into the room, unsure if I should be mature and gently wake Braxton up or scream like a five-year-old when my eyes land on the book in his hand, sending me back six years.

"I can't believe you did this." I snuggle in close to Braxton, laying my head on his chest. It's our six-month anniversary, and he somehow booked us a gorgeous hotel room so we could spend the night together. He ordered us room service, and after eating, we spent time in the private hot tub before he made love to me.

"I'd do anything for you," he murmurs, kissing the top of my head.

We lie in silence for a few minutes before I remember something. "I have something for you."

I reach over and grab the gift bag I brought with me, second-guessing what I got him. "It's nothing as lavish as this"—I wave my hand in the air—"but I saw it in the store, and it made me think of you."

He opens the bag and pulls out a black notebook with gold script on the front that reads: ***Write the words that pour from your heart.***

"It's for your words," I explain. "And to remind you to always write from your heart." He doesn't write half the music Camden does, but when he does write a song, it's always beautiful, powerful, and filled with such emotion.

"I love it," he says, flipping through the blank pages before he sets it down and cups my face. "And I love you. Thank you."

He has the notebook even now. Six years later, and he's still using it.

"Kaylee," Camden says, sympathy evident in his tone. "I can wake him and Gage up."

"Okay, thanks," I choke out, emotion clogging my throat. Without looking back, I run out of the room and out of their suite. I keep running as the traitorous tears spill down my cheeks until I get back to my room. I need to grab my stuff, but instead, I pull my phone out and call Layla.

"Hey," she says. "How's it going?"

"I can't do this," I rush out through my sobs. "Watching him with all these other women... I can't do it." I know what I did all those years ago was horrible, but seeing him like this is too hard, and it hurts too much. Declan was wrong. It is too late for love... It's too late for a lot of things.

Layla's quiet for a second before she speaks. "Do you still love him?"

Dammit, here we go again with the love shit.

"It doesn't matter. I don't have the right to. Not after everything. After the way I hurt him." Declan may believe Braxton would be willing to forgive me, but he's wrong. There's no going back from what I did, and thinking we could be friends was just stupidity on my part. I made my decision all those years ago, and now I have to live with the fallout.

"That was six years ago. Did something else happen?"

I give her a quick recap of last night and this morning.

When I finish, Layla sighs over the line. "I wish I were there so I could hug you."

"I don't deserve it. I did this." I swipe away my tears. "I need to pull up my big girl panties and stop getting emotional. This is a job... possibly my last chance, and I need to handle it professionally."

"True," she says, "but you're still human, and you have feelings."

"Camden's missing you like crazy," I say, changing the subject.

Layla laughs softly. "I swear he's texted me every five minutes since we left LA."

"You love it."

"Yeah, I do." We're both quiet for a moment. "Kaylee, one day you'll find your *Camden*."

Too bad it's not a Camden I want... It's a Braxton.

I'm sitting here high
I can't forget
You wanted my love
I gave it to you

You wanted my heart

I handed it over
You took and took
Sucked me fucking dry
And now I'm sitting here high
I can't forget

After every hit I take
Every memory that surfaces
I wanna forget

Your gray eyes
Your sweet smile
You fucked me over
And now I wanna forget

I watch and listen as Braxton sings a song from their first album. It's not on the set for this tour, yet he's singing it. Camden is the lead singer. Gage is the drummer. Declan is the bass player. And Braxton is the guitarist.

But every once in a while, Braxton and Declan will sing. Braxton's voice is different than Camden's. It's raw and husky, and when he graces the world with it, women go crazy. Like they're doing right now as he sings "I Wanna Forget," a song about me and how much he hates me for what I did to him. I can still remember how people speculated when this song came out. They love to analyze the lyrics and put a face to the words. It makes it more personal when they can point a finger. But Raging Chaos is great about keeping their private life private, so only a few select people know this song is about me.

"You okay?" asks Bailey, Camden's sister and the head of Blackwood's media. She flew into Portland to watch the show and handle a couple of things for the band with Cade, who's on tour with us to film the guys and is working with Layla to create a web series. The fans love it because they get to see below the surface—put a face to the name. Feel and see and hear all the emotions.

"It's nothing I don't deserve," I say, my eyes trained on Braxton as he belts the lyrics with such emotion goose bumps prickle my flesh.

"Nobody deserves to have their dirty laundry aired out for all the world to see."

"Maybe." I shrug. "But that's the risk you take when you date a rock star, right?"

Just as I finish my sentence, the song ends. I expect Camden to take back the microphone, so I'm shocked when Braxton starts to talk. "How about one more?"

The crowd screams, and Braxton laughs, but I can see it on his face that he's not happy. "This one I wrote recently. It hasn't even been recorded yet."

Bailey glances at me in confusion. At the same time, Jill speaks into her headpiece in a rushed whisper, telling me this wasn't planned. I glance around at the other guys, all showing various looks of annoyance.

"It's called 'Unforgivable,'" Braxton says. Gage shakes his head but starts on the drums, and Camden, who took over Braxton's guitar, starts strumming it. I hold my breath, waiting for the lyrics to come, knowing they're going to hurt.

And I'm right because as Braxton opens his mouth and the

words flow off his tongue, wrapping tightly around my heart, it feels as though I can't breathe. Declan was wrong. So wrong. Braxton doesn't just hate what I did. He hates me, and this song proves it.

Young love
Dumb love
Cheating love
Unforgivable love
It was love but the wrong kind
The fucked-up kind
The kind that sets your soul on fire
Leaves you burning with desire
And in the end, all you're left with is heartache and regret

Young love
Dumb love
Cheating love
Unforgivable love

Unable to listen to any more of his words, swallow any more of his truths, or feel any more of his heartbreak, I run, and I don't stop until I get to my hotel room. Then I climb into my bed, throw my blankets over me, and cry. I did this. I created this. I deserve this. But I also really fucking hate this. And my heart... it's not sure if it can take much more of this.

Eleven

Braxton

"HOW LONG ARE YOU IN TOWN FOR?" ALYSSA ASKS, HER VOICE DRIPPING WITH sexuality as she runs her long-nailed finger across my thigh. When Gage and I ran into her and a couple of her friends backstage and they suggested we find somewhere more private to chill, we agreed and came back to our hotel room. We're all lounging in the living room, smoking and drinking and listening to some music. Declan and Camden took off, pissed at the shit I pulled earlier. They've known about the song I wrote, that's why we have the instrumentals for it, but it didn't make the cut when we put out our first album.

I don't know why I felt the need to sing it tonight. Actually, that's not true. I know why. Because every day I'm on tour with Kaylee, I'm softening a little more, my hate lessening. It's so easy to get lost in her beautiful gray eyes and pouty lips. In her melodic laugh. When Declan reamed into me about making

Kaylee get the condoms and lube and then told me she ran out in tears when she saw me in bed with two other women, I had to remind myself what she did. She did this. She set the dominos in motion. And if I want to sing a thousand songs about what she did, I will. Because she deserves it. She deserves to hurt like I hurt and feel the pain the same way I felt it. She deserves to be reminded of what she ruined. I gave her all of me, and she destroyed me from the inside out.

"Tonight's our last night," I tell her, taking a shot of the whiskey we're drinking. Tomorrow, we'll be heading to another state, another city, singing at another show. It all kind of blends after a while.

"We should play a game!" her blond friend says.

"Oh, yeah!" her other friend—this one brunette—adds. "How about *Never Have I Ever*?"

"Isn't that the shit teenagers play in high school?" I ask, praying to fucking God these women are not in high school.

"Yeah, so? It'll be fun," Alyssa says. "And if you're a good boy, I'll let you take your shots off my body." When she says that, my eyes drag down said body, and I can't help but compare her to Kaylee. Where Kaylee is all real, from her blond hair to her pert tits, Alyssa is all fake. She's the type of woman I usually go for, but now, as I take in her burnt tan, bleached hair, and caked-on makeup, which is doing nothing for me, I can't help but wonder if I go for women like her because she's the complete opposite of Kaylee—perfectly real. And then I shake myself from my thoughts because the last person I should be thinking about is Kaylee. She might look real, but she's a damn cheater, which makes her fake as hell.

"We need more liquor," the brunette says with a pout, holding up the almost empty bottle.

"I'll go grab one," Gage offers, taking a hit of his joint and then snuffing it out.

"Actually, I'll send for a bottle," I suggest, already grabbing my phone to call the woman who's at our beck and call.

Gage does his version of an eye roll but doesn't argue. Instead, he relights his joint. My friends might hate the shit I'm doing to Kaylee, but they're loyal enough to keep their mouths shut—except apparently Declan, who seems to be trying to play mediator. But after the show tonight, I imagine he'll have gotten the hint—that I have no desire to ever forgive Kaylee for what she did—and will hopefully leave it alone.

"Hello?" Kaylee says breathily when she answers the phone.

"You asleep?" I ask, hoping I woke her ass up.

"No." She clears her throat. "How can I help you, Brax?"

I pause, wondering if she's been crying and if it's because of the song I sang about her. And for a brief second, I almost consider asking her if she's okay. But then I remember why I sang the song I did and nix that thought.

"We need a bottle of whiskey brought to our room."

While we wait for the new bottle, the girls start the game with the bottle we already have, mentioning stupid-ass shit like, "Never have I ever kissed a girl" and "Never have I ever had a threesome," all three of them giggling and drinking as they admit they've done each sexual thing.

When there's a knock on the door, I yell for Kaylee to come in instead of getting up since she has a key to our room. She walks in, dressed in a loose T-shirt and a pair of yoga pants that show off her curves.

"Here you go," she says, thrusting the bottle toward me. One look at her, and I can see she's been crying. Her eyes are puffy and red, and her cheeks are tinged with tear stains. My natural inclination is to pull her into my arms and hold her close. I always hated when she'd cry. But I don't because she doesn't deserve it. She deserves every single tear she sheds and much more.

"Stay," I suggest when I take the bottle. "Have a drink with us."

She scoffs. "I'm good."

"We're playing a game," Blondie says, oblivious to the tension Kaylee brought with her into the room. "*Never Have I Ever*... Heard of it?"

Kaylee's brow furrows. "The high school game?"

"Yep," I say, opening the bottle and pouring her a shot. "Whose turn is it?" I glance around. "You know what, I'll go." My eyes lock on hers. "Let's see..." I think for a second before the perfect one comes to me. "I got it. Never have I ever...cheated on the person I claimed to love."

"Oh, no, I've never done that," one of the women says.

"Real fucking mature," Kaylee hisses.

"Drink up, sweetheart." I smirk. "Hell, maybe you should have two shots for that one."

Kaylee throws the shot in my face and stalks out, slamming the door behind her.

"How long are you going to punish her for?" Gage asks as soon as she's gone.

"Until she's hurting as much as she hurt me."

"I'M TAKING KAYLEE WITH ME TONIGHT," GAGE SAYS, SHOCKING THE HELL OUT OF ME. We're back in Vegas at the MGM Grand for the award show since we've been nominated for several awards and are performing.

"She's the *help*. You can't find a fucking date?"

"I can." He shrugs. "I'm choosing to take her."

Jesus, first Camden hires her ass, then Declan tries to talk me into forgiving her, and now Gage is taking her as his date. So much for my friends having my back.

"With friends like you guys, who needs enemies?" I grumble, sounding bitter as fuck.

"Layla and Kendall are going," Declan points out as if the fact that her friends will be there is enough of a reason for her to join us.

"Well, she is an easy lay," I say, the words coming out sour.

Gage shakes his head, not bothering to respond.

Because I knew this event was coming up, I asked a friend of mine to join me, not wanting to bring some random chick to the event. She's a musician as well and will be performing.

Since we're all going in one vehicle, we pile into the stretch limo. Kaylee and Gage are the last to slide in, and I can't help but check her out. I seem to be doing that every damn time I see her. She's dressed in a strapless gold shimmery number with a thick shiny belt wrapped around her middle. The dress is tight up top, pushing up her already generous-sized tits, and loose on the bottom. Her hair is down in waves, her makeup light, and when she sits down, the slit in her dress parts, exposing her toned leg and showing off her matching gold heels. She looks fucking gorgeous. She always does, though, and I hate it.

"You okay?" my date, Adrianne, asks.

I glance down and notice my fists are clenched tight. "I need you to do me a favor," I whisper into her ear, my eyes locking on Kaylee.

Twelve

Kaylee

THIS WAS A HORRIBLE IDEA—I SEEM TO HAVE A LOT OF THEM LATELY. WHEN GAGE ASKED me to join him at the Billboards, saying he wasn't up for being the only guy without a date, I couldn't say no. The night we all lost Tori still haunts me. While I was ending my relationship with Braxton, Tori needed me, and I wasn't there. Something I will always regret. And now, Gage is alone, lost and sad, and I would do anything he asked even though I know nothing will bring her back or make it right.

But that doesn't change the fact that this was a horrible idea. I'm sitting in a limo with Camden and Layla, Declan and Kendall—Camden's older pop star sister who Declan is here with—Gage, and Braxton and his date, Adrianne, an up-and-coming pop star who's on tour with Kendall as her opening act. Everyone is chatting amongst themselves, but I can't take my eyes off Braxton, who's looking at me with a mixture of contempt and disgust while he whispers in his date's ear.

She giggles at whatever he's saying, then sits up, taking his hand in hers. "I love your tattoos," she says, playing with his fingers. "What do they mean?"

His eyes leave mine so he can look down at what she's looking at. He goes about explaining each tattoo in detail while she soaks up his attention like a sponge. When she takes his left hand in hers, I hold my breath, waiting for what he's going to say about the tattoo he got with me. I was honestly shocked when I saw that he never had it covered up.

"And this one"—he points at the infinity symbols inked on the outside of his hand, the same one I have in the same spot, and locks eyes with me—"was a mistake."

At his words, I suck in a harsh breath as tears prick my eyes. The shit he's pulled with having me bring him condoms and lube and liquor sucks, the song he sang hurt like hell, and the time he called me a cheater in front of his fuck-buddy groupies was embarrassing, but calling us a mistake...That just about kills me.

"Ignore him," Gage murmurs, leaning in so no one can hear. "You hurt him, yes, but now he's just being spiteful."

"I deserve it," I admit, trying to wipe my tears before anyone else notices.

His glassy eyes meet mine—because he's high...he's always high—and he shakes his head. "No, you don't."

"Aren't you the woman who sexually assaulted Sam York?" Adrianne says, making my head jerk up.

"Excuse me?" I ask in shock as the limo turns quiet, everyone stopping their chatter to listen to us.

"I thought you looked familiar." She eyes me up and down with disdain. "Your face is all over the internet as the woman who made a fool out of herself with Sam."

"That's not what—" Layla begins, but I shake my head to stop her. She's five months pregnant, and the last thing she needs is the stress from coming to my rescue.

"It's fine. I was taught to never defend a lie, and I'm not going to defend myself to her or anyone else." I jut my chin out, hoping to display the confidence I don't feel.

At that moment, the limo stops, and the door is opened. Everyone edges out, leaving Gage and me for last. I take a moment to calm myself before we get out and then put my arm through his, willing myself to make it through the night.

The rest of the evening goes smoothly. The guys win in almost every category they were nominated in, and their performance is on point. They're so talented, and despite how much Braxton's hurt me, I'm so proud of them. They've followed their passion, and it's paid off. The guys are all smiles when they return to their seats after performing, and everyone around them congratulates them while I sit in my seat watching, feeling like an outsider as my thoughts go back to six years ago, before everything went to shit.

"Condo or mansion?"

I roll my eyes. "A regular-sized house."

Braxton rolls onto his back, annoyed that I'm not playing along. "Mercedes or BMW?"

"I don't know." I laugh. "Something to tow our three kids around in."

"You want three kids?" he asks, propping himself up on his hand

and elbow.

"Yeah, I'm thinking two boys and a girl. The girl last so her brothers can protect her."

"I like that. A little girl with blond hair and gray eyes like you." He runs his fingers through my hair that's splayed out around me. We're lying on a blanket in the grass in the middle of Central Park. Today was senior skip day, but instead of going to the beach with everyone else, I packed us a picnic basket and took Braxton out on a surprise date.

"Beach house or ski cabin?"

I shake my head and push his chest playfully. "It doesn't matter as long as I'm with you. I don't care about what car I drive, or how big our house is, or where we vacation. I just want to be happy and be loved by you."

"And you are," he says, touching our tattoos together. "Forever. But our band is going to blow up, and when we do, I'm going to make sure you have everything you could ever want."

"Just you," I insist. "I just want you and me...and a home," I add at the last second. "I want us to have a home that's filled with love."

Braxton nods in understanding, knowing how much I feel like an outsider in my own home, like I don't belong there.

"We'll have that," he promises. "And more. It's going to be fucking awesome. The guys and I will record our album, and then when it blows up, we'll go on tour. You'll come sometimes, right? Join me in different states."

The solemn look in his eyes tells me that even though he's been playing around, he's also serious, so instead of rolling my eyes or laughing, I go along with it. "I will. When I don't have classes, I'll join you."

This makes him smile. "I can't wait." He rolls onto his back again and tucks his arms under his head, staring up at the sky. "I was watching the Billboards the other night, and I just kept thinking, one day that'll be us. The guys and I will be on that stage accepting our award, and you'll be in the audience, cheering me on. And then..." He jumps up and hovers over me, his strong arms caging me in, not caring that we're in a public place. "I'm gonna steal that award and put it next to us in bed while I make love to you in our expensive-ass suite that we'll be able to afford because we'll be rich."

I can't help but laugh at the picture he's painted. "I can't wait," I tell him. "I've always wanted to have sex with a Billboard Award."

I've made sure to watch every award show they've attended, and even though Braxton isn't aware and wouldn't care, I was cheering him on from wherever I was—so damn proud of him for accomplishing his dreams—and wishing I were there with him, wanting the life we talked about and hating myself for being the reason we'd never have it.

After the award show is over, the guys are interviewed, and then we head to the after-party. Gage finds some guys he knows and takes off somewhere I'm sure to get high—or in his case, keep it going. Not wanting to play the third wheel with Camden and Layla, I head out to the back of the monstrous mansion to check out the pool.

I'm turning the corner when I run straight into Sam York.

"Shit, I'm so—" His words are cut off when he realizes it's me. "Well, well, well, if it isn't my cock tease ex-publicist." He smirks, eyeing me up and down. When his eyes meet mine, I can see he's already blitzed out. The guy could seriously put Gage's drug problem to shame.

"Excuse me," I say, attempting to go around him. Only he sticks his hand out before I can get away, stopping me in my tracks. He backs me up against the wall, and I glance around, wishing I would've stayed inside. It's dark out here, and there are no witnesses. I can scream, but I doubt anyone will hear over the loud music.

"You know, it would be easy for me to fix the problem you created for yourself," Sam says, his voice dripping with slime. "Make it all go away." He runs his hand down the side of my body and I shudder in response, hating his touch on me.

Of course, he mistakes my response for liking it and smiles cockily. "What do you say, baby? Wanna convince me to remember the situation differently? I bet your warm, wet mouth can convince me of anything..."

"Get your fucking hands off her."

I hear him before I see him, but I would recognize his deep, gruff voice anywhere. Braxton grabs Sam by the back of his suit and yanks him off me, slamming him against the wall. "Don't ever touch her again. You hear me?"

"What the hell, man? I don't know what your problem is, but she was coming onto me."

"Yeah, that shit might work with the dumbasses who like to kiss your ass, but I know better, and I heard what you were saying. Now, unless you want your pretty boy face to end up all mangled and fucked up, I suggest you walk away. And if I ever hear you speak Kaylee's name again, I'll be coming for you. Got it?"

"What-the fuck-ever." Sam shoves Braxton back. "The bitch is a fucking cock tease anyway. You want her? Good fucking luck." He adjusts his lapels and stalks off, leaving Braxton and me alone.

"You okay?" Braxton asks once he's gone.

His voice is soft, reminding me of the guy I once knew, and all I want is to run into his arms and beg him to hold me so I can inhale his comforting scent. But I lost that right six years ago, so instead, I simply nod. "Yeah, I didn't know he was out here. I was coming to get some air."

"You don't have to explain yourself to me." His tone is back to being cold and distant, and I already miss the warmth from a moment ago.

"I know, but..." I clear my throat and step toward him. "Thank you. You didn't have to do that."

"Yeah, well..." He shrugs and steps around me. "The only person who has the right to make your life hell is me."

I open my mouth to say something—what, I don't know—but before I can put the words together, Adrianne appears.

"There you are," she says, sauntering over. She wraps her arm around Braxton and eyes me curiously. "Everything okay here?"

"Yeah," he says. "I need a drink." Then he glances at me. "You should go back to the hotel. You don't belong here." And with that, he turns his back on me and walks off without once looking back, reminding me that despite him saving me, he still hates me and probably always will.

I need to talk to you.

It's important.

It's about your father.

Kaylee, please call me ASAP.

I STARE AT THE SLEW OF TEXTS FROM MY AUNT, KNOWING WHAT SHE'S GOING TO SAY. I've been waiting for this day for years. Honestly, I'm surprised he lasted this long. Your body can only take so much before it finally shuts down, after all. And my dad's body has taken too much.

I change out of my dress and into something more comfortable and then head out of the hotel and down the Strip. I call my aunt on the way, and she confirms what I already knew. My dad is dead from liver failure. There won't be a funeral because it would be a waste of money. It would be expensive, and nobody would go anyway. She only found out because she's his emergency contact. The hospital called to inform her. He was found without any clothes on in an alley. Some other homeless people must've found him and taken his clothes. Dead people don't need clothes after all.

"A shot of JD, please," I tell the bartender. I've ended up in a trashy, hole-in-the-wall bar, but that suits me just fine. I wasn't looking for anywhere flashy, just somewhere I could drown myself in the alcohol for a little bit.

The bartender comes back with my drink, and I down it in one go, asking for another and then another. I lose track of how many shots I've had, but when I see Braxton taking a seat next to me, I assume I've had so much I'm seeing shit.

"Another shot!" I yell to the bartender.

"You sure that's the best way to mourn a man who lost his

life to alcohol and drugs?"

I glare at Braxton and throw back my shot, slamming it on the bar top. "What better way to honor him than to get lost in the only thing he ever truly loved?"

I expect Braxton to argue, but he doesn't. I'm not sure what he's doing here or how he found me, but I'm guessing someone told him about my dad.

"Did you need something?" I ask him as the bartender places another shot in front of me.

"Nope," he says, then proceeds to order a Jack and Coke.

We sit next to each other for several minutes, drinking, neither of us saying a word. I don't know what to think or what to say. I have so many thoughts running through my head, and I can't make sense of any of them. Which is why I came out to drink. But now, with Braxton sitting next to me, I almost wish I were sober.

My phone buzzes in my pocket for the millionth time, and I pull it out, finding several missed calls and texts from Layla, my mom, and my aunt. All asking if I'm okay and to call them.

"Layla send you?" I finally ask, figuring she probably wanted to go after me herself, but Camden wouldn't let her since she's several months pregnant and Vegas isn't the safest place at night.

"Draw the short straw?" I add with a humorless laugh. When Braxton doesn't answer, I down another shot and glance over at him. He's still in the same outfit he wore tonight—an all-black suit sans tie—and he looks so damn good, it almost hurts to look at him. "I don't need you here. You can let Layla know I'm fine, and I'll be on the bus, ready to go on time. I'm sure Adrianne is waiting for you."

I slide off the stool, stopping for a second when the room spins, and then make my way onto the dance floor, where people are dancing to an upbeat song. I join in, getting lost in the music and making it a point not to look for Braxton. The alcohol runs through my system, numbing my body and mind, and I sway to the beat, letting myself go for the first time in a long time.

At least that's what I think I'm doing. Only my head is running, and my thoughts are all over the place. I don't realize I'm close to losing my shit until a pair of strong hands grips my hips and spins me around. My eyes meet Braxton's for a quick beat before he pulls me against him. My head rests against his chest, and I inhale his comforting scent. And then I let go, sobbing into his shirt while he holds me tight as I mourn the father I lost a long time ago. The man I used to look up to and have spent years loving and hating and missing.

In my moment of weakness, Braxton becomes my strength, silently holding me together. At some point, my legs give out, and he lifts me into his arms, carrying me out of the bar and down the street while I continue to cry into his neck, holding him like he's my only lifeline. I vaguely hear him talking to someone, and then we're in the hotel room in his bed, and he's still holding me.

"Shh, it's okay," he murmurs as he rubs circles on my back, trying to calm me. But I can't stop crying. I've worked myself up, and I can't control it—the sobs, the hiccups, the lack of breath. It's all become too much to handle. Everything is a mess. Nothing is going right. I have no one, and I've never felt so alone in my life. And I only have myself to blame.

"I'm sorry," I mutter into Braxton's chest. "I'm so, so sorry."

Now probably isn't the best time to finally apologize, but I can't help it. For years, my dad hurt me and never once apologized. He did whatever he wanted to do and hurt whoever he wanted to hurt without any remorse. And I don't want to be him. I hurt Braxton, and I need him to know how sorry I am.

He places a kiss on my forehead, and I sigh into him, relaxing for the first time. My eyes flutter open, and I find him staring at me. After everything I've done, it's him who's here for me, holding me and making sure I'm okay. I don't deserve him or his compassion, but I don't have it in me to push him away. I've spent six years missing his touch, his love, wishing for a do-over. I know I'm not getting one, and come tomorrow, it'll be as if this never happened. But tonight, I'm going to close my eyes and pretend that all is right in my world. I'll deal with reality tomorrow.

Thirteen

Braxton

IT'S BEEN TWO DAYS SINCE KAYLEE'S DAD DIED. SINCE HER AUNT CALLED LAYLA concerned and I offered to find her, ignoring the looks everyone gave me. I probably should've been the last person to comfort Kaylee, but when I heard about her dad, all the times she spoke about him came back to me, and I needed to make sure she was okay. Her dad was always a hard issue for her. She loved him, but he wasn't capable of loving anything other than the numbness he craved. I found her grieving, drinking her weight in alcohol, and I put all our shit aside to be there for her.

While she cried and I held her, I imagined us together—her in my bed, in my arms—and I knew once reality hit, it would hurt all over again, but I couldn't stop myself. She's spent two days in my arms, crying, mourning, lost in herself, and I've spent two days soaking her in, rememorizing her scent, the softness of her body. Sometimes, I just want to say fuck it and forgive her so

I can be with her because as much as I hate her, I still love her.

But that isn't what she wanted. If it was, when she cheated, she would've asked for forgiveness. She would've begged and pleaded and apologized. She wouldn't have let me walk away. She wouldn't have gone six goddamn years without saying a word to me.

And then it happened. The moment I imagined over and over again. She apologized. For cheating? For hurting me? I don't know. I guess it's one and the same anyway. I always thought when she finally did say she was sorry, I'd tell her to go fuck herself, but at that moment, all I could do was forgive her. Because the truth is, I'd probably forgive her for anything, and that's not a good thing. But it doesn't change the facts.

"Hey," Kaylee chokes out, looking up at me as if she's just now realizing, after two days, she's lying in my bed. We were supposed to fly to San Jose yesterday, but Camden insisted we stay for Kaylee since we don't have a show until tomorrow night. We had a radio interview to do, but Camden handled it over the phone so we wouldn't have to cancel.

"Hey." On impulse, I tuck several strands of her blond hair behind her ear and then palm the side of her face. She leans into my touch and flutters her eyes closed, sighing contently. I wish we could stay like this, suspended in time, but reality is waiting for us outside. As if needing to remind me, my phone buzzes on the nightstand. I remove my hand from Kaylee's face and check it.

Happy Birthday, son! See you tonight at Henry's... 7:00.

For a moment, I consider canceling just so I can stay in bed with Kaylee a little longer, but I stop myself. My dad's been there for me when Kaylee wasn't. When I was hurt and struggling, he had my back. No matter where we are, he always meets me for my birthday, and I'm not going to choose her over him.

"We have to get going," I say, pulling back and climbing off the bed. I reply to my dad, thanking him and confirming I'll see him tonight, and then go into the bathroom to take a shower and escape the temptation lying in my bed. When I get out, she's gone. The buses are waiting for us, and I go straight to mine, not stopping to see if she made it on hers okay. It's not my problem, and I need to distance myself. She's hurting, and I feel for her, but I can't let her back in. I just fucking can't.

"Hey, man!" Declan pulls me into a hug. "Happy Birthday."

"Thanks. You guys coming to dinner tonight?"

"Of course," Camden says, giving me a one-armed hug.

The drive to San Jose is long as fuck, but I use the time to get caught up on my sleep since I've been up the past couple of days making sure Kaylee was okay. The guys don't mention her, and I don't bring her up. Nothing's changed between us, so there's no point in discussing it.

When we arrive, we get checked in to our hotel since we'll be here for a couple of days. We have shows the next two nights, and then we'll be heading to Denver.

"Are you inviting Kaylee to dinner?" Camden asks as we walk downstairs. It's always been just the four of us and my dad—not even Jill goes, and she's been our tour manager for every tour—so I know it's his way of asking what's going on with us.

"No," I say before we get into the SUV. Simon, one of the bodyguards we take almost everywhere with us, drives us to the restaurant and drops us off at the front. My dad is already seated, so we head straight back. When he sees me, he stands and gives me a hug.

"I can't believe you're twenty-four years old," he says. "I can still remember when you and Camden were twelve, singing karaoke to Nickelback. Now look at you guys."

Camden chuckles and shrugs. "Eh, we're still singing karaoke. Just our own songs and on a bigger stage."

"I saw all your shows are completely sold out," Dad says, pride in his tone. He's always supported us and encouraged me to follow my dreams. While some parents would view their kid being in a rock band as a bad thing, I'm lucky that my dad never saw it like that. All he ever wanted was for me to put my dreams and goals and passions first.

"Yeah, we're damn lucky," Declan says with a smile. "I think a few dates even got added."

My phone buzzes, and I glance at it even though I know it's not Kaylee. She hasn't contacted me in years, and I doubt she has my number. Pulling up my messages, I send a quick text to Jill, asking her to check on Kaylee. Losing her dad hit her hard, and she doesn't have anyone on the tour she can lean on. Layla is back in New York, and her mom couldn't give a shit about her dad—or how his death is affecting her daughter. She's too busy living her perfect life and pretending he never existed.

"Everything okay?" Dad asks.

"Yeah, Kaylee's dad passed away a couple of days ago. Just making sure she's okay."

I regret the words as soon as I say them, but it's too late to take them back.

"Do not let her back in," Dad warns. "The last thing you need is a woman coming between you and your future."

"Some women are worth it," Camden says, taking my dad's comment personally.

"You're still young," Dad says. "Just make sure you think twice before you make any rash decisions. Your music should come first. Women come and go."

"I beg to differ," Camden replies, his jaw ticking in anger. "Layla is forever, and I'll always put her first."

"Ahead of your friends? Your band?" Dad shakes his head as if he can't fathom such a thought.

"Luckily, I'll never be put in the position of having to choose," Camden remarks. "We have each other's backs and make decisions as a group. Like our decision to move back to New York. The guys—"

"New York?" Dad barks, cutting Camden off. "I thought that was temporary."

"It's where Layla lives..."

"And Kaylee," Dad points out, glaring at me.

I sigh, not bothering to argue because clearly, this isn't about me. It's about him and his fear of me ending up like him. Despite how he sounds, I know he means well and is coming from a good place. When I got on the plane to LA after everything went down, he told me countless times how proud he was of me for choosing my future. But what he didn't get—or refused to understand—was that I didn't *choose* it. I was left with no choice. *Kaylee* made the decision for me—for us—when she cheated on me.

"Look, Michael," Declan says, jumping in. "Tonight is about

Brax's birthday, so how about we just focus on that."

Dad nods, thankfully dropping it, and the rest of dinner goes smoothly. The guys are assholes and have people come out and sing "Happy Birthday." After we've eaten the dessert and my dad's paid the bill—he always insists on it when we meet up—the guys and I head to a club in the area to get a drink. I invited my dad, but he said he'd leave the partying to us "kids." He has an early morning flight out and will never wake up on time if he isn't in bed before midnight.

When we arrive at the club, we're taken straight back to VIP, and Gage orders us a bottle. The women flock to us like they always do, and I try to get into it, but for some reason, I'm just not feeling it at all. So after we toast to my birthday, we go back to the hotel.

As we're walking inside, I notice Kaylee coming out of the elevator. She's dressed in gray sweats and a matching hoodie. She's staring down at her phone, so she doesn't see us. I should keep walking, but something pulls me toward her instead. I tell myself I just want to make sure she's okay. Her dad only died a couple of days ago, and Jill never got back to me.

The guys tell me they'll see me later and get on the elevator. If they saw her or know that I'm going to talk to her, they don't say anything.

I'm about to call her name and go after her, but what I see stops me in my place, leaving me confused as fuck and speechless. My dad approaches Kaylee and guides her over to a secluded corner of the hotel. I walk around the outer perimeter, hiding behind the fake trees so I can get close enough to hear. My dad never cared for Kaylee while we were dating, and once she cheated, he made his feelings of disdain abundantly clear, so for them to be meeting up makes no sense at all.

"That's not how this was supposed to go down!" my dad hisses. "You were supposed to let him go, not follow him all over the damn country."

The fuck?

"I didn't plan this. But things happened, and the band... They're my last chance if I want to save my career before it's even started." Kaylee huffs and crosses her arms over her chest. "I didn't even want to be on that damn tour. I only took the job to get my foot in the door, and instead, I was shot in the foot. Now I'm just trying to save my ass. Camden offered me a lifeline, and I took it."

"You're so damn selfish. Just like every other woman," my dad says.

"That's not fair! I haven't even spoken to Braxton since that night." She turns slightly, and I catch a glint of liquid in her eyes. She's tearing up... but why? None of this makes any sense. I hear what they're saying, but I can't help thinking that I'm missing a vital piece.

"What will it take?" my dad asks, standing up straight. "Name your price. What will it take for you to walk away and never look back? Whatever they're paying you, I'll double it."

What the hell? My dad makes a good living, but why would he offer that? All because my ex-girlfriend is our publicist? I know he hates her, but this doesn't make any sense.

"You know what? Fuck you!" Kaylee cries. "I'm not the damn problem here. I did as you said, and he left like you wanted, but he's not happy. Can't you see that? He drinks and smokes and sleeps around. Sure, he has money, but he's not *happy*," Kaylee chokes out. "Don't you want that for him?"

"Don't you fucking go there." My dad steps toward Kaylee, and she takes a step back. My hackles rise, not liking the way he's cornering her. "My son is happy. Don't you dare ruin his future because you're jealous. You did the right thing, now do it again, and walk the hell away."

"And what if I can't?" she asks, jutting out her chin. "What if I want to tell him the truth?"

"Then you're more stupid than I thought," my dad says, "because he's never going to forgive you."

"Maybe... maybe not. But at least he'll know the truth."

"He doesn't need the truth! What he needs is for you to leave him the fuck alone."

"Actually, I would like to know the truth," I say, stepping out from where I've been hiding.

"Brax," Kaylee breathes, her eyes going wide in shock.

"Son... I thought you were going out for your birthday."

"Changed my mind." I shrug. "Now, tell me." I lock eyes with Kaylee. "What the hell is going on?"

"I can explain," Kaylee says.

"Please do."

"Can we go somewhere and talk?" Her eyes flit between my dad and me.

"Nah." I shake my head. "You can just say it right here."

"Okay..." She nods slowly as if she's psyching herself up.

"Braxton, listen—" My dad starts to cut in, but my glare shuts him up.

"Kaylee, talk. Now."

"I never cheated on you," she blurts out, her words making me take a step back. Because what in the actual fuck?

"What in the hell are you talking about?" I bark.

"You weren't going to go to LA, and I didn't want to be the reason you gave up your music career, so I lied." Tears fill her lids and spill over as she looks at me, silently begging me to understand. "I knew you wouldn't leave unless I pushed you away... did something unforgivable."

"So you cheated on me."

"But I didn't. I had Jack take the pictures and post them, so you would think I did. I couldn't do it, and he didn't care because everyone thought we did it anyway. So he took it as a win."

"Why the fuck would you do that?" I mean, I know why. I heard what she said, but I don't understand. That's not the kind of person she was back then... to purposely hurt me. If I hadn't seen the pictures with my own eyes, I wouldn't have believed she cheated.

And then it clicks. "You did this." I look at my dad, who's been quiet this entire time since she started confessing. "You told her to do this."

"I didn't tell her to cheat on you... or pretend or whatever." He waves his hand in the air like there's an annoying fly he can't get rid of. "But I did tell her to let you go." He steps over to me and puts his hand on my shoulder. "I did it for you, son. Because I love you. I didn't want you to make the same mistakes I made. You would've regretted not going to LA to be a part of the band. Look at the success you've achieved. You would've given it all up for *her*."

"That wasn't your choice to make." My fists are clenched at

my sides, my body vibrating in anger. Everything I thought I knew was a fucking lie. I was manipulated, tricked...

"You were young and not thinking clearly," my dad says like he's talking to a child. "I had to do what was best for you."

"Fuck that!" I bark. "You knew how much I loved her. She was young and impressionable, and you used that to your advantage. You knew she would do anything to make sure I was happy because I would've done the same for her."

"Women come—"

"No." I step into his face, cutting him off. "Don't you fucking say it. You need to go now. I need time to think. I can't believe you did this."

"Braxton, please..."

"Go!"

With a sigh, Dad does as I demand and walks away, leaving Kaylee and me alone. Realizing we've made a scene, I head to the elevators, and she follows. The ride up is filled with a silent, stifling tension. I can tell she wants to say something, but she keeps her mouth shut, which is good since I have a million thoughts whirring around in my head, and I don't know where to go from here.

When we get up to her room, she stands in the corner, remaining quiet while I pace back and forth, trying to figure out what to say first. When my anger and frustration finally boil over, I stop and lock eyes with her, settling on the one thought that keeps circling around in my head. "You fucked it all up. You should've come to me and talked to me. Instead, you fucked everything up."

I stare at the woman who was my entire world, wanting to

shake her, wanting her to make me understand why she would do this to me... to us. She didn't have the right to make that decision for me. I loved her and wanted to spend my life with her. And she pushed me away.

"You wouldn't have listened," she whispers, her voice clogged with emotion. "You wouldn't have gone to LA."

"That's not how relationships work!" I pick up a vase and throw it against the wall, making it shatter into pieces. Kaylee jumps in fear, but I don't have it in me to care. The anger and betrayal running through my body has nowhere to go. Somehow, this feels worse than her cheating. Because at least then there was a valid reason we broke up and went our separate ways. Why I spent the past several years hating her, missing her, forcing myself to live without her.

"Braxton," she cries, tears pouring down her cheeks. "I'm sorry."

"You're sorry?" I scoff. "*Sorry?* Fuck being sorry. We were supposed to be a goddamn team. Trust each other!"

"I know, I know," she sobs. "But I just... I didn't want to be the reason you lost everything."

"That's what you don't get," I say, walking over to her. I palm her cheek reverently, needing to feel her. She's the best and worst addiction I've ever had. "You were my everything, and because of your choices, I lost every-fucking-thing."

"So where does that leave us?" she asks, her voice shaky.

I back up, dropping my hand, needing to distance myself from her. "First, I didn't trust you because you cheated. Now, I don't trust you because you lied and hid shit from me." I sigh, mentally and emotionally exhausted. "Guess that leaves us right where we were… absolutely fucking nowhere."

And with that, I turn my back on the only girl I've ever loved and walk away.

Fourteen

Kaylee

"WHERE'S BRAXTON?" I SEARCH THE DRESSING ROOM. "HAVE YOU SEEN HIM?"

The guys shake their heads while they quickly change into clean shirts. When they're on stage, they sweat, and by the end of the show, they're soaked. So before they head to meet the fans for the meet and greet, they always change. But Braxton is nowhere to be found, which is a problem since the winner of the radio contest picked to meet him.

"Dammit, I need to find him," I mutter, racing out of the room and down the hall in search of him. I ask everyone I come in contact with if they've seen him, and of course, nobody has. Honestly, even if they had, I doubt they'd tell me. I'm the bitch who broke his heart, and he's the guy who signs their paychecks. Well, technically the label does, but you get my point.

It's been several days since Braxton found out I didn't cheat, and while I hate to admit it, Michael was right. He's pissed. I mean, I knew he wouldn't be happy that I lied, but I thought he'd at least be less mad that I didn't actually cheat. Nope. If anything, he's madder.

When it's clear I'm not going to find him, I head back to where the meet and greet is being held so I can make up a lie and give the girl who won extra gifts in hope she won't be too upset that she won't be meeting Braxton.

Declan, Camden, and Gage are accommodating and spend a little extra time with her to make up for their fourth bandmate being a dick. Once we get through them taking pictures with everyone, we head back to the hotel since they have another show tomorrow night.

"Is he going to miss the meet and greets for the rest of the tour?" I ask. He's missed every one since the night he found out I didn't cheat on him. Aside from him showing up to perform, he hasn't been around at all. He doesn't even go out.

"He just needs time," Camden says. "He spent years thinking you cheated, and that gave him a reason to hate you. Now... it's all just fucked up." He blows out a harsh breath.

"Maybe I should leave the tour," I suggest, hating that Braxton is hiding out on his own tour because of me. The morning after everything went down, I heard him tell the guys he wanted me off the tour, but Camden told him it wasn't happening.

The guys don't argue, and I know it's because they're stuck between a rock and a hard place. They've told me countless times I'm doing a good job at keeping everything organized and promoting the hell out of this tour. But I'm also the woman who hurt their best friend.

We arrive at the hotel and go our separate ways. Since they

don't need to do anything in the morning, we're all off until tomorrow afternoon for the sound check. Needing to clear my head, I change into my bathing suit and cover-up and head up to the private indoor pool that's only available to the band. After undressing and dropping my towel onto a nearby chair, I dive in and swim laps while I think about what I need to do.

As much as I need this job, it's not fair to Braxton that I stay. I was already selfish enough, between lying to him and taking this job. He's been hurt so much. I was stupid to think I'd tell him the truth, and he'd magically forgive me.

A movement out of the corner of my eye stops me in the water, and I see Braxton. Dressed in a pair of board shorts and T-shirt, he's standing against the pillar watching me.

"Sorry," I say, swimming to the steps to get out. "I didn't know you'd be using the pool tonight."

"You don't have to leave on my account."

"It's fine." I climb out and grab my towel, drying my hair and body off. When I look up, Braxton's standing right in front of me, so close I can smell the fresh scent of the cologne I originally bought him.

"Camden said you suggested you leave the tour."

"I did." I flip my hair up and wrap it in the towel so it's not dripping everywhere.

"I think that would be for the best."

My heart drops, and I nod, refusing to make eye contact with him. I know I set all of this in motion, but it doesn't mean I'm not hurt by it. Pushing Braxton away was the hardest thing I've ever had to do. I threw up for hours afterward and spent days crying, my heart feeling as though I reached into my chest and ripped it out myself. There were times I wanted to run to him and tell him the truth, and moments I didn't think I could move forward without him. But I watched as the band took off, and even though it hurt like hell, I thought deep down I did the right thing. And that's what got me through every day.

"I understand," I tell him as I reach for my cover-up to put it back on since I'm only in a tiny bikini. As I'm finding the sleeves, a hand pulls it away, and I'm forced to look at him, confused.

"What the fuck is this?" he breathes, his fingers wrapping around... *Oh, shit.* I forgot to take it off. "You still have this?"

He fingers the promise ring he gave me all those years ago, and I nod robotically, praying he doesn't rip it from my neck. I took it off the day he left since I didn't deserve to wear it, but I put it on a chain and have been wearing it around my neck ever since.

"Why do you still have this?" he asks, his eyes meeting mine.

"Because you gave it to me."

"And then you cheated." He shakes his head, growling under his breath in frustration. "Dammit, Kaylee. Why did you do it?" He tugs on the ends of his hair, his gaze pleading with me to give him the right answer. But I don't know what he wants or needs to hear. What will make this better.

"I didn't cheat—"

"Lie! Why the fuck did you *lie*?" he asks, his voice raspy and filled with so much emotion that all I want to do is wrap my arms around him and hold him tight.

"I thought I was doing the right thing." That's the only explanation I have because despite it sounding like a cop-out, it's the truth. In my head and heart, I thought I was doing what was best for Braxton and his future.

"You wouldn't have left." Traitorous tears fill my eyes, but I quickly blink them away.

Braxton grips my chin, raising my face to look at him, and the look of hurt in his eyes damn near sends me to my knees. I would do anything to make this right, but there's nothing I can do. The damage has already been done.

"It wasn't your choice to make."

"But your choice was because of me." I palm his hand that's holding my face. "I couldn't let you give it all up for me. What if we didn't work out? What if you regretted it? I know you don't agree with it, and maybe your dad and I handled it wrong, but I did it because I loved you," I choke out. "I still love you." I step closer. "I never stopped loving you."

He steps back slightly, breaking our connection, then his fingers go back to the ring, stroking it gently. "It could've been amazing." He looks at me, his hazel eyes so intense, it's as if they're reaching deep into me and squeezing my soul. "You and me... we could've had everything." He says the words as if they each were once living and are now dead. As if he's mourning the loss of the idea. "All you had to do was believe in us the way I did. I would've done anything for you, *for us*. All I wanted was forever."

He drops his hand and walks away, leaving me staring after him, wishing I would've made so many different choices. Once I know he's gone, I drop into the chair and cry. I hate how often I cry, but I can't help it. It all just hurts so damn badly.

I spend the next several minutes balled up, letting out my

emotions, and once I'm all cried out, I wipe my face and head to my room to pack. It's the least I can do so Braxton isn't in pain having to see me every day.

After booking a flight home for tomorrow morning, I go down to the bar, needing a drink. I find Gage sitting there, drinking straight from the bottle.

"Mind if I join you?" I ask, sliding onto the seat next to him

His eyes meet mine, and I notice they're bloodshot and puffy. *Has he been crying?*

"Hey." I place a hand on his forearm. "Are you okay?"

He tilts the bottle back, downing way too much alcohol, and then without looking at me, he says, "It's been six years... today."

He doesn't have to say anything else. There's only one thing he could be referring to, the only thing that would have him sitting alone in a bar, drinking himself into oblivion, and I feel like shit for not remembering the date.

Since nothing can be said, I don't bother talking, and instead, I sit next to Gage quietly while he drinks more liquor than can be good for his liver. When he's finally so wasted that he can barely keep his eyes open, I text Camden and Declan so they can help bring him up to his room.

"I'm worried about him," I say to them once they've delivered Gage to his room. "It's been six years, and every day, he's getting worse. Drinking more, smoking more. And we all know he's doing other shit behind closed doors."

"I know," Camden says with a sigh. "I've talked to him about going to rehab, but he's not having it."

"Well, maybe you need to make him."

"It doesn't work like that," Declan says. "We can convince

him to go, but once he's there, he can check himself out. He has to want to go, and he's not there yet."

"So you're just going to pretend he's fine? For how long?" When the guys don't say anything, I sigh and walk to the door. "He needs you. You may think you're being his friend, but you're only enabling him. And at the rate he's going, we'll be burying him right next to Tori."

BUZZ. BUZZ. BUZZ.

I wake to the sound of my phone going off on the nightstand. It's Easton. When I see it's only five in the morning, I know something is wrong. That's the only reason he'd be calling me this early.

"Hello."

"Sorry to wake you. It's eight in the morning here."

"It's okay."

"We have a problem."

I should probably tell him that I'm leaving, and my flight is scheduled for this morning, but if it's about the band, I'll do everything in my power to help fix whatever I can as long as they'll let me help.

"A woman posted on social media that she's pregnant with Braxton's baby. She hasn't made any demands, but they never do on social media. They first post to get a feeler out there."

While my head wraps around what Easton's just said—a woman is possibly carrying Braxton's baby—my heart squeezes in my chest as I imagine a completely different scenario.

Braxton and me getting married.

Buying a home together.

Finding out we're expecting a baby.

Filling our home with lots of babies and love...

"What do you need me to do?" I ask, shaking my thoughts from my head. All of those dreams went up in smoke the second I pushed him away, so daydreaming about the what-ifs will only make it hurt that much worse.

"Braxton isn't answering his phone. I need you to find him and ask him if he was with her. I'll send you the info and her picture. Keep him from getting online, please. His initial response will be to lash out at her, which we don't want him to do. Once we know whether her accusation is plausible, we'll go from there."

We hang up, and I quickly shower and get dressed. It's still early, so I can handle this before I need to get going. Technically, this is still my job since I haven't been fired yet. I'd imagine if I was, Easton wouldn't have called me, or he would've at least let me know.

I find Braxton in his bed alone and sit on the edge, watching him for a few seconds before I wake him up. He looks so calm in his sleep, and I would give anything to be lying in bed with him, snuggling against his warm, hard body. When we were together, the times we got to spend the night together were few and far between, but those were some of the best nights of my life. Not just because of the sex, even though that was damn good, but because I always felt safe and at home in the comfort of his arms.

I glance over at the nightstand and see the journal I gave him. Despite the way he feels about me, I love that he still uses it to write his words in—even if some of those words are written with the intent to hurt me. It makes me think that in some way, even though I hurt him, he still cares about me the way I care about him. Otherwise, wouldn't he have thrown it away and gotten a new one that wouldn't make him think of me?

When I shake him, he turns over, and his eyes meet mine in confusion.

"What are you doing?" he asks, his voice gruff from sleep.

"We need to talk." I pull up the social media account that Easton sent over and click on a picture of a beautiful woman. "Recognize her?"

Braxton barely gives her a once-over. "Yeah... so?"

"She's claiming to be pregnant—"

"Good for her..."

"—with your baby."

"Not possible," he says matter-of-factly.

"Condoms break."

"True." He slides up the bed, and the blanket falls, exposing his naked, muscular, tattooed chest and six-pack abs. I can't help but look. It's been a long time since I've seen him up close, and when we were together, he was still more boy than man. Now... he's all fucking man.

"Like what you see?"

My eyes ascend to his face and find him smirking. He lifts his arms, crossing them behind his head, and I swallow down a groan.

"You've gotten a lot of tattoos," I say stupidly.

He chuckles, and the sound wraps around me like a warm blanket on a cold night. I can't remember the last time I heard him laugh, and especially not with me.

"She's not pregnant with my kid."

"Huh?" And then I remember what we were talking about. "How do you know? Condoms aren't one-hundred-percent effective. And we don't know how far along she is."

"It's not possible—"

"Braxton..."

"—because I didn't sleep with her."

"What? But you said..."

"I recognize her, yeah. Did we fuck around? Yeah. But I never stuck my dick in her." His tongue darts across the seam of his lips, and flashbacks of how well he used that tongue on me hit me hard.

"Maybe you were too high or drunk to remember."

"Doesn't matter how much I smoke or drink, I always know who I'm sticking my dick into. And I know I haven't stuck my dick into her."

"Maybe—"

"Kaylee," he says, stopping me from finishing my sentence. "I haven't fucked her or anyone in months."

His admission has me rearing back. "Months?"

He nods. "Months."

"But..." I've seen the women in his bed. He even asked me to get him condoms.

"Months," he repeats.

"I don't understand."

"That makes two of us." He throws his blanket off his body

and stands. "Call her bluff. She isn't pregnant with my kid. And then can you order breakfast, please? I'm starved."

He says it so nonchalantly that I can't help but believe him.

BRAXTON WAS RIGHT. AFTER I REACHED OUT TO FIONA—THE WOMAN MAKING THE accusation—and told her that Braxton would gladly do a paternity test once she was seven weeks pregnant, she tried to go around it, saying she wasn't going to risk harming her precious baby. I was expecting this, so I explained science has come a long way, and a noninvasive test can now be done.

She immediately went on alert, saying if he didn't want to be part of the baby's life, he could pay her off.

Could she be any more cliché?

"Actually, he's excited. He's always wanted a baby," I lied. "Once we run the DNA test and get it confirmed, he'll reach out and discuss the custody details."

A few hours later, her account had been deleted, proving what Braxton said was true—he didn't sleep with her—and leaving me with a shit ton of questions I'm dying for the answers to, starting with... Was his dry spell because of me? And if so, what the hell does that mean?

I push my thoughts away, though, because it doesn't matter. It doesn't change anything. In a few hours, I'll be back on the East Coast, looking for a job. As I pull my stuff out of the small closet I was given on the bus I share with several other tour employees, I can't help but think about how off course my life has gone. Six years ago, I was about to graduate high school and had my entire future ahead of me. I was happy and in love and couldn't wait for what was to come. Now, I'm alone and jobless, and I only have myself to blame.

"There you are," a masculine voice says from behind me. Expecting everyone to be at the venue already, I jump, knocking my suitcase to the floor. The entire contents spill out, and I sigh in defeat.

"What are you doing?" Braxton asks, bending to help pick my stuff up.

"I got it." I grab my panties from him and shove them back into my luggage. "Thanks."

"Going somewhere?"

"Flight is for noon." I stand and set the suitcase back on my bunk. It's tight in the hallway, and when I look up, Braxton is close... too close to me. "Did you need something before I go?"

"Easton said you handled that woman like a pro. She disappeared, deleting all her accounts and shit. And the statement you made on my account was worded perfectly. Thanks."

"Of course. It's my job." I reach down to grab my suitcase to zip it up, but Braxton stops me in my place, his fingers wrapping around my bicep.

"I don't want you to leave." His words come out raspy, almost sounding desperate, and I have to force myself not to read too much into them.

"I think we both know my coming on this tour was a mistake."

"Maybe," he says. "But you're here now, and...the band needs you."

My stomach drops at his admittance. *He* doesn't need me. The band does. I wasn't expecting him to say he needs me, but a small part of me was hoping he would.

"We still have more than half of the tour left," he adds. "And next week, we'll be in Florida at the theme parks." His lips quirk into a half-smile, and a flashback from our past hits me hard.

"Paris."

"Why Paris?"

Braxton shrugs, and I roll over to face him, wrapping my arm around his torso. We started this game of "If you could..." months ago, and whenever we're bored, one of us will throw one out there. Mine was, if you could go anywhere in the world, where would you go? *Braxton's answer was Paris.*

"Tell me," I say, kissing his flesh.

His gaze darts to mine, and he clears his throat. "My mom used to say when you can afford to visit the Eiffel Tower, it means you've made it. I was young when she left, but for some reason, I always remember her saying that."

The mention of his mom leaves me momentarily stunned. In the years I've known Braxton, including all the months we've been together, he's never once mentioned his mom. Layla once said Camden told her she left him and his dad years ago. She was some huge actress, but I don't know who she is. I'm assuming she doesn't use the same last name as Braxton's, which is Lutz.

"How about you?" he asks, breaking the silence.

"Florida."

"Florida?" He laughs and rolls us over so he's on top of me. "Why Florida?" He kisses the corner of my mouth, and I shiver in anticipation.

"Specifically, Tampa and Orlando. I've never been to a theme park." I shrug nonchalantly. "My dad always worked too much. And then the accident happened, and my mom didn't have the money. I've always wanted to go to Disney and Universal and Busch Gardens. Ride the roller coasters and take pictures with the princesses."

Braxton chuckles. "We'll go together. You and me. Once we have the money, we'll ride every damn ride there is and take a million pictures."

"And then we'll go to Paris," I add. "Take a picture in front of the Eiffel Tower."

"Damn right, we will," he says, pressing his lips to mine.

"I can't wait."

"Have you been?" Braxton asks, shaking me from my memory.

"Nope. How about you? Make it to Paris yet?" They've been on several tours, some taking them to other countries, so it would make sense.

"Not yet." He glances down at my open suitcase. "Stay on the tour. Come to Florida with us."

"You going to ride all the rides with me?" I half joke.

"Yeah, I will," he says seriously.

"Brax," I breathe. "What does—?"

"I don't know, Kaylee." He cuts me off, knowing what my question is without me finishing it. "I don't fucking know what anything means anymore. All I know is, when Camden said you were leaving, I had to stop you. I don't know what that means or where we stand, but I'm not ready for you to leave this tour yet. So I'm asking you to stay."

Fifteen

Braxton

I ASKED HER TO STAY, AND SHE SAID YES. I DON'T KNOW WHY I DID IT. I'VE SPENT WEEKS wanting her off our tour, and when Camden said she was leaving, I should've felt relieved. Instead, my heart pounded against my rib cage, and without thinking, I went in search of her. I wasn't sure what the hell I was going to say until I saw her standing on the bus, packing her shit, and then the words just slipped out.

Maybe it was finding out that she never cheated, or seeing her wearing my goddamn ring around her neck, or perhaps it was admitting out loud that I haven't had sex since she came back into my life. It could be a combination of all of the above—but I just couldn't let her go... not yet.

"You asked her to stay?" Camden asks, dropping into the seat next to me. We've just finished our show in Tulsa and are about to leave for Atlanta, where we've got two back-to-back shows before we head to Florida. "She said you asked her to stay."

"She didn't cheat on me."

His gaze swings over to me, and I notice Declan glances up from the magazine he's reading. Gage is passed the fuck out from whatever he's on, but he already knows since I told him the other night while we were at the bar getting drunk.

"What do you mean?" Declan asks.

"She lied to push me away. My dad told her if she didn't let me go, she'd be the reason for my future being fucked, and she knew the only way I'd walk away was if she did something fucked up. So she staged it all."

Declan whistles, and Camden curses under his breath. For the past six years, I've made a damn career out of hating Kaylee because of what I thought she did. And yeah, I'm mad as fuck that she lied, but without her having cheated, it's making it really hard to hate her the way I did.

"So what now?"

"No clue." I drop my head back and scrub my eyes. I'm so damn tired. I hate being on tour, and I've spent years fucking and drinking my way through my heartbreak. And now, to find out it's not true. It's like my life, my anger, was all based on a lie.

"You know she still loves you, right?" Declan says.

"Doesn't matter. It's not enough. She pushed me away, and we can't go back. Too much has happened." I slam my fist into the sofa. "I'm just so pissed. She fucked it all up... and for what? Nothing!"

"For us," Camden says. "For Raging Chaos. We wouldn't be the same without you."

I appreciate his words, but... "I'm not the same without her."

Camden's gaze follows over my shoulder, and when I glance back, I find Kaylee standing in the doorway. Based on the look on her face, she heard what was said.

"And I'm not the same without you," she whispers, her tear-filled eyes meeting mine. It's at that moment that nothing else matters. Not our past or the present, or whatever the fuck the future holds. Nothing else matters but Kaylee and me. I need her in ways I've never needed anyone. From the moment she kissed me on the beach, she's owned every part of me—mind, body, and heart. Our souls are entwined. And when she pushed me away, I might've gotten on that plane without looking back, but my heart and soul stayed with her.

"I, um..." She clears her throat. "I have your schedules," she says, walking over with papers in her hands. She gives Declan his, then Camden. She leaves Gage's next to him. When she steps close to me, extending her hand, I catch a whiff of that sweet, intoxicating rose scent, and something in me snaps, just fucking snaps.

Without thinking, I grasp her waist, throw her over my shoulder, and stalk back to the main bedroom in the back of the bus. I ignore Declan and Camden laughing as I slam the door closed and then drop Kaylee onto the center of the king-sized bed.

"What are you doing?" she gasps as I climb up her body until I'm hovering directly above her.

"I'm about to fuck you. We have a sixteen-hour drive, and I'm planning to spend every fucking minute of it inside you, making up for the past six goddamn years I've been without you because of what you did to us. You got a problem with that?"

"I..." She swallows thickly. "I thought you were mad at me."

"I am," I growl, tugging on her hair so she's forced to look at me. "You fucked everything up." But I also miss the hell out of her, and I need her. I wasn't lying when I said she was the worst and best addiction. I've been craving her for six damn years, and I need my fix.

"I did it for you," she whispers.

"You should've come to me."

"We can't do this. I said I wouldn't sleep with you while I'm your publicist."

"Fine. Then you're fired." Problem solved.

Before she can argue, my mouth connects with hers in a bruising kiss. Her lips are pillow soft, just as I remember, and she tastes as sweet as the most decadent fucking candy. When I try to deepen the kiss, she bites down on my bottom lip, making me groan. I do it back, nipping at her flesh, and she moans into my mouth.

The chemistry between us was always like sparks flying on the Fourth of July. We were young and wanted each other like mad. But now, as she grinds her center against my hard cock, and I devour her mouth, tasting and caressing her, it's as if something stronger has replaced those pretty fireworks, and with one flick, we'll explode.

I break our kiss and yank her shirt off her body, exposing her powder-blue lacy bra. With her tits spilling out the tops, I take a moment to appreciate the sight in front of me. Her smooth, tanned skin. The freckles scattered sparsely across her shoulders. When she goes into the sun, they become more prominent. She hates them, but I love them—have spent too many hours kissing and counting each one.

A glint catches my eye, and nestled between her perfect tits is the ring—the one I gave her. My mouth goes to where the swells of her breasts meet, and I place an open-mouthed kiss to her flesh, making it a point to kiss the ring as well.

Kaylee sucks in a harsh breath, her legs tightening around me, and I pull one of her cups down, revealing her pale-pink nipple. I swipe my tongue across the tip, and it hardens, creating a point. I wrap my lips around it, sucking it into my mouth, and she arches her back, silently begging for more. When she walked onto the bus and admitted she's not the same without me, I imagined taking her back here and angry fucking the hell out of her, but now that I have her in my bed, all I want to do is reacquaint myself with every inch of her.

Pulling the other cup down, I swirl my tongue around the pointed tip. Kaylee's entire body shivers, reminding me how responsive she is to my touch. After removing her shoes, I unbutton and unzip her pants, pulling them down her thighs. Her underwear is the same color as her bra, and it brings me back to when we were together. She always made sure they were matching. She said if she was ever killed or hurt and had to be undressed, she didn't want to be caught in ugly undergarments. I didn't get it, but I loved that it meant she always looked sexy as hell under her clothes.

"Brax," she breathes, her voice husky. "I need you in me." She reaches up to grab my cock, but I swat her hand away.

"Soon, baby."

I turn my attention back on her, kissing my way down her soft, flat torso until I get to the top of her underwear. With an open-mouthed kiss to the hood of her pussy, I inhale her scent through the thin material. Of course she smells like goddamn roses, making my dick even harder.

"Brax," she groans, wiggling impatiently.

"Patience," I chide. "I've waited six years, and I'm not going to rush it."

I hook the sides of her underwear and drag them down her legs, leaving her completely exposed. Unlike when we were younger and she had curls of blond hair down there, she's now neatly trimmed. I spread her legs and have the perfect view of her pink pussy. It's already glistening with her arousal, so I dip down and lick up her slit, needing her on my tongue.

"Fuck, you taste just how I remembered," I mutter between licks, tasting and smelling her arousal. I push a digit into her tight hole, then two. She rocks against me, trying like hell to get herself off, so I stop. Her pleasure is mine. All mine.

Hooking her legs over my shoulders, I dip my face between her thighs and eat her pussy, licking and sucking, devouring it like it's the first sweet I've had after a six-year diet. I flick her clit softly—just enough so she feels it but not enough to get her off. I work her up higher and higher until she's begging and pleading for her release, and then I give her what she wants. She screams my name as she writhes under me, shaking as she orgasms all over my face and fingers.

I've been with a lot of women over the years, but Kaylee is the only woman I've ever gone down on. Those other women were about losing myself in and getting off. This is intimate, personal, and she's the only person I've ever wanted to be this close to.

When she comes down from her high, she sits up and reaches for my pants. "Now, it's my turn," she says, leaving no room for argument as she pushes me onto my back and tugs my pants and boxer briefs down. When my dick juts out, her eyes go wide.

"You're..." Her gaze flicks from my dick to my face and back to my dick again.

"Pierced? Yeah." I smirk, knowing it's one of her favorite things in a book. When we were together, she'd read raunchy as fuck romance and always said she loved when the guy was pierced. She begged me quite a few times to do it, but it would've meant going weeks without being inside her, and no way was that happening.

She glides her hand gently over my shaft where the piercings are. There are two horizontal bars pierced through the bottom of my shaft. They're not big, just enough to add pleasure to sex.

"Will I be able to feel them through the condom?" she asks curiously, but my mind stops on the word condom. Kaylee and I never used condoms, ever. She was on birth control, and I wanted to feel every part of her. But now, she's implying we're going to use one?

"You don't really think I'm going to use a condom with you, do you?" I ask, taking her hand and tightening it around my dick. I stroke it up and down, showing her that she doesn't have to be gentle. I've had these piercings for years, and unless someone were to tug hard on them, they're good.

"You've been with other women..."

"And you've been with other men. But I've been tested, and I'm clean. And I know damn well you wouldn't risk fucking anyone without a condom but me."

Without giving her a chance to argue, I pull her on top of me to straddle my thighs and then lift her onto my dick. She takes me in, inch by inch, moaning as the piercings rub against her inner walls. When she's completely full, I close my eyes, needing a moment to get my shit together because regardless of all the pussy I've had over the years, nobody, and I mean *nobody*, feels the way Kaylee feels—like motherfucking home.

Her hands rest on my chest, and she starts to move up and down, using me to find her pleasure. I open my eyes, watching as her blond hair curtains around us, and her mouth parts slightly, releasing the sexiest damn moan.

"You're a greedy little thing, aren't you?" I ask as she grinds her pelvis against me, stroking her clit while riding me. With her bra still intact, her tits are trussed up, bouncing up and down in tandem with her movements.

She smiles down at me, not denying it, and I grab the back of her neck, pulling her face to mine for a hard kiss. I fuck her mouth with my tongue while she fucks me. And as we both find our release, I know that despite how fucking mad I am at her for what she's done, for all the years we've lost, there's no one like her, and there never will be. Now I just have to decide what to do with that.

Sixteen

Kaylee

ONE MINUTE, BRAXTON WAS GLARING MY WAY, AND THE NEXT, HE WAS THROWING ME over his shoulder, full-on caveman style. I expected the sex to be selfish and for him to take. God knows I wouldn't have blamed him. What I wasn't expecting was for the old Braxton to appear, the one who always made sure I was taken care of several times before he even considered getting off. Unlike when we were younger, when we were learning our own bodies as well as each other's, he played mine like the strings of his guitar with such expertise, it made every guy I've been with over the years look like amateurs.

I should be resentful that part of the reason he's so fluent in the body language of a woman is because he's been with other women, and I am to an extent, but as he pulled me on top of him and I rode him while he fucked my mouth, I felt it, that spark, that chemistry, and I know he did too. I could see it in his eyes. He can fuck as many women as he wants, but none of them will replace what we have.

"Fuck," Braxton curses under his breath as I climb off him. Without a condom, his cum drips out of me and down my leg. I run to the bathroom that's connected to the bedroom and turn the water on while I go pee. I expect him to stay where he is, so I'm shocked when he joins me in the shower. On the bus I ride, one person can barely fit in the shower, but the bus for the guys is custom built with the two bedrooms, two bathrooms, a kitchen, and a living room all bigger than the average New York apartment.

We're both quiet as we wash our hair and bodies. I don't know what to do or say. The ball is in his court. He's the one who's mad at me. It's not that I'm allowing him to string me along, but I don't know where his head's at, and since it's been six damn years, and so much has happened and come to light, I'm giving him a moment to breathe.

When I go to step around him so I can rinse off, he stops me, pushing me against the wall. One hand slaps the tiles next to my head, and the other squeezes the curve of my hip.

"I hate you," he says, and my stomach drops at those three words.

I close my eyes, unable to look at him while he says whatever it is he needs to say, but when he pinches my chin, forcing me to look at him, I have no choice but to make eye contact with him.

"I hate you," he says again, his eyes alight with silent chaos stirring in his hazel orbs. "I hate that you lied. That you didn't talk to me. I hate that you let me go instead of holding on. That it took six years to learn the truth, and it was only because I overheard you and my dad. That you didn't believe in us. I hate that the moment my mouth was back on yours, that I was back inside you, it felt so damn right..."

His admissions cause me to choke up, and I thank God the water is spraying over us, so he can't see the tears racing down my cheeks.

"I fucking hate that no matter how much I hate you, I still fucking love you." He grabs my chin a bit tighter, and I release the sob I can no longer keep in.

"Fuck, I love you so damn much." He releases my chin and strokes the side of my cheek with the backs of his knuckles. "I never stopped. And I don't know what the hell to do about that. So yeah, baby. I hate you...because no matter how much I don't want to, I can't stop loving you."

His mouth crashes down on mine, and the taste of him, of his tongue plunging into my mouth, sends me into an emotional frenzy. My arms lock around his neck as he lifts me and slams my back against the wall. He breaks our kiss, and when his eyes meet mine, they're filled with a myriad of emotions—love, hate, confusion, desire. And I feel every one of them down to my marrow.

My legs cup his hips, and he drives into me, his thick, long, pierced shaft massaging my vaginal walls in the best way possible. As he bottoms out in me, he releases a pained groan, telling me he's battling with himself. He both loves and hates me. Likes and loathes me. He wants me but wishes he didn't—and I don't blame him. I did this. I hurt him, and while there's a chance whatever we're doing won't leave this room, this bus, I'll take Braxton any way I can get him if it means I simply have a piece of him.

I fist the chocolatey strands of his hair and bring his face to mine for a passionate kiss as we lose ourselves in each other. And as we both find our release, I tell myself that I'll accept whatever this is, for however long it is. As much as I've longed for this day—never thinking it would ever come—I know I have no right to make any demands. So I'll just roll with it and see where it goes.

When Braxton pulls out of me and I slide down the wall to my feet, he's silent. We finish showering, and he hands me a towel so I can dry off. I stay in the bathroom while he goes out to the bedroom to get dressed. I towel dry my hair and brush my teeth with an extra toothbrush I find under the sink, all while obsessing over what's going to happen next. I literally just told myself whatever it is, I'll go along with it, but it's hard when I don't know where Braxton stands.

Needing my clothes, I step into the bedroom but find it empty. He must've gotten dressed and gone back out with the other guys. I search for my clothes, which I know were scattered all over the floor, but I can't find a single article. What the hell? Since I can't leave naked, I pull open a drawer that I know is Braxton's and find a pair of boxer briefs and a T-shirt to throw on.

I stand in front of the closed door for several seconds, trying to get up the courage to do my mini walk of shame. The guys are going to know what we did, especially since I'm sure Braxton walked out there before me with wet hair.

Once I've formulated my plan—run through the bus as fast as possible without making eye contact and go straight to the other bus—look, I didn't say it was a good plan, just a plan—I grab the doorknob, ready to bolt, when the door pushes open, making me stumble back.

"What are you doing standing in front of the door?" Braxton asks, eyeing me up and down. He's in a pair of basketball shorts sans shirt, and I wonder, not for the first time, what all the tattoos mean. He explained a couple to his bitch of a date, but he has several she couldn't see under his shirt that are all exposed right now.

"Crazy," he says, using my nickname to get my attention, "what are you doing?"

"I was getting ready to leave. I, umm, couldn't find my clothes, so I borrowed these." I run my fingers over his Rolling Stones shirt. "I'll give it back."

"You can't go anywhere," Braxton says with a smirk. "The buses already left. We have an eleven-hour drive."

"Oh, shit," I breathe. "I can..." I glance around, unsure what exactly I can do.

"You can get your ass back in the bed and take those clothes off," he finishes for me, shocking the hell out of me. "I threw your clothes in the hamper to be washed."

I do as he says—climbing onto the bed but keeping my clothes on—while he follows, slamming the door behind him and then stopping on the side of the bed.

"Grabbed us some sustenance." He holds up a couple of drinks in one hand and what looks like a Tupperware bowl of food in the other. "Figured we should hydrate and replenish some of those calories before I take you again."

He drops the items he's holding onto the nightstand and

climbs onto the bed. "Shirt off," he demands, lying next to me and tugging on the hem of his shirt to help me pull it over my head.

"I don't have my bra," I screech as the shirt comes off, exposing my breasts.

"That's the point." Braxton dips his head and latches onto my nipple, biting and then licking the pain he just caused away.

I moan, and he backs up, chuckling. "Food and drink first."

"Or..." I push him onto his back and scoot down, turned on all over again and intent on using every minute we have to my advantage. "I can just eat and drink you." I tug his shorts down, and his pierced dick pops out, semi-hard.

I wrap my fingers around his shaft and lick the tip, making Braxton groan. "Yes," I murmur. "This seems like plenty of sustenance to me." And then I proceed to suck him down like the best tasting lollipop.

"LET'S GO!" CAMDEN SHOUTS THROUGH THE DOOR. "WE'RE HERE!"

I roll over, completely spent, refusing to open my eyes. How the hell did eleven hours fly by that quickly?

And then I remember how they were spent.

Braxton in me. On me. All over me.

I stretch my limbs and wince at the slight pain between my legs. It's been a while since I've had sex and to the extent we had last night. I'm pretty sure we fucked in every position and on every surface in the bedroom and bathroom.

And when we weren't fucking, we were touching and talking. Our topics were scattered—going from what his tattoos mean to what rides I'm excited for when we get to the theme parks to the songs he's been writing—but neither of us seemed to care. We never broached the subject of us, and I didn't push. Instead, I just enjoyed the night for what it was.

"Brax, Kaylee, we gotta go!" Camden yells, annoyance laced in his words. "We have a radio interview."

His words have me sitting up since I'm in charge of that part of the tour. The blanket covering me slides down, and I quickly remember I'm still naked—and have no clothes on this bus.

"Brax..." I shake him gently since he's still passed out next to me, equally naked.

"Guys!" Camden says again.

"We're coming!" I yell back. "Just, uh... give us a few minutes."

There's grumbling on the other side of the door and then footsteps leading away.

"Brax," I say again. This time when I say his name, he groans and rolls toward me, pulling me into his arms. I'm not expecting it, so I screech in shock, and he covers my mouth to silence me.

His other hand slides down my hip and cups my pussy, and his mouth latches on to the side of my neck, nipping and sucking on my flesh.

"We have to go," I mumble from under his hand.

"What? I can't hear you," he says, humor in his voice. "Did you say you need some morning sex?"

He pushes two fingers into me, and I moan, my eyes rolling back. "We have to go," I say again even though my words are indecipherable.

"I agree," he says, a mischievous grin on his sexy face. "A good morning dicking is exactly what you need."

He uncovers my mouth, and I snort out a laugh. "We need to—"

My words are cut off when his thumb goes to my clit, massaging it gently.

"Maybe...we can be a few minutes late."

"WE HAVE ONE MORE QUESTION TO ASK BECAUSE IF WE DON'T, WOMEN ALL OVER THE city will come after us."

We're at the radio interview—and shockingly—I have no idea how—we actually arrived on time. After Braxton gave me two orgasms and a "good morning dicking" as promised, we showered, and then he ran to my bus to grab my clothes so I wouldn't have to do the walk of shame from one bus to the other. We parted ways once we were dressed since I needed to work and met back up in the SUV to grab breakfast and go to the scheduled interview. We haven't spoken a word about last night, and thankfully, although they know what went down, the guys haven't said a word either.

"Are any of you off the market, aside from Camden, since we know he's officially taken?"

The questions are always the same and have to be preapproved by the guys, so nothing pops up unexpectedly. I've listened to them answer this question a dozen times over the course of the tour, but now, as I wait for Braxton to answer, because he's always the one who answers it first, I can't help but hope his answer will be different than his usual.

"The only woman warming my bed is Melanie," he says, referring to his customized one-of-a-kind guitar.

Despite telling myself not to expect anything to change between us after last night, my heart sinks. It's not like I expected him to announce that he spent the night inside me, but I guess I hoped he'd make some kind of comment indicating something had changed.

Gage and Declan both give their standard responses, and then the interview ends. Since the first of the two shows aren't until tomorrow, the guys have the rest of the day to themselves to do what they want. Jill's already checked everyone into the hotel, so I grab the keys and give them to the guys, reminding them that we'll be leaving early in the morning and then take off to my own room.

As I'm pressing my key to the door, a warm body comes up behind me, sending butterflies scattering around my belly. "How many orgasms do you think I can give you in eight hours?"

"I don't know," I rasp, freezing in place.

Braxton plucks the key from my fingers and presses it to the door, unlocking and then opening it. "There's only one way to find out."

Guess *Melanie* won't be warming his bed tonight either.

Seventeen

Braxton

"YOU WANT TO EXPLAIN WHAT THE HELL HAPPENED ON THE BUS?" CAMDEN ASKS. We're in the dressing room at the venue, about to go on for our first of two back-to-back shows. It's the first time we've been alone since I hauled Kaylee over my shoulder and spent the next several hours inside her—only stopping long enough to do a scheduled interview.

"Like you didn't hear what happened on the bus over and over again," Declan says with a smirk.

"And on the other side of the wall in the hotel," Gage adds dryly, taking a hit of his joint before offering it to me.

"So what, you two are back together?" Camden asks.

I shake my head at Gage, not in the mood to get high, and think about Camden's question. I'm unsure what to say because despite spending the last day and a half in Kaylee, I don't know what's going on between us. Do I want to get back together with her? Yeah. But at the same time, the shit that went down is fucked up, and I need time to process it all. Should I have fucked her before figuring my shit out? Probably not. But our chemistry was never the issue, and when she told me she wasn't the same without me, something in me snapped, and I had to have her, consequences be damned.

When I don't answer him quick enough, he glares my way. "Great, so should I tell my dad we need to start looking for a new publicist now?"

A gasp from behind me has me turning around. Kaylee is standing in the doorway, a pained expression written all over her face.

"You're really firing me?" she asks softly.

"You told her she's fired?" Camden barks. "What the hell, man?"

"I thought you were joking." Tears fill her eyes, and before I can stop her, she runs out of the room.

"Dammit!" I'm about to go after her when Jill pops inside to let us know we have to go on. "I need to find Kaylee."

"Not now, you don't," she says. "You need to get your butts on the stage in two minutes."

I consider ignoring her and going after Kaylee, but I can't let the guys down. She can't go anywhere right now anyway, so I know she'll still be here after the show. She might be upset, but she takes her job seriously, and she wouldn't flake on her duties—even if she does think she's been fired.

"What the hell were you thinking firing her?" Camden says as we walk down the hall leading to the stage.

"I didn't fire her... well, not seriously." I wave him off, not wanting to explain it all right now. We have a show to get through, and the last thing I need is to fuck up because Kaylee is all up in my headspace.

The venue is dark so we can get situated, and a few minutes later, the lights come down on us. The crowd screams in excitement when Camden speaks, and then Gage starts in on the drums. The next couple of hours fly by, one song after the next, but the entire time, I can't get Kaylee off my mind and the hurt look on her face when she thought I'd actually fired her. I might be a dick, but I wouldn't do that to her. Sure, I mentioned I didn't want her on the tour, but that was before the past couple of nights. And even when I made the comments before, I never acted on them. It was just me talking shit out of hurt and anger.

The misunderstanding reminds me that despite how perfectly I fit inside her, we haven't been around each other for several years. We've both grown up and changed. While we know each other, we also don't. And I have to figure out what I want because the last thing I want to do is hurt Kaylee. She might've hurt me, but I wouldn't do it back just to spite her. I meant what I said. I love her. I always have and always will.

But a part of me is still pissed at what she did, so I need to figure out if I can let that go and whether we have a chance at a future. Hell, I don't even know what she wants. Maybe she just needed a good dicking, and now that she's gotten it, she's done with me. The thought pisses me off. She was upset about the possibility of her being fired, but she hasn't once asked about where we stand.

By the time Cam is thanking Atlanta for being amazing, I've worked myself up and am desperate to find Kaylee. Without waiting for the guys, I push past the crew in search of her. I don't find her in the dressing room or anywhere backstage. Figuring she must be on the bus, I head outside, but before I get there, I find her talking to Jill. Her eyes meet mine, and I'm about to drag her somewhere private, but she plasters a smile on her face and says, "Ready for the meet and greet?" Dammit, I forgot about that.

"We need to talk."

"We need to get you to where the fans will be waiting shortly."

"We have time," I argue. "It always takes a good half hour."

"Then you should probably use that time to change your shirt."

Without waiting for me to respond, she turns on her heel and leaves me standing there stunned silent. So it's going to be like that? Fine. I'll wait until we're done. Then I'll lock her ass in her hotel room until she's ready to talk.

Since I've already missed a couple of the meet and greets recently, when I let my emotions get the best of me, the last thing I want to do is miss more of them. So I go through it with a smile stuck on my face. The fans pay good money to meet us. They're the reason we get to do what we love and are able to make a damn good living at it.

But the second it's over, I'm out the door and off to find Kaylee. Since I was in her room last night, I already have a key. I storm inside and find her in bed, acting like she's already asleep.

"That's cute," I say as I lift her into my arms.

"Brax!" she shrieks. "Put me down!"

"No," I say, suddenly feeling a hell of a lot calmer now that

I have her in my arms. "You're not going to run away when you hear something you don't like without even having a goddamn conversation."

Needing to have this discussion out of bed so I can focus, I carry her into the living room and set her down on the couch, then sit a few feet away from her on the same couch.

"If you would've asked before you ran away, you'd know that Camden was only asking if he should ask his dad to find a new publicist because he assumed you'd be quitting after we had sex."

"And why would he think that?" she asks, jutting her chin out in a challenging manner. Fuck, I've missed this woman so much. I love everything about her. How she can be both soft and hard and give me shit while still showing how much she cares.

"Because he asked if we were back together, and I didn't answer him."

"And...?" she says, throwing the ball straight into my court.

"And..." I tug her over to me, pulling her onto my lap to straddle my thighs. She's soft and warm and smells amazing. "I don't think we should rush shit. It's been a long time, and we've both changed, but I want to see where things go. I wanted you all those years ago, and I still do."

"I want you too," she agrees. "But you're right. It's been a long time, and things have changed."

I cup the side of her face and kiss her supple lips. "I can't wait to get to know you all over again."

"WHAT IS THIS?" KAYLEE GLANCES AT ME.

"A box."

She playfully rolls her eyes. "For me?"

"Open the damn thing."

She doesn't need to be told twice as she undoes the ribbon and tears the box open to reveal a shimmery black dress with matching heels. Since we were on the road to Jacksonville, I couldn't go to the store myself, so I had the hotel concierge handle it, but I made sure he sent me pictures so I could pick which one I wanted.

"It's beautiful," she says, awe in her voice. "What's the occasion?"

"I'm taking you out."

The smile that spreads across her face, along with the hearts in her eyes, makes it worth the effort. She's always been one to appreciate a thoughtful gesture. It's as if she's never expecting it, so when it does happen, she's that much more excited about it.

"Go get ready. I'll be back to pick you up at six o'clock."

Technically, we're sharing a room since I have no desire to sleep in a separate bed than her—regardless of us taking shit slow—but all my stuff is in my room, so I head over there to get ready. I made reservations at a Japanese restaurant since Kaylee mentioned she loves it. After taking a shower and shaving, I get dressed then go out to the main room to wait until it's time to pick up Kaylee. Camden and Declan aren't there, but Gage is sitting out on the private balcony.

"What's up?" I say, sitting in the chair next to him.

He offers me a hit of the joint he's smoking, but I shake my head, not wanting to be high when I pick up Kaylee. He shrugs and takes another hit before he takes a sip of his drink. While we sit in silence, I glance at him. He's the same age as the rest of us, but he looks older, more tired, and I'm worried about him. We all smoke and drink, but Gage is intoxicated more than he's not. We all know why that is, and because of it, we've looked the other way. But I can't help wondering if we're only hurting him by not forcing him to deal with his shit.

"See something you like?" he finally says when he catches me staring.

"I'm worried about you."

He chuckles humorlessly and shakes his head. I expect him to argue, to defend himself, tell me I'm a dumbass and to mind my own business, but all he does is take another hit of his joint.

"Where are you off to tonight?" he asks after a few minutes.

"Taking Kaylee out on a date."

A small smile graces his lips. "That's good, man." He takes a swig of his drink and then stands. "You both deserve to be happy."

"So do you," I say as he walks inside. The slight tenseness in his shoulders is the only sign that he heard me.

At six o'clock, I walk over to Kaylee's room and knock on the door. When she opens it, donning the dress and heels I bought for her with her blond hair down in waves and her face full of makeup, I consider saying fuck it to going out and taking her straight to bed instead.

"Don't even think about it," she says with a playful smile as if she could hear my thoughts. "I didn't get this dressed up not to be taken out." She steps toward me, patting my chest. "And if you're a good boy, I might even let you take the dress off me at the end of the night."

"And what about the heels?" I ask, glancing down and admiring the way they make her legs look even longer and more toned. "Can I take those off too?"

She shakes her head. "I think those will stay on," she murmurs. "I've always had a fantasy of being fucked with heels on. Like in the romance books... digging them into the guy's ass. Maybe you can help me fulfill that fantasy."

"I'm the *only* one who'll be fulfilling any fucking fantasy you have," I growl.

"We'll see." She shrugs and walks around me, the door shutting behind her.

Since we're not in LA, the chance of me being recognized is less, but since there's always the possibility, I have Justin, my personal bodyguard, drive us to dinner and escort us into the restaurant. The sight of the big, burly guy might draw more attention than if he weren't here, but I can't take the risk, especially with Kaylee.

As promised, we're seated outside in a private area overlooking the river, and the server has signed an NDA so nothing will get posted—seems like overkill, I know, but it's necessary if I want our date to remain private.

After taking our drink order, the server disappears, leaving Kaylee and me alone. She's quiet, clearly lost in thought, and I watch her for several beats, admiring how beautiful she is.

"What's going through your head?" I eventually ask, wanting to know all of her thoughts.

"I never thought we'd be here."

"In Jacksonville?" I joke, making her side-eye me.

"I spent so many nights wishing you would show up in Boston, and then when I got kicked out of school and ended up back in New York, I would constantly look for you... at the coffee shop we used to go to... at the beach. When I would visit Layla's mom, I would look for you at the Blackwood house even though I knew you were on the other side of the country."

The day she "cheated," I found out she was attending Boston, and I thought maybe that was why she did what she did, to push me away, but a few months later, Camden mentioned she was back in New York, and I always wondered what had happened.

"Why did you switch from Boston to NYU?"

"When I let you go, it was the hardest thing I'd ever done," she says quietly. We talked about what happened, but we've yet to discuss it in detail since we went from me hating her to being pissed at her to fucking the hell out of her.

"I knew it would be hard, but when Layla and I got to Boston, I missed you so much." Her eyes meet mine. They're glassy and filled with raw emotion. "I messed up. Drank too much, partied too hard to hide the pain, and I failed out."

The server drops our drinks off, and we both order. Once he's gone, she continues. "I tried to get a job working for a marketing firm, but nobody would take me seriously without a degree, so after I worked and saved up enough money, I went back to school. It took a little while, which is why Layla graduated before me."

"But you still graduated."

"Yeah, but it all felt like I was just going through the motions. I would see you on tour, in pictures on social media, laughing and having the time of your life, and it felt like my heart was being stomped on… but it also made me so happy because even though it hurt to let you go, every time I saw those pictures, I felt like I did the right thing."

I'll never agree with what she did, but I also get it. Because she's right. Had she not done what she did, I wouldn't have gotten on that plane to LA. I had already told the guys I wasn't going, and Easton was searching for a guitarist for the band.

"Anyway," she says, perking up slightly and plastering a smile on her face. "I just can't believe, after everything, we're here on a date, getting a fresh start." She smiles softly—a real one this time that has my heart pounding against my rib cage. "I'm really glad we're getting this second chance."

When our dinner arrives, our conversation takes on a lighter tone as we flit from topic to topic, catching up on the years we've been apart. You'd think since we haven't spoken or seen each other in so long, it might be awkward, but it's not. As Kaylee tells me about her time in school, some of the places she's worked at, and the various concerts she's attended—which leads to us debating over what good music sounds like—it's as if time has never passed.

After dinner, we take a walk along the river, holding hands while talking about our upcoming time off. We'll be going to the theme parks between shows in Tampa and Orlando, and then the entire band and crew will have a one-week break for the Fourth of July.

"I was planning to go back to New York," she admits sheepishly. "At the time, we weren't talking and…" She shrugs.

"Well, now we are." I guide her over to a darkened area that leads to an alley between two buildings. I can see Justin's following us, but he keeps his distance, so we have our privacy. "Gage, Declan, and I rented a place next to Camden. His parents and sisters are coming down as well, and so is Layla's mom. It'll be fun."

"I don't know," she says cheekily. "I'd hate to intrude and ruin your fun..."

I back her against the wall and, with our fingers threaded, lift her hands over her head. "Ruin the fun?" I part her legs with my knee and rub my thigh along her center. "I plan for you to *be* the fun." I bring my lips to the curve of her neck and suckle on her soft flesh, making her moan.

When she pulls her hands out of mine, I release her, kissing my way up to her earlobe. Her arms snake around my neck, and she hops up, making me catch her as she encircles her legs around my waist, her heels digging into my back. "I say we start the fun now," she murmurs, grinding herself against me.

"Not here," I say, nipping at her lobe. "When I fuck you, I want you in nothing but those damn heels."

"Well, then what are you waiting for?"

Eighteen

Kaylee

"UNCLE BRAX!" FELIX YELLS, RUNNING OVER AND LATCHING HIS LITTLE ARMS AROUND Braxton's legs. While Camden grabs Layla's and Felix's bags, giving his wife a quick kiss, Braxton carries Felix over to the SUV waiting for us. The bodyguards surround us so nobody can get close, but several people stand around taking photos that will end up on social media within minutes. I'm already messaging Bailey to warn her so she can keep an eye out for anything that shouldn't be posted. Camden and Layla are big on not allowing pictures of Felix to be posted, and if anyone does post them, they demand them to be taken down.

"I'm so excited!" Felix shouts as Braxton buckles him in. I can't help smiling as I watch the two of them together. Braxton might be this badass, tattooed, and pierced rock star to the world, but the second Felix is in his arms, he turns into a complete softy.

Layla's eyes meet mine, and she smirks, having caught me staring. "Bet he'd make a great dad," she whispers.

"Don't get any ideas. We're taking things slow."

"Yeah, okay." She scoffs. "I was on the phone with Camden and heard you guys taking things slow."

My face heats in embarrassment, which has Layla cackling. The drive from Jacksonville was only three hours, but it was spent with Braxton inside me the entire time. I tried to be quiet... I swear I did. But the guy has made it his personal mission to pull as many orgasms out of me as possible every time we're together, and despite the bus being luxurious and worth millions, it's still just that... a bus. And when I try to remain quiet, Braxton takes it as a challenge to make me scream that much louder.

"Mommy said we're going on fifty hundred rides!" Felix announces, and I've never been so thankful for a subject change in my life.

"Fifty hundred rides, huh?" I say. "That's a lot of rides."

"Uh-huh," he agrees. "You gonna go on the rides with me?" Felix asks, flashing his expertly staged puppy dog eyes that he knows I don't stand a chance against. "Mommy can't 'cause she's too fat."

Braxton snorts out a laugh, then quickly schools his features. "She's not fat, buddy. She's pregnant... with your little sister."

"Her belly is super fat," he argues. "She won't fit on the rides."

"Well, that's true," he concedes. "But it's not nice to call her fat. She's pregnant."

Felix shrugs. "Okay, but you and Kaylee will go on the rides with me, right?"

"Of course we will," I tell him. "I've never been on the rides either."

"Where's Gage?" Layla asks, looking around.

"At the hotel. He's not feeling well," Camden says.

The truth is, he went out on a bender last night and nearly got alcohol poisoning. I was afraid we were going to have to take him to the hospital, but thankfully, we didn't need to.

Layla sighs. "We need to—"

"You don't need to do anything," Camden says, cutting her off. "You're pregnant and shouldn't be stressed."

"But—"

"But nothing." He gives her a kiss. "You're here to have a good time. It's our last trip with Felix before we bring our little girl into this world." He rubs her belly, and her shoulders visibly lower. "Gage is at the hotel room, sleeping it off. He had a rough night, but he's fine."

Nobody in the SUV believes a word he's saying—not even himself—but until the guys do something, there's nothing any of us can say. Gage is functioning and performing, but he needs help. Unfortunately, until he hits rock bottom, I don't think the guys will interfere. Damn men... so stubborn.

"OKAY, SPILL," LAYLA SAYS, GLANCING OVER AT ME WITH A DOPEY SMILE ON HER FACE.

We've spent the day at the theme park, riding every ride with Felix until that cute little Energizer Bunny's batteries finally died. He passed out in the stroller, not waking when he was put in the vehicle or when Camden carried him up to the room. We're all sunburned and exhausted, but it was a great day.

After everyone got settled in their rooms, Layla dragged me down to the hotel spa for some pedis and "girl talk"—her words, not mine—leaving Camden and the guys to keep an eye on a sleeping Felix.

"That sounds messy," I joke, inwardly moaning at how good it feels to have my calves massaged.

When she glares my way, I laugh. "I don't know what to say."

"How about starting with how the hell Braxton went from hating you to acting like you two are in high school all over again?"

I flinch, hating that Layla isn't caught up to speed. I wanted to tell her everything, but I felt like it would be best explained in person since Braxton wasn't the only person I lied to. I thought maybe Camden would tell her, and I was half expecting a pissed-off phone call, but I should've known he'd leave that to me. Camden is the least gossipy person I know.

"Kaylee, talk to me," she says softly, her voice laced with hurt.

"I never cheated on Braxton."

Her brows dip in confusion.

"I lied to push him away so he would go to LA."

Her eyes go wide. "Kaylee..."

"While Tori was..." I swallow thickly, unable to finish my sentence. Even all these years later, I get emotional just thinking about her—we all do. "I was pretending to cheat on Braxton."

"Oh, Kay..." She sets her hand on mine. "I get it, I do. But..." She releases a harsh breath. "So he found out the truth?"

"Yeah, he overheard his dad and me talking. I was threatening to tell him the truth."

"His dad?"

"It was his idea. He has this issue with women. I guess he gave up a huge opportunity for Braxton's mom, and she ended up leaving him. He doesn't really talk about her, but his dad didn't want him messing up his future for a woman."

"So where do you guys stand? It's clear, you guys are..." She waggles her brows playfully, making me laugh.

"We are," I admit. "We're taking things slow."

She quirks a brow.

"I mean, not slow... I don't know. We're just seeing where things go. We're on this tour, and I think it's easy to get lost in each other while we're sharing a space. But once we're back at home, we'll be able to figure things out. For now, I'm just enjoying reconnecting with him."

"You've always loved him."

"Yeah, but I never thought I'd be given this second chance, so honestly, I'm just going with the flow. Getting to know him all over again."

"I'm happy for you." Layla squeezes my hand. "Look at us finding love. Did you hear the news about Camden's sister?"

"Kendall?"

"Nope, Bailey." She grins. "She's getting married to her fiancée, Cynthia, at the beach."

"Stop! That's awesome."

We spend the rest of our pedicures catching up, and it feels good to be able to relax and talk with Layla. For years, before she was with Camden, she was married to a grade A asshole who didn't let her do shit, so it's nice getting to spend time with her again.

"When I get home from the tour, we need to make this a weekly thing."

"I agree." Layla smiles. "I've missed you. Maybe we can go on a double date."

"We'll see. Let's not get too far ahead of ourselves."

"Ahead of ourselves?" she says. "I was watching you guys all day. Braxton is just as obsessed with you as he was all those years ago."

"Maybe." I shrug, not wanting to get my hopes up because I feel the same way about him, which scares the hell out of me. I already lost him once—completely my fault—and I don't know if I could go through that again.

After our toes are pretty and our feet are soft, we head back up to our rooms for the night. The guys have a show tomorrow, and then we're heading to Orlando for a show, spending the day at Disney, and then driving down to Miami for their final show before their much-needed break.

When I step into the room I'm unofficially sharing with Braxton, I find him sitting outside on the balcony, scribbling words into the journal I gave him years ago.

"Writing anything special?"

He glances up and smiles at me before he puts the pen down and pulls me into his arms. "I'm writing something I haven't written in a long-ass time... a love song."

"OH, WOW, THIS PLACE IS GORGEOUS!" I BREATHE, STEPPING OUTSIDE WHERE THE infinity pool overlooks the beach. When Braxton said they were renting a place on the beach, I had assumed they were staying in a hotel of some sort—taking up an entire floor. I didn't realize they were renting an entire freaking house. And not just any house, a damn mansion, complete with a private beach.

"Camden's place is to the left, and his parents and sisters are one more over. Between the three houses and all the property they're on, we're completely secluded from everyone else."

Braxton wraps his arms around me from behind, and I sigh into him, excited for the next several days. No buses or meet and greets or radio interviews. Just Braxton and me and our friends and the beach.

"Too bad we're sharing this house with Declan and Gage," I say, grinding my ass up against his front. "This pool would be the perfect place to go skinny-dipping in."

Braxton groans. "I can totally make that happen." He fists my hair, tugging my head to the side, and suckles the side of my neck. "As a matter of fact, I can make it happen right now."

"How?" I gasp when he nips at my lobe.

"We're alone." He licks the curve of my ear, sending a chill down my spine. "They left as soon as we got here. A friend of ours opened a new strip club and invited the band to the opening. They'll be gone for hours. It's just you and me."

"You didn't want to go?" I ask since he implied whoever it is, is his friend as well.

"Why the hell would I want to spend the night with a bunch of strippers when I have you?"

His words cause my heart to swell and give me an idea. "Sit

here." I direct him to one of the chairs near the table on the expansive patio that houses an outdoor kitchen complete with a massive grill.

When he drops into the chair, confusion marring his features, I grab my phone and quickly hook it up to the Bluetooth speakers, then scroll through my music until I find the perfect song—"Problem" by Natalia Kills.

I click play, and as the instrumentals start, I saunter over to Braxton, stopping just out of reach. He frowns, and I smirk. And then when I begin seductively rocking my hips from side to side, his eyes go wide.

As the woman begins to sing about a couple dripping in sweat as they fuck, I slowly pull my shirt over my head, then unbutton and unzip my shorts, sliding them down my thighs. Instead of kicking my Vans off, I make it a point to bend all the way over, my breasts damn near spilling out of their confines as I unlace and tug each shoe off.

"Jesus, fuck," Braxton hisses, grabbing his crotch and rearranging himself. "Get over here, Crazy."

"Nuh-uh." I shake my head. "You aren't allowed to touch the strippers," I tease, making him groan. "Pull your dick out. I want to see how hard it is."

He does as I say, undoing his pants and tugging them down enough to pull his dick out. It's dark outside, but thanks to the floodlights, I'm able to see everything. His shaft is hard and veiny, and the metal piercings glint in the light. My mouth waters, remembering what he tastes like...what he feels like.

The music picks up, and I sway my hips as I glide my hands down my neck, along my collarbone, and over my breasts. I reach behind and unclip my bra, letting the material slide down my arms. With my eyes locked on Braxton, I reach up and squeeze my tits, making it a point to pinch my nipples.

"Kaylee," Braxton growls, fisting his cock and stroking it roughly. I can tell he's losing his patience, so I pick things up, removing my panties and then bringing my hand to my mound, teasing myself as I walk closer to him.

"I could be persuaded to give you a private lap dance"—I lean forward, making sure not to touch him—"if the price is right."

"How much?" he asks, playing along when I step back and continue to dance slowly to the beat of the song.

"I don't know if you can afford me." I pinch my nipple some more, and his gaze turns molten with lust.

"I'm a rich fucking man," he says, his voice gruff. "Name your price."

"You," I say, stopping in my place. "I want you."

"Done." He reaches out and grabs the curves of my hips, pulling me toward him to straddle his thighs. Our mouths connect in a searing-hot kiss at the same time his dick enters me. I ride him to the beat of the song, hard and rough, while he fucks my mouth the same way until we're both coming apart in each other's arms.

"Wow," I gasp, out of breath. "It's hot out here." My hair is sticking to my neck, and I can feel droplets of perspiration dripping down my skin.

"I think I can fix that for you," Braxton says, settling his hands under my ass and standing. I assume he's going to carry me back inside, so I'm stunned in shock when he heads straight for the damn pool instead.

"Brax—" I start, but before I can finish my warning, he's jumping into the pool with me clinging to him. The water is cold as fuck, but with it being a hundred damn degrees out, it feels good.

"Now, we can go skinny-dipping," he says with the sexiest boyish grin on his face.

"I WANT TO GET A TATTOO."

"What?" Braxton asks, setting his writing journal down and laughing.

For the past hour, we've been lying on the oversized couch, our legs entwined while Braxton writes, and I read. But at some point, I got distracted and have been eyeing his ink instead. He's explained what each one means, and I love that he's gotten one to symbolize or represent milestones in his life over the years. When the band recorded their first album, when they went platinum, when they went on their first world tour... For every occasion, he's gotten inked, like a photo book of memories that people can see but only he understands.

"A tattoo. I want to get another one... with you."

"What do you want to get?"

"I was thinking a daffodil. I read that they represent new beginnings, a fresh start. And I feel like with this job and getting a second chance with you, it's sort of like that. You don't have to get the same thing. You can get whatever you want."

"I like it," he says, pulling me into his arms. "And I love that we're getting a fresh start."

"So you'll get one with me?" I perk up in excitement.

"Of course. I'll have to think about what I want to get—"

"Yay! Let's go."

"Wait, now?" He laughs, and I pout playfully, nodding. "Some things never change," he adds with a chuckle, standing and pulling me up with him.

"What's that supposed to mean?"

"You're still as crazy as ever." He shakes his head and pulls his shirt over his head, covering his sexy body. "And I'm still just as pussy-whipped."

"Is that a bad thing?"

"Nah." He grips the curves of my hips and tugs me toward him, so our bodies are flush against each other. "It's not a bad thing at all." He drops a kiss to my lips and then to my nose before he backs up and smirks. "Let's go get some ink."

I thought we'd have to find a place, but it turns out Braxton already knows someone and when he calls and asks if we can come by, of course the guy says he's available. You'd be stupid not to be when someone as famous as Braxton says he wants to come in.

When we get there, we're taken back to a private room, and Braxton and Guy bullshit for a few minutes catching up—apparently, he's done a few pieces for Braxton in the past—before he asks what brings us in today.

Braxton explains I want to get a daffodil inked, and I show him what I'd like. Since he specializes in freehand ink, I agree to let him do his thing. I get it on my hip, and when he's done and shows it to me, I'm in awe of how beautiful it is. Instead of one, he inked three and explained they reminded him of the past, present, and future when I told him daffodils represent a fresh start. They couldn't be more perfect. And Braxton agrees when I show them to him.

"What are you getting?" I ask when Braxton has a seat and lifts his shirt.

"You'll see." He winks and lies back while Guy gets the station cleaned up from my tattoo and ready to do Braxton's.

While he gets tattooed, Guy gives me free rein to his music, so I play deejay, going from song to song while Braxton bitches about my taste in music.

"We used to have similar taste in music," he points out.

"I've evolved. You should try it."

Guy shakes his head, and Braxton laughs.

When Guy announces he's done, I pause the music so I can see the ink. Braxton gets up and steps in front of the mirror to check it out, and I join him so I can see too. My eyes go straight to his rib cage where the fresh ink lies. There are several roses, shaded in black and gray, with the stems and thorns inked as if they're being woven under and over his skin. It's so lifelike, it almost hurts to look at them. I can practically feel the irony in the beauty and pain between the roses and thorns. My eyes sting, remembering that he would constantly tell me that he loved the way I smelled like roses, my signature lotion scent.

"*She's under my skin*," I read out loud the words that are etched along the outline of the roses.

"She's under my skin, like the thorns of a rose. You know loving her is going to hurt, but you're blinded by the beauty of the rose." Braxton's eyes lock with mine in the mirror, his hazel to my gray. "It's from a song I've been writing..."

"About me."

"Yeah."

"I hurt you."

He turns to me, and it's then I realize we're alone. Guy must've left to give us privacy. "Love hurts, but the beauty that comes with loving you is worth the pain."

Nineteen

Kaylee

"MOMMY, COME MAKE A SANDCASTLE WITH ME!" FELIX YELLS, SCOOPING UP AND throwing sand every which way.

We're hanging out at the beach, lounge chairs under us and umbrellas above us. It's hot as hell outside, the sun as unforgiving as a woman scorned, but the guys have armed us with cold drinks and snacks that will quench our thirst. It's been like this every day since we arrived, and I'm dreading when the vacation is over. A woman could get used to this.

"I have to get up, don't I?" Layla groans, half-joking, her hand going to her very big bump—which makes sense since she's six months pregnant.

Before I can answer, she's already standing, looking adorable. From the back, you wouldn't even know she's pregnant since she's all belly, but from the front is another story.

"Layles, go lie down," Camden demands. "I got this." He

jogs over to where Felix is and drops down next to him. If you didn't know their story, you'd think Camden was Felix's biological dad—that's how good he is with him.

"You heard the man. Lie back down." I pat the chair next to me and sip my delicious fruity alcoholic beverage Bailey made me. The woman was probably a bartender in another life.

Layla slowly lies back down, situating herself so she can get comfortable. "It's probably for the best. Had I actually gotten down in the sand, I'd probably never get back up."

We all laugh at her dramatics even though she's dead serious.

"You all ready for tomorrow?" I ask Bailey, who's cuddling on a blanket with Cynthia. They decided on a small ceremony, just close friends and family, and since Cynthia's family doesn't condone her choice of partner, that makes the party even smaller.

"Yep, my mom handled everything. All we have to do is get dressed and show up."

"Do you think Kendall will get here in time?" Layla asks, concern etched in her features.

"With my sister?" Bailey scoffs. "You never know. I love her, but she's so damn flaky."

"She's not flaky," her mom chides. "She just beats to her own drum." Sophia says it nonchalantly, but I can see a small amount of sadness there, and I briefly wonder what that's about. But before I can give it much thought, there's a commotion behind us, and as if speaking her name has summoned her, Kendall appears.

Sophia jumps up and runs over to her daughter, hugging her tightly as she jokingly reprimands her for being away for so long. While Sophia is obviously older than Kendall, the two look more like sisters than mother-daughter. They both have the same thick blond hair and creamy complexion. The only difference in their features is while Sophia has emerald eyes, Kendall's are a bright blue.

"I can't believe you made it," Bailey says, getting a bit choked up. I imagine getting ready to be married will do that to a person.

"I wouldn't miss my baby sister's wedding," Kendall retorts, wrapping her arms around her sister. Phoebe, their other sister, joins them, and then their dad does as well. When Camden sees his entire family is together, he gets up and goes over to them. Layla joins them next, along with Felix and Cynthia.

I watch as they embrace each other, kissing each other's cheeks while they smile and laugh.

"Why the frown?" a masculine voice asks. I look over and find Braxton sitting on the edge of my lounge chair. He had run up to the house to use the bathroom.

"I want that." I nod over to them. When Braxton quirks a brow, not understanding, I explain, "I want a family."

I don't have to say anything more because he gets it. He listened to me when I was younger talk about how much I missed my family. Sure, I still have my mom, but when she looks at me, I think she sees my dad, which makes it hard for her to be around me.

"Sometimes, I think having had a family and losing it is worse than never having had one at all," I admit softly.

"I get that," he says, squeezing my leg.

"What's going on?" Declan asks, joining us.

"Kendall's here," I say. "Flew in for Bailey's wedding."

Declan's gaze darts over to where the Blackwood clan are

talking. "She, uh, here with anyone?"

Braxton rolls his eyes. "Man, when the hell are you going to ask her out? It's obvious you like her. Have since you were a damn kid. You guys hang out all the time. I know you write music together. Your ass has been friend-zoned, and if you don't speak up soon, it's where you'll remain."

Well, that's something new. I mean, I get it. Kendall is freaking gorgeous. But she's also Declan's best friend's sister and several years older. When we were in high school, Camden would talk shit about Declan having a crush on his sister, but I never knew it was more than that.

Declan doesn't say anything back. He just punches Braxton in the arm before walking over to where everyone is and wrapping his arm around Kendall, drawing her into his side. She smiles up at him and kisses his cheek. He must say something funny because she throws her head back with a laugh that has Declan grinning like a fool.

"Declan likes Kendall?" I ask even though it's obvious now that I'm watching them together.

Braxton laughs. "He's had it bad for years. Started out as a crush, from what Camden said, and eventually turned into more."

"So why doesn't he ask her out?" Declan is hot. With his long dirty-blond hair, midnight-blue eyes, and scruffy face, women practically cream themselves when he graces them with his presence. He's not my type. I prefer someone more rugged—i.e. Braxton with his tattoos for days and dick piercing—but Declan definitely isn't hard on the eyes.

"He's a romantic." Braxton shrugs. "And Kendall is a

heartbreak waiting to happen."

"True." You'd have to be dead or living under a rock not to know about the dozens of men she's dated, dumped, and then wrote songs about. "But maybe she just needs to find the right guy."

"THERE'S A MUSIC FESTIVAL UP THE BEACH. WE SHOULD TOTALLY GO." KENDALL IS lying out in her teeny-tiny bikini while Declan remains near but not too close, drooling from afar. I can't help but laugh at how obvious his feelings are now that I know, and I wonder if Kendall realizes.

"Really? Which one?" Declan asks.

"The Miami Summer Music Festival. It's mostly up-and-coming artists, but I bet it'll be rocking."

"And which *artist* are you interested in?" Camden says dryly.

Kendall laughs. "Can't I just be *interested* in the music?" Her parents snicker, and she rolls her eyes. "Whatever."

"I'm down," Easton says. "We actually have a few people performing there. We can check out the talent. I bet there'll be a few unsigned artists."

"You up for it?" Camden asks Layla.

"Sure." She shrugs. "But I'm not sure Felix will be." She glances down at her little boy, who's curled into her side and sleeping soundly, the sun having knocked him out.

"I can stay with him," Patricia, her mom, offers. "I'm wiped."

"Can I stay too?" Phoebe asks, looking up from her phone.

"Sure, sweetie," Patricia says, smiling at her.

After agreeing on when to meet, we head back to the house, shower, and get ready. Since it's an outdoor festival, I dress in a pair of denim cutoff shorts with one of Braxton's *Chaotic Tour* shirts that's a bit too big, so I've knotted it at the corner to show off a bit of my skin, and a pair of Vans.

Braxton was using the other bathroom, and when he comes out dressed in his ripped to shreds skinny jeans, a Raging Chaos shirt, and the same damn Vans as me, I can't help but laugh.

"What?"

"We're matching."

He glances down at himself and then takes me in. "You look hot in my shirt."

I roll my eyes playfully. "Of course that's all you'd notice."

He shrugs unapologetically and hooks his arm around my neck. "Let's roll."

We meet up with the others and walk down the beach to where the festival is being held. It's completely sold out, but of course, between the Blackwoods being who they are and the band being mega famous, we get in without a problem.

We spend the next hour or so checking out the various bands from the VIP section since the guys and Kendall can't exactly hang out with the rest of the crowd without being mobbed. They range from rock, like Raging Chaos, to R&B and pop, similar to Kendall. Most are newer in the music industry, but they're all extremely talented.

Of course, when you're famous, you're never really off, so when we go backstage, because Easton wants to find out about the possibility of signing a couple of the artists, and one of the guys mentions it would be awesome if Raging Chaos would surprise everyone by jumping on stage and performing a couple of songs, the guys agree.

Since it's the perfect opportunity to promo them, I pull out my phone and quickly log into their social media, clicking to go live. Fans love when musicians show up and do shit like this. They play one song and then start in on another, making the crowd go insane.

Wanting to zoom in on them, I walk over to the side of the open stage where I'll have a better view. I'm not paying attention, solely focusing on the band, so when I bump into someone, I'm a bit taken aback.

"Well, look who it is," Sam York slurs. He's too big to be performing tonight, so he must be in Miami partying for the Fourth of July weekend. He stumbles toward me, and I immediately retreat, not at all comfortable with being around him alone.

"C'mon, baby doll," he says, getting me into a corner before I can get away. "We can take this somewhere private, and I can make all of your problems go away." With his bloodshot eyes and slow movements, it's clear he's drunk and high—so, pretty much the norm for him.

"Not happening," I say, glancing around and wishing someone would walk over here. That's what I get for stepping away from everyone to get a better video of the band performing.

"Ahh, so I see you're still the same cock tease you were while you were working for me," he hisses.

Realizing my phone is still in my hand—and live—instead of shutting him down, again, I take the opportunity to set shit straight. The phone isn't facing him, so nobody can see us, but they can hear what we're saying.

"Really, Sam?" I say, making a point to speak his name. "Thought I was the one who sexually assaulted you? Now I'm a tease? Which is it? I can't be both."

And... like the drunk and sloppy dumbass he is, he falls right into my trap. "You're such a fucking cock tease little bitch. I've seen the pictures of you and that trashy rocker. Is that what gets you wet? A guy like—"

Before he can finish his accusation, he's being shoved against the wall by Braxton.

"Who the fuck do you think you are talking to her like that?"

Shit! They must've finished performing. "Brax, stop!" I say, pulling him by his arm. "Don't do this. Not now," I plead.

With my phone still live, we can't chance that being recorded. Thankfully, he listens and lets go of Sam, who cackles like an idiot, thinking he's won.

Wrong. So fucking wrong.

"Hey, Sam," I say, pointing the phone at him. "Say hello to everyone... We're live. And thousands just heard everything."

"You fucking bitch!" He steps forward like he's going to come after me, but Gage steps in front of him.

"Back the fuck up before I fuck you up."

And with that, I end the live.

"Sorry," I say to Braxton once we're away from Sam. "I didn't mean to use your page..."

"Hey, fuck that." He puts his arm around me and pulls me into his side, kissing my temple. "I'm glad you got that shit on camera. He deserves it."

"Yeah, he does," Declan agrees. "And now that the truth is out, your reputation will be cleared."

"Working with musicians is exhausting," I say half-jokingly. "After this tour, I'm planning to find a nice boring office job in marketing and advertising."

Since it's almost nine thirty, we make our way out of the festival and go back to the house so we can watch the fireworks from there. We have the perfect balcony overlooking the water, so Braxton and I say good night to everyone and head up to our room.

Just as we open the French doors, the first firework goes off, bright reds and blues exploding in the dark sky. I step up to the railing, and Braxton cages me in from behind, his arms wrapping around me and his hands landing on top of mine. I glance down as he threads our fingers together, and for the first time in a while, I feel content.

It feels like the past several years have been a constant uphill battle, a mountain that I've been climbing on my own—my own doing, of course—but tonight, right here in Braxton's arms, it feels like I'm no longer alone. I have friends who care about Braxton and me. We might not be officially together, but what we're doing is a step forward. When I'm with him, I feel complete.

"What's going through that beautiful head of yours?" Braxton asks, leaning to the side so he can look into my eyes.

"Nothing. I'm just happy."

He nods once, then dusting my hair to the side, he places a soft, open-mouthed kiss to my sensitive pulse. I try to focus on the beautiful fireworks, but my attention is half gone when his kiss turns into sucking. He quickly strips my shirt and bra off, then undoes my shorts, pushing them down my legs along with my panties. The warm breeze hits my overheated body, and a chill races through me, dotting my flesh with goose bumps.

His mouth goes back to my heated skin, licking and sucking, nibbling to the point I'm squirming in want with my lady parts aching. A gorgeous heart-shaped white firework bursts into the sky as Braxton separates my legs and drives his fingers into me.

"Oh, fuck," I groan as he pumps them in and out of me, working me up into a frenzy. All too soon, his thumb flicks my clit, and I'm spiraling over the edge.

As I come down from my orgasm, I hear his belt jingle and his fly lower. His shirt lands on the ground next to our feet, and a second later, he's entering me from behind. My body thrusts forward, my tits hanging over the railing. One of Braxton's hands digs into the curve of my hip and the other wraps around my front, pinching my nipple as he drives in and out of me. His mouth latches onto my neck, and I moan in pleasure, loving the way he knows exactly how to turn me on and get me off.

As our bodies connect in the most intimate way, our flesh hot, our skin dotted with sweat, the fireworks continue to light up the sky—gold and silver flecks raining down and disappearing into the black ocean.

"It's never been like this," Braxton murmurs into my ear huskily. "Never felt like this... *Fuck*," he growls as his thrusts turn savage, hitting me deliciously deep.

I should probably be upset or jealous that he's comparing me to the other women he's been with, but I don't have it in me to be. Because right here, right now, he's with me. He wants me.

And regardless of all the other women he's been with, I'm the one who does this to him.

"Only... Fucking... You," he growls as he lets go, his warm seed shooting inside me and coating my walls, sending me into another climax that's so strong, my knees damn near buckle.

He stills, his body still connected to mine, and drops a soft kiss to the top of my shoulder that somehow feels more intimate than the sex we just had. "Only you, Crazy," he whispers, pulling out as the fireworks finale lights up the sky. "Only fucking you."

Twenty

Braxton

THE MUTED SUNLIGHT SLIPS IN THROUGH THE BLINDS, MAKING KAYLEE BURROW HER face into my neck, her pillow-soft breasts pressing against my side. I don't move, not wanting to wake her up, just simply enjoying the quiet moment. In a rock star's world, quiet isn't something we get a lot of, especially not on the road, so when we do get it, we tend to soak it up and revel in it as long as we can.

When her stomach rumbles, her eyes pop open, and she giggles. "Morning."

"Morning." I kiss the tip of her nose. "Hungry?"

"How'd you guess?" She sighs. "I can't believe this is our last day on vacation. I say you quit your job, and we buy this house and never leave." She cuddles into my side, and I wrap my arm around her tighter. I know she's only joking, but the idea sounds damn good.

"Can't leave the guys hanging," I say, pinching her chin and raising her face to look at me. "But we can definitely come back soon." And if she wants me to buy a fucking beach house, I'm not opposed to doing so. The thought has me taking a deep breath because it's the first time since we've been doing what we've been doing that I've thought about us as more than just right now and at the moment.

I know I love the woman, always have, but I meant what I said at the time, that we needed to take shit slow. I didn't think having sex would affect us, but I should've known that sex with Kaylee isn't like sex with those groupies. Every time I fuck her, my heart is part of it. I can't simply think with my dick where she's concerned, and that's scary as fuck because even though I love her, she still hurt me—hence, the thorn-covered roses inked into my side.

Kaylee lied, pretending she cheated on me to push me away. She let me believe for six goddamn years that she fucked another guy. She knew it broke me, but she never tried to put me back together. I want to forgive her, want to move forward, but it's hard as hell to do that when her putting me first meant putting my feelings last.

"Hey, you okay?" Kaylee asks, snapping me out of my thoughts.

"Yeah." I sit up, gently moving her off me. "Wanna go get breakfast? Then we can figure out what we want to do today."

"Sure." She nods, her smile forced because she can sense my tension. She knows me as well as I know myself. It doesn't matter how much time we've spent apart. "We have to be ready to go to the airport tomorrow at five o'clock."

Since we're in Miami for the week, the buses drove to Tennessee, where we'll be performing next, and we're taking a flight there instead of having to endure the fourteen-hour drive.

After we both take showers, we head downstairs and find Declan sitting at the bar, drinking a cup of coffee.

"We're going to breakfast," Kaylee says. "Wanna go?"

Declan shrugs, making Kaylee frown. "Okay, you're going. I'm not leaving you here to pout." She grabs his cup and sets it in the sink. "You don't get to be upset about Kendall when you refuse to tell her how you feel."

Declan glares. "And risk her *stiffing* me? Fuck that. This guy will be gone soon enough." He's referring to the real reason Kendall wanted to go to the music festival—the guy she's recently started talking to was playing there.

"And then will you tell her?"she asks.

Declan shrugs."I don't know... maybe."

"Where's Gage?" She glances around, looking for him.

"Probably in his room." Declan stands. "I'll get dressed and then we can go."

"Drag Gage out too. He shouldn't be holed up in his room. He's sinking into a depression."

Declan's eyes meet mine because she isn't wrong. We've all noticed him getting worse, but he usually does around the anniversary of Tori's death—although it doesn't usually last a damn month—and it doesn't help that we're on vacation, giving him too much time on his hands. Hopefully, once we're back on the road playing, he'll snap out of it. We only have a few weeks left on tour.

I know it sounds like we're choosing to play over getting

Gage the help he needs, but the guy is stubborn as fuck, and he'll never stay in rehab if he feels like he's letting down the band. It's all he has, all he lives for, and taking that away from him isn't the way to get him to focus on getting clean.

Once Declan and Gage are ready, we head out. Since we're in a busy city and Kaylee wants to walk, we have my bodyguard, Justin, with us. He mentioned a while back that he could use the money, so we offer him overtime to join us whenever we're going somewhere that's out of his contractual time.

"I read this place has the best Cuban coffee," Kaylee says, walking up to some hole-in-the-wall place.

"We're eating here?" Declan says, sounding like a stuck-up prick. The guy has probably eaten pussy dirtier than this place.

"Places like these always have the best food," Kaylee argues. "Besides, I'd rather give my money to a small business than some chain."

Without waiting for Declan to reply, she pulls the door open and goes in. If the smell of the place is anything to go by, I'd bet my left nut the food is delicious. We order iced *café con leches,* a bunch of pastries Kaylee wants to try, and some sandwiches, then we find a picnic table at a park near the beach.

"Damn, this is good," Declan says, taking a sip of his drink and then stuffing a bite of his sandwich into his mouth.

"Of course it is." Kaylee mock-glares. "It's like New York. You have to find the hidden gems. Once I—"

"Braxton? Is that you?"

The feminine voice calling my name has all of us turning our heads. Nobody's noticed us yet, so if someone did, shit's about to get crazy. But the way it's said, it's not like the fans usually say it.

It's more like she's unsure, startled.

"Ma'am, I need to ask you to please ..."

Whatever Justin is saying becomes a buzz in my ears as my gaze lands on the person who called my name. She's several years older than the last time I saw her, than the pictures I've seen her in. Crow's feet line her eyes, but she's still beautiful with glossy brown hair and bright hazel eyes. Everyone used to say I was my dad's twin, from our hair to our facial features. Even our body type is similar. But my eyes, they're not my dad's... they're my mom's. She's dressed in a flowy floral sundress, her skin a bit red from the sun.

As I take her in, I notice she's not alone. Standing with her is an older gentleman, a boy who looks to be in his teens, and two girls, identical, several years younger. When my eyes scan over them, trying to figure out what I'm seeing, I land on the boy's eyes: hazel, like mine... like my mom's.

"Braxton," my mom breathes, making me focus back on her. "It's been so long..."

"Nineteen years." I was five when she walked away and never looked back.

She winces, almost as if she's ashamed of how long it's been. "This is my husband, Scott, and our children. Shane is eighteen, and Julia and Jessica are—"

"Eighteen?" I hiss, cutting her off. "He's eighteen?" It's not difficult to do the math in my head. "You said you didn't want a family, that you weren't cut out for being a mom. You left!" I bark, making her flinch.

"Now, son..." her husband starts to say, which has me turning my glare on him.

"Fuck you. I'm not your son. Hell, I'm not her son either." I turn my attention back on her. "It's been nineteen years since I've seen you or heard from you. You left and immediately started a new fucking family? Why?"

Tears well up in her eyes, but I don't give a fuck. She did this, not me. "Why?" I repeat.

"I left for you," she whispers. "Your dad and I—"

"For me?" I cut her off, a humorless laugh escaping. "You left for me?"

"Braxton...maybe let her explain," Kaylee says softly, her hand going to my arm. It's meant to be comforting, but all I can think about is how when I found out she lied to me, she said the same shit. *I did it for you.*

"Fuck you," I hiss, shaking Kaylee's hand off me. "You didn't do it for me. You did it for you. You left and got yourself a whole new family."

Denise—because fuck that, I'm not calling her Mom—shakes her head, liquid spilling down her cheeks, and I can't be here another second. My body buzzes with pent-up aggression, my heart pumping with raw emotion. I need to get the fuck out of here before I do something, say something...

I turn on my heel and stalk away. I hear voices murmuring behind me, but my head is too fuzzy to know what they're saying.

"Brax, wait!" Kaylee yells, trying to catch up to me. "Talk to me, please."

"Not now, Kaylee," I bark. "I need some space."

When I get to the house, I grab the bottle of liquor sitting on the counter and take it up to my room, slamming the door behind me. Seeing my mom and her perfect little family and hearing her tell me that she left for me is just too much.

My dad told me why she left—she didn't want to be a wife or a mom. She wanted to act, wanted to live that life, and we were only holding her back. She broke his heart, so he moved us back to New York to get away from her.

Yet soon after, she remarried and had three damn kids. Not once, in all the years since she left, did she ever reach out. I never looked her up because I didn't want to face what I might find. I was afraid I would find her happy, living her life without a single regret of walking away from Dad and me, but I never thought for a second I would find out she moved on so quickly and started a whole new life.

Fuck, my dad. I wonder if he knows. If he did, it would probably gut him.

I take a swig from the bottle, the alcohol burning as it slides down my throat and warms my insides.

"Braxton!" Kaylee yells through the door, banging on it.

I ignore her. I know she didn't do anything, but hearing another woman who I loved tell me that she did what she did*for me*, something that hurt me, tore me up inside, has me raging, and I can't be around her right now.

"Braxton, please," Kaylee begs. "Open the door. Your mom is here and wants to explain."

Well, that gets my attention. I don't want to talk to the bitch who walked away, but maybe I need to hear her excuses so I can have all the facts when I tell her to go the fuck away for good.

"Where is she?" I ask when I swing the door open.

"Downstairs."

Pushing past Kaylee, I take another swig from my drink and

go downstairs, finding Denise sitting on the couch alone.

"Where's your perfect little family?"

She flinches, wiping her eyes. "I wanted to talk to you alone."

"So talk." I sit on the coffee table across from her.

"When I met your dad, I was young, barely eighteen. I came from a poor family, and he was older. I wanted to go to LA to pursue acting, but then I got pregnant. While he was finishing law school, I stayed by his side, focused on raising you, but I had dreams too..."

"Dreams that were more important than your son?"

She shakes her head. "You were my entire world. A friend of mine told me about a film doing auditions in Manhattan. I didn't think I'd get the part, but I still went for the heck of it. Weeks went by, and I assumed I didn't get it, but then I got the callback. They wanted me. One movie turned into two, and the next thing I knew, I was being offered the chance of a lifetime to star in a huge production. The only problem was they needed me in LA...

"Your dad wasn't happy. He was up for partner at the firm he was working at, but I needed this... for me. So we agreed I would go, and we'd visit each other when we could. I wanted to take you with me, but he said no, said that living on set wasn't the life for a child, and I agreed. So you stayed with him. I was supposed to come back after filming, but then I was offered another role in another movie. The pay was more than your dad made, and I told him I would be a fool not to take it."

She sighs and shakes her head. "I think he resented that I was making more money than him. Anyway, after I told him I wanted to take the job, he agreed to move to LA, giving up his chance at making partner. And for a while, things were good. He found a law firm to work at, and I thought we were happy.

"And then one day I came home and found him with the nanny. I lost it. Told him I was going to file for divorce. I kicked him out and told him we were done."

What the fuck? Nothing she's saying makes any sense. This is nothing like what my dad has told me over the years.

"I had a friend of mine pick you up from school while I was looking for a new nanny, but when she got there, she was told you were already picked up. Your dad had taken you back to New York. Because I was contracted to finish the movie, I couldn't go after you, and before I could file for divorce, your dad filed first, claiming I abandoned you and was an unfit parent."

Fresh tears spill from her lids, and just as I'm about to reach for her and comfort her, she says the words that have me stopping in my tracks.

"I let him have you." Her admission causes my heart to drop. I always knew she walked away, but her confirming it makes it feel real.

"You gave me up without a fight?"

She sniffs. "I did it for you. A long-drawn-out custody battle wouldn't have been good for you. I was young, and your dad was a lawyer—a damn good one. I met with an attorney, and he told me the chances of me winning were slim."

"And I wasn't worth it to you to fight for..."

"No," she gasps. "I regretted it every day. I asked him several times to reconsider, but he was so mad. He said he cheated because I was never home. He blamed me. He was so angry and wouldn't let me near you."

"So instead of trying to fight for me, for your kid you gave birth to, who you were supposed to love and raise and protect and mother, you walked away and started a new family."

I stand, not wanting to hear another word. "Glad we got the facts straight."

"I never stopped thinking about you," she cries. "I just... I didn't know how to fix it. I missed you every day. I had planned to come to you once you turned eighteen, and then your band hit it big, and I'll admit, I was too scared. I thought you would think I was only coming to you because your band was successful."

"You seem to have excuses for everything," I say dryly. "You claim to have loved me, but it wasn't enough to fight for me. You missed me, but it wasn't enough to seek me out. You said you walked away for me. Well, I claim bullshit. You did it for you. Because you were scared and weak, and you didn't love me enough."

"Braxton, please," she pleads, but I raise my hand. I'm done. Just fucking done.

Without another word or sparing her another glance, I walk away from her, the same way she walked away from me all those years ago.

I'm back in my room, one bottle emptied, another half gone, when there's a knock on my door, followed by Kaylee begging me to let her in.

Knowing her ass isn't going to stop until I open the door, I stumble over to it, unlocking and opening it.

"Finally... I—"

"I said I needed space earlier, and I meant it."

"That was before your mom—"

"Doesn't change shit," I slur. "I need fucking space."

Her face falls, and I almost feel bad. "What does that mean?"

"That means what I said. I need time... space to figure my shit out."

"Let me be here for you, please." She places her soft hand on my arm, and I catch a glimpse of the tattoo she got when we were together.

"You said forever..."

"Huh?"

I grab her hand and twist it so she can see the ink. "You said forever, but the second shit got rough, you lied and pushed me away. Just like my mom did."

"That's not the same thing."

"Really? How is it any different? She walked away... for me. You pushed me away... for me. You both promised forever, and as soon as the first bump in the road hit, you forgot the promises you made."

"Braxton..."

"I don't wanna hear it. I've heard enough fucking excuses for one day. What I want is to be by myself and drink until I'm so drunk I forget about today."

Before she can argue, I slam the door in her face and head back onto the balcony, where I do exactly what I said—drink until I'm so drunk I can't remember anything but the porcelain toilet I spend half the night throwing up in.

Twenty-One

Kaylee

"IS HE OKAY?"

Declan shrugs, closing the hotel room door behind him. "He passed out."

"I'm worried about him."

It's been several days since Braxton ran into his mom and lost his shit, and he's spent every waking moment drunk or high—or both. I've tried to talk to him, but he keeps pushing me away, refusing to let me in. Not that it would matter if he did, because he's always so drunk, he wouldn't be able to have a conversation anyway. But I can't imagine all this drinking is good for his liver.

My thoughts go to my dad and how his drinking led to his death.

"We need to get him help."

"He needs time," Camden says, walking over and joining us.

"Like Gage? You guys keep saying that about him, and it's been six years. I get you guys are rock stars, but that doesn't mean you have to go out like them."

Camden sighs. "They're grown-ass men, Kaylee. We can't make them do anything they don't want to do. And Braxton isn't Gage. He's hurt right now and lashing out, but he isn't going to be like this forever. He just needs a damn moment."

"Fine." I shrug, walking away from them.

When I get to my room, I call Layla, needing to vent.

"How are you?" she asks when she answers the phone.

"Better than Braxton."

"That bad, huh?"

She saw the aftermath the next morning when we all had to go to the airport. Braxton was still drunk, and she had to keep Felix away from him, telling him that Uncle Brax was sick.

"It's been days, and he's only getting worse. And the guys are enabling him."

"They mean well," she murmurs.

Since I don't want her caught in the middle, I change the subject. "Evolution reached out."

"The PR company?"

"Yep. They wanted to apologize. They're probably afraid now that the truth is out, thanks to me going live, I'll throw shade their way."

"Which they would totally deserve."

"True, and I'm not interested in working for them anyway. Working with musicians is not my cup of tea. But at least it seems my reputation has been somewhat restored."

"And with the pay from working on the tour, you'll have

money in the bank so you can look for the job you want."

"Exactly."

There's a crash and then, "Mommy!"

"Shoot, Felix just knocked the lamp over doing some new dance. I gotta go. Hang in there. Braxton loves you. He's just struggling right now. We'll talk soon. Love you!"

"Love you more."

We hang up, and since I have the entire night to myself, I pull out my laptop to search for jobs in New York to apply for. Life's too damn short to settle for something you don't love doing.

"HAVE YOU SEEN BRAXTON?"

Camden flinches and shakes his head. "I'm sure he's around here somewhere..."

"Well, he needs to be around here now," I say, irritation evident in my tone. He almost missed a show because he was passed out and nobody could find him. He's skipped two meet and greets and blew off a radio interview. This is quickly becoming an issue.

I get it. His mom messed up. I messed up—although I was hoping we were moving past that, I mean, we even got tattoos that symbolized a fresh start—until he compared me to her, saying we both promised him forever, only to walk away while claiming we were doing it for him. She hurt him... I hurt him. I one-hundred-percent get it. But instead of him dealing with it, he's choosing to avoid it all by remaining drunk and high twenty-four seven. I imagine he's even pissed at his dad since he lied as well, but as far as I know, he hasn't confronted him yet.

"Let's just do it without him," Declan says.

"Again? Fans have posted, calling him out. It's supposed to be all of you. Rumors are going to start circulating."

"We'll talk to him on the bus. But right now, they're waiting for us."

"Fine!" I throw my hands in the air and stalk off, determined to find him. As I'm checking out each of the rooms, I see Gage come out of the room all the way at the end.

"Hey, the meet and greet is starting. Is Braxton in there?"

Gage's bloodshot eyes meet mine. "Yeah," he slurs, "but—"

His words are cut off by the sound of giggles. Fucking giggles. "Motherfucker!" I storm into the room and find Braxton sitting on the couch with a bottle of JD in his hand, taking a large swig while two women are sitting on the other couch, making out like they're in a damn porn film.

"Are you fucking serious right now?"

Braxton glances at me, and then his gaze goes to the women who are still kissing and feeling each other up. His eyes go wide for a split second before he schools his features.

"They're with Gage," he says nonchalantly, looking around. "Speaking of which…where is he?"

"Going to the meet and greet, like you're supposed to be."

"Don't feel like it." He shrugs.

"So they're not here for you?" I nod toward the women still going at it.

"Nope."

"Then you won't mind me doing this..." I stalk over to them and fist each of their manes. "Get out. Now."

They both screech but stumble off the couch. "We were invited!" one whines.

"And now you're uninvited." I push them toward the door, open it up, and shove them out before I slam it closed again.

"What part of space did you not understand?" he says, glaring at me over the bottle.

"Seriously?" I walk over to where he's sitting and grab the bottle from him, the liquid sloshing out over my hand. "It's enough already. I get you're upset, but it's been days, and all you're doing is getting drunk."

Up until this point, he hasn't moved, his features completely devoid of any emotion. But the second the bottle leaves his hand, he jumps up in my face, grabs the bottle from me, and sends it flying across the room. It smashes against the wall, glass and liquid exploding under the pressure.

"It's enough? What are you, my fucking mom?" he half barks, half slurs since he's three sheets to the wind. "Although, I'd bet you two would get along really well. Both of you fucking martyrs."

When he gets in my face, the scent of the alcohol sends me back to when I was a kid... when my dad would get so drunk, he'd start throwing shit, which would lead to him beating the shit out of my mom.

The flashbacks have me stumbling backward, the reality of the situation hitting me like a slap to the face. "You asked me to communicate," I say to him slowly, my eyes locking with his. "Well, this is me communicating loud and fucking clear. I will not be with someone who uses drugs and alcohol to deal with the shitty parts of life. So figure your shit out, and then get back to me."

I open the door, but before I can make my escape, he makes sure to get the last word in. "That's right, Kaylee. Run. Run like you always do. I wouldn't expect anything less. Not from you or from my *mother*."

I want nothing more than to turn around and hug him, comfort him, because I know he's lashing out. He's been hurt. But I can't and won't ever be someone's punching bag. I watched my mom do it for years. I don't believe Braxton would ever put his hands on me, but when people are under the influence, shit gets twisted. My mom never thought my dad would hurt her either. She made excuse after excuse until she was in a hospital bed. She was fighting for her life after having been beaten and finally had no choice but to admit that the man she loved, who she swore would never hurt her, did just that.

So I do what I have to do and walk out the door.

Back at the bus, I pack my stuff and then book a flight to New York. I find Camden as they're coming out from meeting with the fans and pull him to the side.

"I have to go. If that means I'm fired—"

"Whoa, stop," he says. "Did something happen?"

"He threw a bottle of alcohol across the room. I just... with my mom and dad..." I choke out, my throat filled with raw emotion so thick I'm unable to finish my thoughts. This isn't how I saw Braxton's and my relationship progressing, but I should've known nothing in life is ever that easy. And the worst part is that I had finally got him back. Felt him, smelled him, touched him, kissed him…We made love under the stars while fireworks went off, and then the next morning, it all went to shit.

"I get it," Camden says, squeezing my shoulder in a comforting manner. "Honestly, I think it's probably for the best."

"You think I'm making it worse."

"I think as long as you're here, he's going to keep doing this. Maybe if he sees you're gone, he'll wake the hell up."

"Or he'll think I ran." Like he accused me of doing earlier.

"You're not running. You're walking away from a situation you don't deserve to be in. Braxton had a bunch of shit dropped on him, and he's got to wade through it on his own. He never actually dealt with what happened with you two, and now with his mom…I think space will be good for you both."

My heart aches at his words, but he's right. Braxton went from hating me for cheating to being pissed that I lied to pulling me close and us almost acting like it never happened. It was easy to do because when things are good between us, they're damn good. The problem is we've never dealt with the bad. I want to deal with it together, but I can't do that if he's not in a place to be with me.

"And don't even worry about a recommendation or your pay being deducted. You'll be paid in full, and Blackwood will give you a good rec. You did good on the tour. You kept us organized and in line. The promo for the tour exceeded everyone's expectations. It was a success, and we only have a couple of weeks left."

"Thank you. I'll type up everything that's coming up and email it to you and Jill."

"Sounds good. Give my wife a kiss for me when you get

home, yeah? I hate not being there while she's pregnant."

"Since I'm between places, I'm actually planning to beg her...and you to let me crash." I wince, making Camden laugh. Since I was going to be gone for a couple of months, I gave up the room I was renting, throwing all my stuff into storage. I thought I had another couple of weeks to get it all figured out, but I guess not.

"I'm sure she'll love having you crash. And it'll make me feel better knowing she's not all alone with Felix. She won't admit it, but I know she's been doing too much and pushing herself. She's acting like she isn't less than three months away from giving birth."

My heart swells at the love shining in through the annoyance in his tone, proving that while my best friend drives him nuts, he loves her crazy ass.

"You might not be saying that once you're home and I haven't found a place yet."

Camden laughs. "You're welcome any time. Besides, our bedroom is on its own floor." He winks and then envelops me in a hug. "Give him time... he'll come around."

"Maybe," I say back, noncommittedly.

I call Layla on the ride to the airport, and of course, she's ecstatic about me staying with her temporarily. I could stay with my mom, but we haven't been close since she remarried. I actually get where Braxton was coming from when he learned his mom had a whole new family. Our situations aren't the same, but the feeling of your parent starting a new life, one that you feel like you're an outsider to, is something I've felt for years and can completely relate to.

While I wait for the plane to take off, before we're required to turn off our phones, I check my messages no less than a dozen times, hoping Braxton will text me. Of course he doesn't, and as I switch it off and the plane starts its takeoff procedures, I can't help but feel like maybe I made a mistake by crossing over that imaginary line with him. The past six years sucked, for sure. Watching him from afar, wishing we could have another chance, hoping for the opportunity to make things right, wanting to be with him again. But now, I almost wish I was still on the other side, hoping and wanting, because now that I've had him again, it hurts worse, knowing what we might never have.

Twenty-Two

Braxton

THE FLORAL SCENT LINGERS… EVEN AFTER DAYS…MAYBE WEEKS. I HAVE NO CLUE what fucking day it is of her being gone, but I can still smell her. The fragrance of fresh roses clings to the pillows and sheets. If I had allowed the linens to be washed, the smell would disappear, but I've refused. It probably makes me a masochist, getting lost in the scent of a woman I pushed away, not wanting the smell to go away. And during the few minutes when I wake up and am faintly sober, I regret not having the sheets burned, but as soon as the alcohol flows through my system, I crave her scent. It's like the sweetest, most addictive drug—one sniff and I'm hooked.

"Yo, we're here," Camden yells through the door. Usually, the guys and I take turns in this room, but they let me have it when Kaylee was here, and I've continued to sleep in it since she left.

Fuck, she left.

Sometimes, my heart fucking aches. I miss every damn thing about her—the way she would run her fingers through my hair, lightly scraping her nails on my scalp. When she would wake up and smile softly, all sleep drunk and happy. The sight of her in my shirts that weren't long enough to actually cover anything, so when she would walk, her peach of an ass would peek out.

That same ass I'd spend hours squeezing and grabbing and fucking. She loved to be fucked, slow, fast, hard, soft. She would take me any way I wanted. Unlike some insecure women, she's comfortable with her body, with me seeing and touching her body. And after we would have sex and both of us were sated, she'd cuddle up next to me, and we'd talk until she'd eventually pass out.

Other times, I hate her... for the same reasons that my heart hurts. Because she came back into my life, gave me all of herself, and then walked away.

Because I'm not enough for her.

Not enough to fight for.

To stick around for.

Just like I wasn't enough for my mom.

She left. Didn't fight. Moved forward.

Just like Kaylee.

And they both did it for me.

The thought has me reaching for the almost empty bottle and downing what's left, not giving a shit that it's still morning. I have no idea where we are or what city we're in. And I don't give a shit. It's all the same anyway. Drive to a new city, perform the same songs, and then move on. And I could play in my sleep.

"Brax! Let's go!" Camden beats on the door harder, so I roll off the bed and stumble to my feet. I unlock the door, cracking it open slightly. The light filters in, and my skull pulses against my brain.

"We have an interview with NiteLife," he says, pushing the door farther open. "Let's go. You need to shower and"—he grabs the bottle that's apparently still in my hand—"quit drinking! Fuck, man. It's been nearly two weeks, and you've spent it drunk and high. We get it. Your mom fucking sucks, and Kaylee hurt you." He grabs my face and forces me to look at him. "You're making a big mistake, and when you realize it, it's going to be too late."

I snap my head out of his touch and back up, too hungover and not drunk enough to deal with him. "The only mistake I made was letting her back into my life."

"Oh, what-the fuck-ever," Camden spits. "You forgave her until your mom showed up. Now, instead of dealing with your shit, you're taking it out on everyone." He walks back toward the door. "You better figure your shit out soon before she moves on without you. Women will only put up with a man's shit for so long."

"Who the fuck said I want her back? I'll be ready to go in a few minutes."

Instead of arguing, he rolls his eyes and leaves me to get ready. Once I've showered and gotten dressed, I grab my wallet and phone to stuff into my pockets when my phone lights up with an incoming call from my dad. I've been avoiding him since I saw my mom, knowing if I answer, words are going to be said. He fucked up getting Kaylee to help get me to LA, but

I forgave him—for the most part. Now, I find out the shit he pulled with my mom. If he tells me he did it for me, I might lose my fucking head—more than I already have.

When it rings again, I send it to voicemail and then type out a text, letting him know I'm in the middle of something important and I'll call him soon.

The drive to the studio is short, and once we arrive, we're taken to a waiting room that looks similar to a hotel living room. It has a few plush couches and a table and chairs with a spread of food and drinks. There's a bathroom off to the side and a vanity with a shit ton of makeup and hair products.

While we wait to be called out, Gage sprawls out on the couch, closing his eyes since he can't drink or smoke without the other guys giving him shit. Camden sits at the table texting his wife, and Declan sits next to me on the other couch, writing away in his notebook.

Since we left the beach, he's been quiet lately, and I'd bet it has something to do with Kendall kissing that guy she was there to see at the festival. He gets moody every time she starts dating someone new.

I glance over, and sure enough, words like *asshole*, *heartbreak*, and *never mine* are scribbled on the page.

"It might not seem like it now, but you not telling her how you feel is for the best," I mutter.

He glances up at me. "What?"

"Women are nothing but a heartache waiting to happen, and Kendall is no different." She may be chill as hell and fun to hang out with—coming across like one of the guys—but she's still a woman who has no problem stringing men along before she drops them like flies.

"You're only saying that because you're half drunk and hurt."

"No, I'm saying that because it's the truth. Look at Tori..." Declan glares in warning, one I don't heed, and I feel Gage's eyes on me, but I don't care. "What she did to Gage was selfish as fuck. Did she give a shit about him when she destroyed him? No."

"Shut your fucking mouth," Gage barks.

"No. It's the truth, even if you don't like it. She claimed to love you and look what—" Before the rest of the words are out of my mouth, Gage storms over to me and grabs me by the front of my shirt, pulling me up.

Because I'm still half drunk—as Declan pointed out—and hungover, I'm slow to realize what's happening, so before I can block, his fist meets my face, knocking me back on my ass. My face stings from the brute force of his punch, and I can taste blood in my mouth.

"Punching me won't change anything," I point out. "She was a fucking liar, just like—"

"Braxton, stop!" Declan barks, jumping between Gage and me.

"—my mom and Kaylee."

"Enough!" Camden yells, pushing Gage back while Declan remains in front of me.

"Why?" I say, standing and walking over to where the alcohol is. I grab a bottle, crack it open, and chug it down. "It's the truth. Women want love and affection. They lure us in and make us dependent on them. They want loyalty and the promise of forever, and for what? So they can string us along and then fuck us over? Fuck that and fuck them."

I don't know what comes over me, but suddenly, everything feels like it's been built to the highest point and placed on my back. I can't stand, can't walk, can't carry all these fucked-up feelings anymore. The pain, the anger, the resentment. It's all become too much, too heavy, and I need it off me, off my back.

And before I realize what I'm doing, I'm swiping everything off the table, as if all that shit is the weight on my shoulders and in my heart. Fruits and bread go flying every which way. Glass bottles shatter when they hit the floor. Realistically, I know what I'm doing isn't helping in any way, but the release feels good, so I continue destroying everything around me.

At some point, my vision goes blurry, and then hands are on me, pushing me against the wall.

"Brax, chill out," Camden says, his voice calm as always.

"I..." I open my eyes and look around at my best friends, who are more like brothers. They're staring at me with genuine concern and sympathy in their eyes. "I feel sick." I push Camden out of the way and just barely make it to the toilet to throw up the entire contents in my stomach, which is mostly liquid since I've been drinking more than I've been eating.

"You can't keep going like this," Camden says, keeping it real like he always does. "We can't." His gaze swings over to Gage, and my heart plummets into my now empty stomach because his tone makes me realize I'm only adding to the stress Camden carries since he's the person who handles everything for the band, and that's not fair.

"I'm sorry," I choke out.

He nods. "We need to get your face covered before we go

out there."

Declan grabs a makeup artist, who quickly covers the bruise that's already forming on my cheek, and then we go out and handle the interview like the pros we are.

On our way to the hotel, I consider calling Kaylee, but I don't know what to say or where we stand. We'll be home soon, so I decide it would be better if I wait until we can talk face-to-face. I'm not sure what I want at this point, and I know I need some time to figure it out. Even if it means we go our separate ways—a thought that feels like my heart is being squeezed by barbwire—I don't want to have that conversation until I'm sober and thinking clearly. Camden was right. I did forgive her—at least I thought I did—until the shit with my mom happened, and then I lumped her into the same category with my mom.

When we arrive at the hotel, we all go our separate ways. I head to the gym to get a much-needed workout in, hoping to sweat some of the lingering alcohol out of my pores and work on getting back into shape—not that I've fallen too far, but up until the past couple of weeks, I'd been working out once, sometimes twice a day for years.

While I'm running on the treadmill, Fallout Boy's "Sugar, We Goin' Down"—yeah, I prefer old school music, sue me—blares in my ears, forcing me to think about shit. The song cuts off for a second, indicating I have an email. I slow down to check it, since only work and personal shit go here, and press the stop button when I see it's from Easton with the subject: Denise Cohen.

When I was drunk and curious one night, I learned through a search of my mom that she met her husband, Aaron Cohen, while on the set of a movie he was producing—while she was still with my dad. They were married shortly after my parents' divorce was finalized, and soon after came Adam, my apparent half brother. Her husband is worth millions, and after she got pregnant, she took a few years off to be home with their son. She appeared in a few more movies before she got pregnant again with the twins, who I guess I'm also related to. It's crazy... I went from thinking I was an only child to finding out I have three half siblings. She's since remained out of the public eye, her husband the sole provider.

Braxton, a woman named Denise Cohen has reached out to Blackwood in search of you. She's claiming to be your mother and would like a way to get ahold of you since all your social media and email is through us. Would you like me to give her your info?

-Easton

I stare at the screen, unsure what to think. The woman went years without reaching out, and now she wants to, what? Keep in touch? I'm not sure what she can possibly have to say after our last chat. I thought I made how I feel pretty damn clear. I can't imagine anything she has to say will change my mind, but at the same time, the masochistic part of me wants to know.

Easton,

Yeah, that's the woman who brought me into this world and then walked away... You can give her my personal email. Thanks.

I'm lifting free weights when my phone goes off with another email. This time, it's from Denise. Not wanting to read this in the middle of the hotel gym, I go back to my room, take a quick shower, and then open it.

> Braxton,
>
> Thank you for allowing me to contact you. First, I would like to say I'm sorry. I know it's years too late, but I am truly sorry for not fighting harder. I have no excuses except that I was wrong. I took the coward's way out, and I will always regret not fighting harder. I could've contacted you so many times over the years, but I allowed my fear of rejection to stop me, and that's completely on me.
>
> I'm not writing you today to ask you to forgive me, but for Adam. You see, while my husband, Aaron, knew about you, offering many times to help me reach out, I never told our kids about you. I used to tell myself it was because it hurt too much, but the truth is, I didn't want to have to admit what I did... I gave up my son. Because then my kids would ask questions, and my guilt couldn't handle that.
>
> After Adam found out about you, he was upset that he had a brother I never told him about. My hiding the truth about you hurt him, and I don't know how to make that right. I know finding out about having siblings was a shock to you, but I just want you to know that if the day ever comes that you want to get to know them, I know they would love to, and it wouldn't have to have anything to do with me. Although I hope we can talk some more one day, but I'll leave that up to you...

She goes on to give me Adam's contact info as well as hers and then signs it: With love, Denise.

My first thought is the kid only wants to get to know me because of who I am, but at the same time, I have an eighteen-year-old brother who isn't at fault for what went down. Since I'm nowhere near ready to reach out to him, I store his info in my phone and then turn it off, needing to go for a walk so I don't end up getting lost in the bottom of a bottle. I have no desire to email Denise back. She's had years to reach out, so she can wait until I'm damn well ready to respond, if I ever do at all.

Right now, I only have one person I need to focus on: myself. Everybody else can fucking wait.

Twenty-Three

Kaylee

"I'M NOT SURE WHAT TIME I'LL BE—"

"Cam!" Felix yells as the front door opens, and in walks Camden, dropping his bag onto the ground.

"Oh my God!" Layla gasps, springing to her feet and waddling her cute butt over to Camden. "You're home early!"

"Only a day," he says, wrapping his wife and stepson up in a hug. "The bus was having issues, so we ended up flying in instead."

"I missed you so much." She sighs into him, and he drops his arm around her shoulders as they walk back into the living room.

"I made up a new dance," Felix tells him, not giving him a second to get inside and decompress. But if Camden is annoyed, he hides it well, smiling at Felix and giving him his attention, despite, I'm sure, wanting to give his attention to Layla.

"Well, c'mon and show us," Camden says, dropping onto the couch with Layla still stuck to his side.

"Welcome home," I say, standing and hooking my purse over my shoulder.

"You're not leaving on my account..."

"No, I have somewhere I need to be."

"Where?" he presses.

"Café Latte. If you want some alone time later, I can watch Felix for you guys."

"Thanks," Camden says. "Maybe another night. Tonight, I just want to be home with my family."

Layla beams at him like he's hung the moon while Felix starts up the song I've watched him dance to no less than a hundred times in the past week. As I walk out, quickly glancing back at them, I make a mental note to find a place as soon as I find a job. They might have said I can stay as long as I need to, but after Camden being gone for two months, and Layla about to give birth soon, they need this time alone, as a family. Which means it's important I find a damn job.

When I arrive at the coffee shop where Ralph Martinez, the owner of Evolution PR, asked me to meet him, I look for him before grabbing a cup of coffee. I immediately spot him from his pictures on the company website and walk over to him.

"Mr. Martinez?"

"Please, call me Ralph. Kaylee?"

"Yes."

"What would you like to drink?" he asks, standing like a gentleman and pulling my seat out for me. He's dressed in a sharp suit that probably costs as much as the rent here in

Manhattan.

"Iced vanilla latte is good," I tell him, keeping it simple.

"Anything to eat? Those chocolate chip muffins are calling my name." He smiles wide, and a single dimple pops out of his left cheek. He's cute in a wholesome way, but he does nothing for me... not like Bra—

I inwardly sigh and shake *him* from my thoughts. It's been over two weeks since I walked away, and he hasn't once tried to reach out.

"What the heck, I'll take one," I say, suddenly in need of something sweet. Emotional eating is a real thing.

"Sounds good."

While he's at the counter ordering, I check my phone for any messages or emails, telling myself that I'm not looking for anything from Braxton.

When a throat clears, I glance up, thinking it's Ralph, only, instead, it's the man who's been in my every thought.

"Brax," I breathe, shocked to see him standing here. "What are you doing here?"

"Camden said you were here."

"You asked him where I was?"

"He said you were staying with them, and I went by there to talk to you."

"Why didn't you call me?"

"Thought it would be better to talk in person."

My insides knot, unsure if that's a good or bad thing. I take him in, and despite Layla mentioning he was drinking heavily after I left, he looks good—sober and well-rested. He's dressed in a simple T-shirt and jeans, Vans donning his feet and a hat covering his head.

"Here you go," Ralph says, making me dart my eyes from checking out Braxton over to him. "One vanilla latte and a chocolate chip muffin." He sets them on the table in front of me, not realizing that Braxton is standing next to our table, staring daggers at him.

"Brax—"

"Are you serious right now?" Braxton says, not giving me a chance to explain. "You're on a fucking date?"

I shake my head, but he's already jumped to conclusions. "This is Ralph—"

"I don't give a damn who he is. Is this what you're into now? *Suits*?" he spits, making it clear a man in a suit is not a good thing.

Ralph's brows rise at the dig. "Something wrong with a man in a suit?"

"Nope." Braxton shrugs as I quickly stand and grab his arm, needing to haul him away before things get worse. "Just wasn't aware Kaylee was into guys with sticks up their asses."

I know damn well he doesn't feel that way since many of the people he works with at the label wear suits, but it's the only thing that he can think of to talk shit about since he doesn't know who this guy is.

"Braxton," I hiss. "Stop it. You're embarrassing me."

"I'm embarrassing you?" he barks out with a laugh. "It's only been, what? Two weeks and you've already moved on? You're embarrassing your damn self."

"Please give me a moment," I beg Ralph, who's now frowning.

"Nah, you don't need to give her anything. Go sit and enjoy

yourself. We're done here." Braxton shakes my hand off his arm and stalks out, leaving me stuck wondering if I should stay where I am or go after him.

"I'm not sure what's going on," Ralph says, standing, "but maybe you should go handle that. The last thing I want is to get in the middle of..." He waves his hand, unsure of what exactly he just walked into the middle of, and I don't blame him. He's an important man, who has no time for immature shit.

"I'm really sorry."

"It's okay. Really, I just wanted to apologize on behalf of Evolution. When I heard about what happened, I wanted to clear the air myself. If you need a letter of reference, please contact my secretary, and she can get something for you."

In the emails, he mentioned the possibility of a job opportunity in their marketing department. While I wasn't even sure I would take it if it were offered, having not wanted to work for the company who didn't have my back when all that shit went down with Sam York, the fact that it's now off the table because of Braxton has me fuming.

"Take care, Ms. Thomas."

He leaves without taking his drink or muffin with him, and after I throw it all away, I head out, dialing Braxton's number so I can bitch him out. The first couple of times, he sends my ass to voicemail, which only makes me even madder.

On the third attempt, he answers. "Date over so soon? Hope it didn't end on my account."

"Where are you?" I hiss.

And that's when my eyes land on him, leaning against the black SUV with his bodyguard, Justin, standing next to him.

"Don't you move!" I hang up and stalk over to him, watching as he pockets his phone, and his eyes jump up to meet mine.

"What the hell is your problem?" I say once I get over to him.

"Maybe you should've mentioned you moved on, then I wouldn't have intruded." He shrugs, all cockily, like he's got this all figured out

"For your information," I say slowly, "that was the owner of Evolution PR."

His mouth pops open slightly.

"For a guy who's so big on *communicating*, you're seriously the shittiest communicator there is." I poke my finger against his chest. "That was a potential interview, and you just ruined it because you wouldn't listen to me. So maybe, the next time, before you bitch at other people for not communicating, take a look at yourself."

I back up and hit him with one more glare. "Because of you, I lost a job opportunity, so thanks." And because this seems to be our thing, I walk away without waiting for him to respond.

Not wanting to intrude on Cam's homecoming, I go for a walk through Central Park, stopping and sitting on the bench so I can search for job listings on my phone. I apply to several places, even some I don't really want but will take if it means getting my foot in the door, and then send an email to Ralph's secretary, asking for the recommendation letter I was promised since it can't hurt to have.

Once I've sent it, I turn off my phone and people watch, trying to get lost in the beauty and craziness of the city so I can forget about how messed up my life is. When I was growing up and imagining what my life would be like, I never thought I would be so lost at my age.

When I was little, I imagined becoming a wife and a mom. When I got a little older and would sit with my dad, working with him for hours, I imagined going to college and becoming a marketing badass. When he got injured and turned to drugs and drinking, I imagined escaping to college and eventually following in his footsteps—pre-injury. I wanted to make him proud and show him what he was missing out on.

And when he left and my mom found new love, starting a new family, I imagined starting my own. Creating a life and a home that I felt happy and welcome in.

Yet here I am, about to turn twenty-five years old, living in my best friend's home, and once again feeling like an outsider. It's not her fault, and if Layla knew how I felt, she would do everything in her power to make me feel at home. But the truth is, there's nothing she can do because when I see her and Camden and Felix, I don't want to be a part of their family. I want what they have. I want my own house and my own husband who loves me. I want our own kids, our own family. I want a kick-ass career, to go to work and then come home and have someone to discuss my day with.

The problem is, every time I imagine it—the husband, the children, the house, the love—I only see it with one man: Braxton. So many times over the years, I attempted to move forward, went on dates, tried to envision it, but nobody ever fit into that picture but him.

I want him, in the house, with the kids. I want little hazel-eyed babies running around. I want date nights and rides on the motorcycle he told me he bought because he loved his dad's. I want family trips and hot sex... God, sex with Braxton is so damn good. And the way he loves to hold me afterward like he can't get enough...

I don't realize tears are running down my face until the liquid slides down my chin and along my neck. I swipe them away, hating how emotional I am when I did this to myself.

When the sky looks like it's going to burst with raindrops, I reluctantly head home, where I find Layla and Camden cuddling on the couch with Felix spread out on the floor, all of them watching a movie—like the cute, perfect little family they are.

Because Layla didn't fuck everything up like I did.

"Hey, you're home," she says, sitting up slightly. "Wanna watch the movie with us? It just started."

"I have jobs to apply for," I say, plastering a smile on my face.

As if she can sense my unease, she simply nods. "Okay, well, if you change your mind..."

"Thanks."

"Did, umm, Braxton find you?" she asks carefully.

"Yeah." I want to tell them that the next time they think it's a good idea to tell my... well, whatever he is... where I am, they should warn a girl. But then I'd have to explain all that went down, and I'm not in the mood, so instead, I let it go and go to my room so I can continue my pity party for one.

I'm lying on the bed scrolling through social media when my phone goes off with a text from Layla saying everyone is going out to dinner and that I'm invited. Because I know she'll give me shit if I say no, and because, at some point, I'm going to have to face Braxton since we're friends with the same people,

I agree to go.

"WHERE'S GAGE?" I ASK DECLAN, GIVING HIM A HUG AND IGNORING THE TENSION between Braxton and me that's so thick, it would be hard to cut with even the sharpest knife.

"At home." He shrugs. "Probably sleeping the tour off."

We find our seats, and I'm shocked when Braxton comes over and sits on the other side of me. We obviously didn't leave things on good terms earlier, so I'm not sure why he's not sitting on the other side of the huge table.

To keep it from getting awkward, I make it a point to talk to various people throughout the meal, afraid if it goes silent, Braxton will find a way in, and the last thing I want is to argue with him here in front of everyone.

"Hey, Kaylee," Easton says, grabbing my attention. "We received your résumé from a recruiter."

"Oh," I breathe. I filled out a form with an online recruitment company, hoping they might be able to find places hiring that I couldn't. Since the companies are the ones who pay their fee, if they hire someone they find, I figured it couldn't hurt.

"I must've selected the wrong info, or our wires got crossed," I explain. "I'm actually not looking to do anything in PR. My goal is marketing and advertising."

"That's where we're hiring." He smiles. "With so much changing with social media, YouTube channels gaining more popularity, and platforms like TikTok and interactive apps, we're doing a complete overhaul. When I took over, I was focused on the artists and let the marketing side of things go, so our aim this coming year is to bring Blackwood into the twenty-first century, so we stay relevant and on top. We saw a huge increase in Raging Chaos's following when Layla took over and created the YouTube series, so we're planning to take that approach with some of our established clients as well as the new ones we're in the middle of signing."

"That's smart," I agree, having learned a lot about marketing and advertising through social media while in school. "The days of simple television, magazine, and radio ads are long gone. Now, it's all about social media. Look at Kylie Jenner. She's created a billion-dollar empire from her Instagram. Obviously, there's more to it than that, but one of her posts will bring in like a hundred-thousand dollars. People think she's simply posting, but it's all a marketing gimmick."

"Exactly," Easton agrees. "A few of Blackwood's marketing execs aren't on board, wanting to keep it traditional, so when I spoke to the team, a few made the decision to retire early, opening up positions."

"People hate change."

"And change is necessary." He shrugs. "I'm sure you have a few interviews lined up, but we'll be calling you on Monday to schedule one. Bailey will be running the department since she's familiar with the social media aspect, but she needs a team of marketing and advertising experts to work with her. And before you think it's a pity interview, it's not. I'm looking for young employees who are tech-savvy and willing to learn."

He's right. That was my first thought, but I know Easton

doesn't do pity. He owns a multibillion-dollar recording label that houses some of the top artists in the world. You don't get to that level without making smart decisions. Which means if he's considering me, it's because he believes I might be a good fit, and I would be a fool to turn down an interview with his company. "That sounds really good. Thank you for considering me."

The rest of the meal is spent with everyone getting caught up since the guys have been gone. Bailey and Cynthia tell everyone about the week in Hawaii they spent for their honeymoon, alternating between the pool, beach, and spa.

When the check comes, Easton, of course, insists on paying. We walk out to the front, and after everyone says their goodbyes, I start heading to Camden's SUV when a hand grabs my wrist.

"Can we go somewhere and talk?"

Layla glances back, then quickly turns around, pretending to give us privacy.

"Please," he says softly, so he doesn't cause a scene. "I just want to talk."

I stop and look at him for a moment, wondering if that's smart, since every time we *talk*, it ends in us fucking or fighting, but I decide he's right. We do need to talk. We both have things we need to say, and it might as well happen now so we can get it over with. Neither of us is going anywhere, so it will be good to clear the air.

"Okay, sure. We can talk."

Twenty-Four
Braxton

WHEN KAYLEE AGREES TO TALK TO ME, I SIGH IN RELIEF. WE'VE BOTH FUCKED UP, DONE shit neither of us is proud of, but being without her these past couple of weeks has proven one thing: I can't be without her—and I don't want to be.

Since it's hard to go anywhere without being spotted, we go back to my place, but instead of taking her to my bedroom, we go out onto the balcony. I flip on the lights and guide her over to the lounge chairs. Neither of us says a word for several minutes, both of us lost in our thoughts. So much has happened. It would probably be easier for us to walk away from each other, but I can't do it. I love her and always have.

Just as I'm about to tell her what I'm thinking, she speaks first.

"Without trust, we have nothing. And it's clear you don't trust me. For you to think after everything we've been through, when you were inside me only a couple of weeks ago, I would run to another man without so much as talking to you first proves that.

"And if I'm being honest, I don't know if I trust you either because every time you get upset, you end up drinking and getting high, and I can't be with someone like that.

"What you did at the hotel, the drinking and yelling and throwing shit? It's what my dad did before he started to get violent..."

Her sad gray eyes meet mine, and I've never felt like more of a piece of shit than I do at this moment. I was so caught up in my anger, my hurt, I didn't even stop to think about how it would affect her because of her past. In my drunken head, it was just a fight. I was pissed and reacted, but for someone who was raised in an abusive household, it went deeper than that for her.

"Kaylee, I'm—"

"You're what? You're sorry? That's what he would say, the morning after...he would apologize and beg my mom for forgiveness. Sometimes, he would bring her roses and breakfast, and she would fall for it every time...because she loved him."

I hate that she's comparing me to her father, but I get it, so I don't argue. Instead, I nod in understanding.

"I can't be her," she says, her words cracking with emotion. "I *won't* be her." The decisiveness in her eyes and in her tone fills me with pride. I have no doubt she loves me, but I believe she would walk away before she would allow what happened to her mom to happen to her, and I love her that much more because of it.

"I don't want you to be her." I edge closer and take her hands in mine, kissing the tops of her knuckles.

"So where do we go from here?"

"We fight." I lock eyes with her. "We fight for each other because we love each other. And we'll get through this." I entwine our fingers and tug her into a standing position, guiding her back into the house. I head straight for the kitchen and, with her hand still in mine, use my other one to open each of the cabinets, pulling bottles of liquor from them and dumping them into the trash. Next, I clear out the fridge.

Once that's done, I take us upstairs to my room, where I grab the few bottles and a couple of joints on my dresser and drop them into my garbage.

"I'm not an addict," I tell her. "But I do use it as an escape, and I will never do that again. If I have to see a therapist or go to AA to prove it to you, I will." I grab her other hand and pull her close to me. "I won't lose you over alcohol and drugs."

"It's not that easy," she argues.

"No, it's not," I agree. "But I love you, and you love me, and I'll fight for you, for us, every damn day if you fight right alongside me. And some days, when you don't feel like you can fight, I'll fight for us both." I release her hand and cup her face. "And I know you'll do the same."

"We fight," she breathes, tears welling in her eyes.

"We fight."

Our mouths come together at the same time, ravaging each other, needing the connection. Her arms encircle my neck, and I pick her up, twirling us around and setting her on top of the dresser. Her legs part, and I step between them, deepening the kiss. I've missed her so damn much, her lips, her touch, her scent.

Her hands glide down the sides of my neck and over my shoulders. She makes her way under my shirt, her cool hands sliding up and down my abs before she moves down to my pants. It feels so good, being with her, kissing her... I want more, but if we're going to make shit work, we have to change how we handle shit. What's that saying? *Doing the same thing over and over again while expecting different results...*

I pull back, breaking our connection. "I want this, and I want you, but I don't want to fall back into our usual pattern of having makeup sex."

Her eyes widen slightly in shock, and trust me, I get it because I've never imagined saying those words, but I don't want her for now. She's my goddamn forever, which means we need to make different choices.

"You said we need trust, and I agree. I think we should work on that. Getting to know each other without the sex."

The gorgeous smile that spreads across her face tells me I made the right suggestion.

"Okay," she says, leaning forward and giving me a chaste kiss before dropping onto the ground, her body rubbing against mine on the way down. "So I guess I'll see you later?" She steps around me, edging toward the door.

"Now, wait a second..." I snag her hand and pull her back to me. "I didn't say we couldn't hang out. We have a perfectly good hot tub..."

She laughs. "Which will end with us fucking in it."

True. "Okay, we could go out."

"Where?"

I think for a moment. It's hard for a person like me to just go out without being bombarded. New York is better than LA, but it can still get crazy if you're spotted. "Lush." A friend of mine owns the club, and he caters to people like me who are in the spotlight.

"Oh! I've been wanting to check out that club, but it's super hard to get into."

"Let's go. We can go dancing and—"

"Drinking?" She raises a brow.

"I was going to say dancing and have a good time."

She winces. "Sorry."

"Don't be." I wrap my arms around her. "I'm not an addict, Kaylee. I know those are just words, and it'll take time for you to see that, but I'll show you. I want to take you dancing. We never got to have that."

"Have what?"

"Dating. We did it when we were younger, but not once we were adults. We've been on tour for months. Now that we're home, I want to date you... woo the hell out of you."

She giggles, the sound so damn beautiful. "You've been hanging out with Camden for too long."

She isn't wrong. Camden and his dad love that damn word, and we always give them shit for it, but look at them, both happy and in loving relationships with families of their own. Maybe they're onto something.

"I'm gonna woo the fuck out of you, baby," I tell her, kissing her roughly.

"I can't wait."

AFTER TEXTING JUSTIN TO LET HIM KNOW I'LL NEED HIM TONIGHT, I GET DRESSED AND then we head to Camden's place, so Kaylee can get dressed. Camden and Layla end up joining us because her mom took Felix for the night, so we pile into the SUV and head to Lush. I text Declan and Gage to let them know where we're going in case they want to join, and then shoot Brody Fields, the club owner, a message, letting him know we'll need a VIP table if that's possible. I probably should've asked first, but it was all last minute. A few minutes later, he replies that he'll have it taken care of.

Clubs like his are already popular, but they know that once we're in there and post our location on social media, it's free advertisement for them. It's why celebs can go anywhere and do anything for free. Why famous people get stuff sent to them in the hopes they'll post about it. I can't even tell you how many guitars I've been sent by various companies, hoping I'll post about their products.

When we arrive, it's after ten o'clock, and the line to get in is around the damn corner. With two of our guards flanking us, we walk straight to the bouncer, who immediately recognizes us and lets us through with a single nod.

The hostess takes us directly upstairs to a roped-off area and lets us know our server will be by momentarily to take our orders.

Without waiting for her to arrive, I snag Kaylee's hand and pull her over to the dance floor. She's dressed in a tight little shimmery dress with tall as fuck heels, her blond locks down and messy. Her fingers delve into my hair, and my hands grip the curves of her hips, grinding against her. This club isn't like most. It's not as loud and crazy. The clientele is a bit older and on the wealthier side. The music is more sensual, the lights lower.

The song transitions from one to the next, and I tighten my hold on Kaylee as our bodies sway to the beat. My knee is nestled between her thighs, so close to her cunt that I can feel her warmth. I drop my face into the crook of her neck and suckle on her heated flesh, then kiss my way across her exposed skin. My hands skate down to the swell of her ass and give it a slight squeeze.

She shivers in my arms, and I chuckle, loving the effect I have on her. The fact is, it doesn't matter what we do—our attraction, our chemistry, is so goddamn potent that the possibility of it ending in sex is always present.

When she sighs into me, squirming a bit, my lips meet the shell of her ear. "Are you turned on?"

"You know I am." Her thighs tighten around my leg, squeezing it like her pussy does to my dick when it's inside her. I lift my knee slightly, rubbing it against her center. When she moans, I know I've hit the right spot, so I keep doing it. Her moans get louder the closer she gets to her orgasm, and when she detonates around me, I crash my mouth to hers, muffling the sound, just in case. The music is loud, but I don't want to chance it. Her body trembles, and I can feel the wetness between her legs even through my jeans.

When she comes down, sagging into me, I end the kiss, and her sated eyes meet mine. "I want you now."

I grin at that, loving that an orgasm isn't enough for her. She wants *me*. "Not tonight."

"Yes, tonight," she argues. "I bet there's a bathroom somewhere..." Her gaze darts around the area.

"I'm sure there is, Crazy, but we're not finding out." I palm her neck and kiss her softly. "No sex... not until I woo you."

We spend the next few hours dancing and hanging out with our friends. Declan shows up but doesn't stay for long, saying he's not in the mood to play the fifth wheel. When Layla says she's tired and ready to go home, we all head out. I want to ask Kaylee to come home with me, but I don't, wanting to mean what I said. Instead, when I kiss her goodbye, I thank her for tonight and tell her I'll text her later.

Twenty-Five

Kaylee

“WOW! YOU DID ALL THIS?” TEARS FILL LAYLA’S EYES AS SHE TAKES IN THE PRIVATE room filled with pink-and-white balloons and streamers. There’s a three-tier pink-and-white cake with a princess-crown topper, dozens of matching cupcakes and cake pops, as well as several kinds of pastries.

Tables with pink linens and comfy chairs are spread out throughout the room, and a couple of servers are walking around, offering everyone coffee and tea since the shower is being held at The Tea Room.

“When you were pregnant with Felix, you didn’t get a shower.” I shrug. “You deserve to be spoiled a little.”

She nods in understanding, wrapping her arms around me. “Thank you.”

“That’s what best friends do, especially ones who take over their best friend’s guest room.”

"Oh, stop it," she chides. "You know I love having you close to me."

It's been almost a month and a half since I've moved in with Camden and Layla, and while they keep saying I'm welcome to stay as long as I want, I need to seriously find my own place. I've started working at Blackwood, and with the pay they offer, I'll be able to afford rent without a problem.

"I know, but my plan is to be out before the baby comes."

She pouts slightly but doesn't argue.

"This all looks so great," Kendall says, giving us a hug. "I can't believe I'm going to have a niece soon." She rubs Layla's belly since she doesn't mind. She actually encourages it. "Have you thought of any names?"

"A few," Layla says, "but we haven't decided yet."

"Well, whatever you don't use, you can use for the next baby," Sophia says with a laugh.

"Funny," Layla says back. "Don't say that in front of your son, though. He's already asking how long we have to wait for me to get pregnant again." Everyone cracks up even though we know she's not kidding.

"Saw you were spotted out with Declan last night," Bailey says to Kendall when we're all seated with plates of sweets and cups of coffee and tea.

"Yeah, so?" she says, taking a sip of her coffee. "We're good friends."

I groan inwardly at the word friend and glance at Layla, catching her wince as well. The last thing Declan wants is to be Kendall's friend, but unfortunately, he's been friend zoned.

"We've been writing together," Kendall adds. "I think I'm

going to pitch one to Dad."

"That'd be cool," Bailey agrees. "Won't be the first time a pop and rock star collaborated."

"Exactly." Kendall's phone goes off, and when she looks at it, she smiles.

"Declan?" Bailey pushes, clearly on a mission. Her wife, Cynthia, nudges her, but she ignores her.

"No." Kendall types out a message, then looks up. "I've started seeing someone. He's an attorney here in New York. It's not serious or anything, but I really like him."

That's what she always says... until she finds something wrong with him and dumps his ass. It's why Declan won't speak up. He's afraid he won't be able to hold on to her. From the outside, Kendall looks like the perfect pop star. She's beautiful and sweet, but underneath, there's something imperfect, something that eats away at her. Nobody goes through men like one changes their underwear unless they have a hidden insecurity. The problem is, until she deals with it, she'll keep doing what she's been doing for years.

"Does that mean you're sticking around for a while?" her mom asks.

"Yep. I was actually meaning to tell you. I've rented a place near the studio. Since everyone is here, and Layla is about to give birth to my niece, I should be here too."

"That makes me so happy," Sophia tells her daughter even though you can see it in her features that she won't believe it until she sees it.

After we finish eating, we play a few baby games, and then Layla opens her presents. I watch as she oohs and aahs over every outfit and item she unwraps, imagining what it will be like one day when I'm pregnant.

My thoughts go to Braxton and how amazing things have been lately. He meant what he said about wooing me. We've been going on dates almost daily, but since the night at the club—when he got me off with his damn thigh—we haven't taken it any further than that. He picks me up and drops me off like a gentleman, and while we're out, we talk and get to know each other all over again. I've already known I love Braxton, but with every day we spend together, I find myself falling for him all over again.

As if he can sense me thinking about him, my phone pings with a text from him: **So I was thinking... What would you think about going away, just the two of us, this weekend?**

Butterflies attack my belly, knowing what he's asking—implying. And he's leaving it up to me.

Braxton: Nothing has to happen...

I love that he's added that, that he made the decision for us to focus on us and has stuck to it. It's been a month, and not once has he had a drink or smoked. We haven't fought at all, and while I know it won't always be perfect, it's been nice getting to know each other all over again without the drama. We've talked about the past, about his mom and dad, and we've agreed to put it all behind us. This is our fresh start, and even though we'll always have history, we don't want it to taint our future.

Braxton: Kaylee... did I fuck up?

Shit! I never messaged him back, lost in my thoughts.

Me: You didn't mess up. I would love to go away with you,

and it's the perfect time since I won't want to go anywhere after Layla has the baby... at least for a little bit.

I don't mention anything about his *nothing has to happen* comment. There's nothing to say. If it happens, then it happens—and really, I think at this point, if it does, then it's okay.

Braxton: Pick you up at 8:00. Pack light and a bikini.

"What's got you smiling like a crazy person?" Layla asks, nudging me.

"More like who... Braxton."

"Well, duh, but what did he say?"

"We're going away for a couple of days, so you'll get your house to yourself."

Layla rolls her eyes. "You know I don't care about you being there, but good for you."

"ARE YOU SERIOUS RIGHT NOW?" I SQUEAL, RUNNING OVER TO THE MOTORCYCLE parked in the driveway. "I haven't been on one since..."

My eyes meet Braxton's, and he smiles. "Good. You don't belong on the back of any man's ride but mine."

He takes my bag from me and stuffs it into the saddlebag, then hands me a small helmet. He gets on and then helps me as I wrap my body around his. Once we're situated, and my arms are wrapped tight around his torso, he takes off down the drive and onto the road, going slow until we're out of the Blackwood's community. Since they live just outside of the city, it doesn't take long to get on the main road and away from the crazy traffic.

The second I see the sign, I know exactly where we're going: The Hamptons.

The ride there takes a couple of hours, but it flies by. The wind is too loud to talk, but we don't need to speak to enjoy each other's company. While he drives, I cuddle up against his back, my hands finding their place under his shirt and resting on his muscular stomach. Every once in a while, he finds my thigh and squeezes.

When we pull up to the gorgeous beach house, I notice it's not the Blackwood's, which makes sense since Easton and Sophia use theirs a lot during the summer.

Braxton grabs our bags, and I follow him up to the house. He types in a code on the door, and then we enter. The house is as beautiful on the inside as the outside, decorated with a nautical theme in various shades of blues and whites. I immediately spot the pool and hot tub outside and know we'll be spending a good amount of time out there. With it being close to fall, this will probably be our last trip where we'll be able to hit the pool and beach. Soon, it will be cold as hell, and instead of a bikini, I'll be stuck sporting my snow jacket and UGGs.

After exploring the house, we settle in the master bedroom and quickly change into our bathing suits. Braxton is wearing a pair of board shorts that hang off his hips in that delicious way that only guys with sexy abs can pull off.

I packed a couple of suits but go with the risqué one since we're alone. Braxton's gaze goes straight to me when I walk out of the bathroom in a light pink bikini with cherries peppered all over the fabric, but it's when I turn around, and he sees the way the bottoms curve between my cheeks, leaving nothing to the imagination, that I hear the sharp intake of breath.

"Tell me you don't wear this fucking thing in public," he murmurs, his voice husky. The heat from his body radiates against me from behind, his hands roaming my exposed flesh.

"It's my tanning suit," I admit. Every woman has one... the one that gives us the least number of tan lines, but we'd never wear it while walking around—unless we're alone and want to turn our boyfriends on, that is.

"Fuck, Crazy," he mutters. His mouth lands on my naked shoulder, biting down playfully. His tongue darts out to soothe it while his hand reaches my ass cheek, taking a handful and squeezing it. "How are we supposed to take shit slow when you wear shit like this?"

"I think we've taken things slow enough." I reach behind and cup his cock through his board shorts. "I'm ready to speed this up a bit."

He dusts my hair to the side and trails open-mouthed kisses up my neck until he gets to the tie in the back holding my top on. With a kiss, I feel him tug, and the material falls away. My breasts hit the cold air, and a shiver scatters through my body, causing my nipples to instantly harden.

"Your tits are so perfect," he says, his hands coming around and cupping both of them. I glance up, just now realizing there's a mirror on the back of the door, giving us the full view of what he's doing to me.

As his thumb and middle finger pinch and pluck my nipples, I take us in through the mirror. His inked to my not, his hard body to my soft. Without heels on, he towers over me by almost a foot, something I've always loved because it makes me feel safe and protected in his arms.

His heated gaze meets mine, and I squirm in my spot, wanting nothing more than for him to take away the ache that's now throbbing between my legs.

"Are you ready to go swimming?" he asks, stopping his ministrations and tying my top back on.

"I'm ready for you to fuck me," I say, not caring how crass I sound.

He chuckles softly. "Not yet." He twists me around, so our fronts are flush against each other. "Once I'm inside you, I won't want to leave."

"I'm completely okay with that," I breathe, fully aware of how desperate I sound. But really, can you blame me? It's been a long-ass time, and my vibrator has got nothing on this man.

"Soon." He brushes his lips against mine, then bites down on my bottom lip, sucking it into his mouth before he lets go. "It's a beautiful day and probably one of the last before the cold weather moves in. Let's enjoy it." He kisses the tip of my nose and then takes my hand, guiding us downstairs and out the back.

Braxton hooks his phone up to the dock, and a second later, music is playing around us. He's right, it is beautiful outside, and as much as I want to be holed up in bed with him, I love spending time with him. We head straight for the pool, both of us diving underneath and immersing ourselves in the water. It feels good, the perfect temperature.

When I'm swimming from the deep end to the shallow end, Braxton hooks his arm around me and pulls me into him, his mouth connecting with mine in a passionate kiss. My legs encircle his waist, clinging to his muscular torso like a jellyfish, and for several minutes, we make out, our tongues dancing and our bodies grinding against one another. It feels good to just be with him.

When we both come up for air, he pushes the wet strands of my hair out of my eyes.

"Hey, beautiful," he murmurs with a smile. I love seeing him happy, alcohol and drug free. His hazel eyes are bright and filled with love. He hasn't said the words since we've been back together, but I can feel them in everything he does and every look he gives me.

"Hey back." I run my fingers through his messy, wet hair. "This is nice… being away. Between planning the baby shower and my new job, it's been kind of crazy lately." Good crazy, but still crazy.

"No matter how busy life gets, we'll make time like this." He kisses the corner of my mouth. "How was the baby shower?"

"It was good. That little girl is going to be so spoiled. I can't wait to give her all the lovin'."

Braxton chuckles. "Do you still want three kids? Two boys and a girl, so they have each other and will be protective of their little sister?"

My heart swells that he still remembers what I said even after all these years.

"Yeah, three kids would be perfect. What about you? How many do you want?"

"I want whatever you'll give me," he says, wading us through the water until my back hits the wall.

"So what if I wanted seven?" I joke.

"Then we better get to it." He winks. "But seriously, though,

I'd be good with however many you want. I agree having two or three would be perfect, so they never feel alone. I always had the guys, but it would've been nice to have someone in my house I could talk to and get into trouble with." He hits me with a gorgeous smirk that has me tightening my legs around him.

"Speaking of which... How's Gage?" Ever since they returned home from the tour, he's been acting weird. We've always been close. Even during the years I didn't see them, we would keep in touch, but every time I text him, he gives me one-word answers, which has me worried.

Braxton frowns. "He met someone..."

"What? Who?"

"We don't really know much. A few days after we got home, she showed up and hasn't left. They're usually in his room, only coming out to eat, and sometimes they go for walks, I think. I've seen them hanging out on his balcony a lot. She doesn't really talk much, but she seems nice. Kind of... sad, though. I feel like there's a story there, but we're trying to give him his space. It's the first woman he's hung out with since..."

"Yeah," I breathe, my heart clenching at the thought of Tori. She was one of my best friends, and her death... fuck, it was just so tragic. "Is he still using?"

"I'm not really sure. He's been so wrapped up in her that he's rarely around. I can't imagine him not smoking, but if he's doing anything harder, it hasn't been in front of us."

"Kendall's dating some new guy... A lawyer."

Braxton shakes his head. "Poor Dec."

"It's his own fault for not telling her how he feels. He should've learned from Camden not to do that."

"True." He presses his mouth to mine. "I knew the moment you kissed me all those years ago that you were the one for me."

"And do you still feel that way?" I ask, knowing the question shows my insecurities, but in my defense, we haven't talked about our future, aside from fighting for each other—and now, when we were talking about babies...

"I do," he says without hesitation. "I know what it feels like to be with you, and without you, and I know you're the one for me." Pinning me to the wall with his body, he brings his hand up and cups my face. "I love you, and any future I see has you in it."

I can't help the smile that splits across my face at his words. "I love you too, and I feel the same way."

Braxton's lips glide against mine, and I sigh into him, feeling like I'm finally content for the first time in a long time.

Twenty-Six

Braxton

"BRAX!" KAYLEE SHRIEKS, CACKLING LOUDLY AS SHE SPLASHES ME WITH THE SALT water.

"You're going to get it," I warn, wiping my face and swimming toward her. We've spent the past two days between the pool, the beach, and the bed. We have to leave tonight so she's back for work tomorrow, but she wanted to spend the afternoon at the beach one last time before we go.

"I'm sorry!" She laughs, obviously full of shit.

While we were lounging under the cabana on a large beach blanket, I fell asleep and woke up completely covered in sand. She thought she was funny, but I had the last laugh when I grabbed her and carried her out to the water, throwing her ass in it.

"You're not, but you will be," I taunt, pouncing on her. She tries to swim away, but she's not fast enough, and before she can escape, I grab her and lift her into my arms.

"Brax, please. I really am sorry." She's laughing so hard her words come out in a breathy gasp. I fucking love it. The melodic sound. All I want is to listen to her laughter every day. See her smile. Her face light up. I can't get enough of it... of her.

"Nope. You should've thought about what you were doing." When I get to an area where I can stand, I haul her over my shoulder, smacking her ass as I walk us out of the ocean and back over to where our blanket and cabana are, dropping her onto the ground once we're there.

Holding her so she can't run, I lie on my back and haul her on top of me, kissing her lips while I shove her bikini bottoms off her, leaving her completely bare.

"What are you doing?" She gasps when I grip the backs of her thighs and haul her up until her legs are on either side of my face, hovering over me and giving me the perfect glimpse at her pink lips and swollen clit.

"Doling out your punishment. Now sit on my face."

We're on a private beach and haven't seen more than a handful of people walk by in the two days we've been here, so I'm not too concerned about getting caught. Besides, if someone does walk by, nobody will know it's me anyway since her pussy is covering my face.

"You want me to...?"

"Sit." I pull her down so her pussy is almost suffocating me and inhale deeply, loving the scent of her arousal mixed with the ocean.

When I start to lick her, she's shy at first, but then her hands come down, her fingers separating her lips, so I have better access. As I suck her clit, she rocks back and forth gently, working in tune with my tongue. And then, her fingers delve into my hair, and she uses her grip to grind herself against my mouth, finding her pleasure. She comes long and hard all over my tongue, moaning through her release as her juices flow into my mouth and down my face.

"Fuck, baby, you taste so good." I give her pussy an open-mouthed kiss, and she trembles around me, coming down from her orgasm.

She lifts up, and I'm not sure where she's going—maybe to clean off, maybe to ride my dick, I don't know—but I'm not done with her yet. So grabbing her hips, I flip her around so she's back on my face, only this time, her hands land on my thighs, as if she's on all fours, giving me a different view of her pussy and now ass.

"Braxton," she breathes, ready to argue that she already came, but before she can finish her sentence, my mouth is back on her pussy, licking her juices. She shocks the hell out of me when she once again starts riding my face, this time bouncing up and down while I fuck her with my tongue. She moves forward and back, and when she moves forward again, my tongue slides to her puckered hole to give it some attention.

"Oh, shit!" she screams. "Do it again."

This time, I thrust my tongue into the tight hole, making her moan. "Yes! Yes, that feels so good. More, please," she begs. "I want it in my ass."

She sure as hell doesn't have to tell me twice. I haven't been with her in over a month, so I'll take her any way she'll let me have her.

"Flip back over," I demand, slapping her ass a couple of times.

She does as I say, her legs coming back around to straddle my face. My finger swipes at her juices from behind, and I push it into her asshole, making her moan in pleasure. Her hands go to her tits, plucking and pinching her nipples, while I eat her pussy and finger-fuck her ass. Her moans get louder, her body jerking up and down, and then I feel it. Her pussy tightens and then releases, and she gushes, motherfucking gushes all over my goddamn face.

"Oh, fuck!" she screams, her head tilting back in ecstasy as she rides out another orgasm.

When she looks down and sees the mess she's caused, her eyes go wide, her cheeks tingeing pink as she scrambles off my face.

"Nope, don't you get embarrassed." I grab her hips so she can't go far. "That was the hottest thing I've ever seen in my life."

She drags her bottom lip between her teeth, and I grab her nape to pull her down for a kiss. I expect her to be disgusted by her orgasm all over my face, but instead, she moans, deepening the kiss. Since she's already in position, I reach down and pull my dick out, then thrust up into her sensitive pussy.

She moans into my mouth, taking every inch as I try like hell not to nut too soon. It's been too long, and she feels too good. I could stay right here in her for the rest of my life.

"Fuck me, please," she begs, so I do. I fuck her deep and fast. I would love for her to come again, but she's already come twice, and I'm not sure if I can pull off a third. But still, I try. I rock into her, my piercing hitting her walls in the way I know she loves, and minutes later, she's gripping me like a vise, coming for the third time, and this time, she drags me along with her.

When we've both come down, she opens her eyes and sighs, wearing a sated smile on her beautiful face. "I think we should say 'fuck the world' and move here. You can give me orgasms all day while we lie out by the pool and beach."

She drops down next to me and cuddles into my side, and even though she's only joking, a part of me wishes we could do just that. Because right here, with Kaylee in my arms, is all I fucking need.

The thought both excites and scares the shit out of me because the last time I lost her, I lost a big piece of my heart. And while I'm now older and stronger, my heart a bit tougher, when it comes to Kaylee, I'm still weak as fuck. I have no doubt if she walked away again, a huge part of my heart would go with her. And I'm not sure if there'd be enough left for it to function properly.

"What's going through that head of yours?" she asks, running her nails down my torso. She stops where my newest tattoo is—the one I got of the roses and thorns to symbolize our love—and gently brushes her fingers along it, tracing the outline of the roses.

"That I'm not sure I can handle losing you again," I admit truthfully.

Her fingers still, and she props herself up so she can look into my eyes. "You'll never have to worry about that. I love you, Brax. You're my forever, and nobody is going to come between us again."

Bailey: Pictures leaked of you and Kaylee on the beach.

I read the text, my mind going straight to her sitting on my face earlier and quickly hit call.

"What pictures?"

Bailey laughs. "Hello to you too."

Bailey, Camden's sister and our social media guru at Blackwood, handles everything for the band, monitoring what gets posted and making sure nothing pops up that can cause us to be seen in a bad light. Image is everything in our business, and with social media being so huge, it's easy for a simple picture to be taken out of context.

"What pictures?" If there are any of Kaylee naked, I will kill whoever invaded our privacy—even if it's my fault for dropping my guard so I could give her several orgasms on the beach under our cabana.

"You guys at a restaurant in The Hamptons..."

I release a breath of relief. "Oh."

"You've been spotted, so don't be surprised if you're accosted anywhere you go."

"We're about to leave, so it's all good."

"The paps are speculating, saying with two out of four band members with hearts in their eyes, this might be the band's undoing."

"They're fucking dumbasses." I scoff.

"True, but we should probably put out some kind of press release. I'm going to talk to the PR department and see what they think."

"All right, well, let me know. We'll be home tonight, and Kaylee will be at work tomorrow morning."

"Sounds good."

We hang up, and I'm about to join Kaylee in the shower when my phone pings with an incoming email to my personal account from Adam Cohen, my half brother.

I click on the email and read it once, then again, unsure how I feel about it. I'm reading it for a third time when Kaylee comes up and wraps her arms around me from behind.

"Whatcha doing?" she asks, kissing the side of my neck. "I thought for sure you'd have joined me in the shower."

"I was planning to, but then I got a text from Bailey saying that pictures were taken of us." She stills, and I know she's thinking what I thought. "Of us having dinner." She sighs in relief.

"People are talking shit, saying the band's going to split up because two of us are in relationships."

"Like what your dad was afraid of."

I pull her around so she's draped across my lap. "My dad was wrong."

"Have you spoken to him?"

"No, I've been avoiding him, and before you try to shoulder the blame, it's not because I found out he guilted you into pushing me away. He lied about my mom, and I'm not sure how I feel about that."

Kaylee nods. "I get that. But maybe you two should talk. Throw it all out on the table. He's still your dad."

"Yeah." I scrub my hand over the side of my face. "I also got an email from Adam."

"Your half brother?"

"Yeah, he's going to college in New York and would like to meet up to get to know me."

"And how do you feel about that?"

"I'm not sure." I stare down at the email. "Just yesterday, we were talking about wishing we weren't only kids so we would have siblings to connect with. Now I have one who wants to get to know me. On the one hand, it's not his fault, but on the other..."

"He's part of the person who hurt you."

"Yeah."

"Well, you don't have to do anything now. If he's here for college, he'll be around for a good four years."

"True. If I wanted to meet him, would you go with me?"

"Of course." She frames my face and kisses me. "We're in this together, Brax."

"STOP FIDGETING."

"I'm not fidgeting. Chicks fidget."

"Then I guess you're a chick because you're totally fidgeting." Kaylee grabs my hand and entwines our fingers, bringing them to her lips. She softly kisses my knuckles, and I instantly calm. I shouldn't be this nervous to meet a stranger. I mean, I meet fans every day. I take pictures with them, sign shit during the meet and greets while on tour, and converse with them. But this is different. Because this stranger is my flesh and blood.

"Hey, sorry I'm late," Adam says, stepping up to the table. "My class got out, and I had to ask the professor a quick question, which turned into a twenty-minute conversation, and then I took the wrong train and.... Fuck, transportation is nothing like in LA. I mean—"

"Breathe," Kaylee says, smiling at Adam. "It's all good. We only just got here. Please, sit."

Adam does as she says and takes a deep breath. "Sorry, when I'm nervous, I ramble."

"That's okay. Braxton fidgets like a chick."

She winks at me, reminding me why I love her so damn much.

"I'm Adam," he says, extending his hand toward her.

"I'm Kaylee. It's nice to meet you."

He smiles warmly at her, then has a seat and glances at me, his features turning nervous. I take a moment to look at him, to see if we look alike, but aside from both of us having hazel eyes, nothing would prove we're siblings without a DNA test.

"So Adam," Kaylee begins, breaking the awkward silence. "What are you majoring in?"

"Umm..." He clears his throat, his eyes darting over to me. "Well... music. But please know me reaching out has nothing to do with that. I'm not like trying to start a band or anything. I'm double majoring in music therapy and education, so it really has nothing to do with what you do.

"I wanted to meet you because, up until recently, I didn't know who you were. I knew I had a brother out there, but Mom wouldn't say who you were. I mean, I knew your name, heard the whispers, even though she thinks she hid it from us, but not your last name. And shit, I'm totally rambling again." He sighs, sounding utterly defeated. "If you don't want to get to know me, I'll completely understand. I just thought since I was here and you're here... I have two sisters, but they're a pain in my ass. Well, I guess technically, they're your sisters too. They're cool, but I've always wanted a brother..."

"Breathe," Kaylee says again with a soft laugh.

"Sorry." He winces.

The server walks over and takes our drink orders, and then disappears. We're in a semi-private room at a bistro Kaylee loves. If I decide to pursue a relationship with Adam, I'll choose who knows and when. I'm not leaving that shit up to the damn media.

"You have nothing to be sorry about," I say, finally speaking. "Music therapy sounds awesome. When I was in school, music was cut out due to lack of funding, and it sucked. We actually donate to quite a few charities that work with schools who use music as therapy.

"As for Denise, I'm not ready to discuss her. I'm not sure I'll ever be ready. I know she's your mom, so if that's an issue for you, I get it. I'm here because, like you mentioned, we're brothers, and until I saw you guys in Miami, I had no idea you existed, but now that I know, since you're eighteen and living near me, if you want to pursue a relationship, I'm open to it."

Adam nods in understanding. "For the record, she used to tell my dad how much she missed you and—"

I put my hand up, halting whatever it is he's about to say. I can't go there. I just fucking can't. He doesn't get it because he was raised by two parents, and neither of them walked away. "I appreciate you trying to make shit right, and I get you wanting to defend her, but she walked away when I was a kid, *by choice*, and I'm not sure if I can ever forgive her. If you'd like to get to know each other, I'm down. But it needs to be separate from anything you have with her."

"I understand. And I do." After a beat of awkward silence, he asks, "So where do we go from here?"

I squeeze Kaylee's hand because fuck if I know where the hell we go from here.

"You guys can text, call, hang out, get to know each other," Kaylee says, saving me. "It doesn't have to be overnight. Just take it day by day." She glances at me. "Sometimes, taking it slow is the best way."

Twenty-Seven

Braxton

Dad: Tell me this isn't real... <insert link>

Bailey: Call me ASAP

Camden: You met your brother?

Adam: Please call me...

I CLICK ON THE LINK MY DAD SENT AND FIND SEVERAL PICTURES OF KAYLEE, ADAM, AND me at lunch. Based on the location of the pictures, somebody working at the bistro must've taken them and sent them to the media. And based on the in-depth article, they did their research and aired all our dirty laundry. It's been a couple of weeks since we met up, so it must've taken them that long to put all the pieces together.

"What's wrong?" Kaylee asks, walking out of the en suite

bathroom wrapped in a towel.

"The entire world knows about Adam... and my mom."

Her brows kiss her forehead. "Adam...?"

"No, I don't think so. Looks like one of the servers must've snapped a couple of pictures."

"I'm sorry." She walks over and steps between my legs. "Is there anything we can do?"

"Nah, I gotta call Bailey. Also, my dad saw..."

"Shit."

"Yeah, but honestly, he has no room to say anything, not after all the lies he's told. I'm still pissed at him. My mom might've walked away, but he had a hand in it."

"Which is why you need to talk to him."

"I will." I stand and rest my hands on her hips. "Later. Today is apartment hunting day. Unless I can convince you to just move in here..."

"Not happening." She pecks my lips. "I have no desire to live in this bachelor pad." I open my mouth to argue, but before I can speak, she adds, "And we agreed to take it slow. Moving in together is *not* taking it slow. Besides"—she cups my face with her soft hands—"I need to do this on my own. I've never been independent. I've either lived with my parents, or in a dorm, or with Layla, or had roommates... I want a place to call my own."

I already know this since we've had this conversation before, and I get it, but you can't blame me for trying one last time. Waking up every morning with Kaylee in my bed, in my arms, is the best damn way to wake up, and we both know, even if she gets her own place, there's no way I'm sleeping without her.

But I also get that she needs to do this for herself. Because if she moves in with me, she's not proving that she can do it on her own, and if we get a place together, it's taking a huge step forward in our relationship. So for now, I'm going to let her do what she needs to do, support her independence, and in time, if I have it my way, enough of my shit will be there that she'll realize I'm not going anywhere.

"All right, Crazy"—I smack her peach of an ass—"get dressed and let's go find you the perfect place to live."

While she gets dressed, I call Adam to let him know I'm aware of the situation. We've been talking and texting almost daily, getting to know each other, and we have a lot in common. He even asked me for help with a project he's working on in music appreciation, and I was able to help him.

"What do we do?" he asks.

"That's up to you. I can make an official statement, sweep it under the rug, or deny the claim." When he goes quiet, I say something I never thought I'd say, "You're my brother, and I don't want to hide you. If you're okay with it, I'd like to make a statement that we're brothers. Generally, once the rumors are put to rest, the media calms down, but it will mean you'll be in the spotlight. People who recognize you will ask questions. This will affect you more than it will me, so if you want me to deny it, I'm okay with that. It won't change anything between us."

While I'm waiting for him to respond, Kaylee comes out dressed, wearing a knowing smile. Her ass heard everything I said.

"If you're okay with it, I am too. I mean, I don't want you to think I'm trying to—"

"Stop," I say, cutting him off. Too many times, he's mentioned not wanting to take advantage or use me. I practically had to beg the kid to let me help him with his homework. Sure, there's a chance he has a hidden agenda, but if I thought that about everyone, I'd drive myself insane. "It's all good. Just don't be surprised if you get people trying to talk to you who normally wouldn't."

"What are you saying? I'm not cool enough without my famous big bro?"

"Uh..."

"I'm kidding, man," he says with a laugh. "I know I'm plenty cool without you."

I snort out a laugh. "Yeah, okay, cool guy. I gotta go. Kaylee is making me go apartment hunting with her but won't let me move in." I jokingly glare her way, and she rolls her eyes.

Adam laughs. "Good luck with that."

We hang up, and I call Bailey next, letting her know how we're going to move forward. She tells me she'll speak to our in-house PR team and type up something for me to post.

Since the paps have been acting like fools lately, I have Justin join us. We spend the morning checking out several apartments in Kaylee's price range. When I see the places she can afford to rent based on her salary, it damn near kills me not to beg her to let me help her, but I keep my mouth shut—while I text Easton and tell him he needs to give my woman a fucking raise, even if he needs to take it out of my earnings.

Easton: What's wrong?

Me: Kaylee's looking for a place to rent. It's all shit, and she won't let me help.

Easton: Give me a few minutes.

I was only joking, but hell, I'm not going to stop him if he can make something happen.

"What do you think about this one?" Kaylee asks, standing in the kitchen of the fifth, maybe sixth place we've seen. The place is small, everything is outdated, and it smells like fucking mothballs.

"It only matters what you think."

She frowns, hating that answer, but in my defense, I'm not going to lie to her, and there's nothing I can do to help.

"I'm going to look around." While she does that, my phone goes off again.

Easton: Who's the real estate agent?

I give him the info, and he gives me a thumbs-up—if he weren't my boss, I'd send him a middle finger. Everyone knows you don't thumbs-up people unless you want to piss them off.

Kaylee is checking out the kitchen for the fourth time—I'd bet trying to convince herself it's not as bad of a shithole as it is—when the real estate agent says, "I actually found another place that's in your price range. It just became available."

"Oh, really?" Kaylee asks, hopeful.

"Yeah, let's go check it out."

As we're walking out, Easton sends me another text: **It's been handled.**

I don't know what he means by that, but ten minutes later, when we walk into a luxury apartment building, complete with a guard on duty, I figure it out.

We step inside the place, and it's not big—two bedrooms,

two and a half baths, with a kitchen, living room, dining room, and a nice-size loft upstairs that can be used as an office—but everything is up to date with hardwood floors, stainless-steel appliances, and a balcony where you can put a couple of chairs and a table and enjoy the view.

"Are you sure this is in my price range?" Kaylee asks, sounding unsure. I don't blame her, especially not after seeing the places we've seen all morning.

"It is. The owner bought it as a write-off and just wants to get it rented."

While they talk, I text Easton: **What did you do?**

Easton: Do you really want to know?

No, I don't. Because if I know, I'm an accomplice, but if I know nothing, then I can honestly say I have no idea.

Me: Nope.

Easton: Didn't think so.

After Kaylee asks a dozen times if the real estate agent is sure the rent is what it is, and the real estate agent assures her it is, Kaylee has no choice but to say she wants it. There's no way in hell she's going to find anything half as nice as this place on her budget. I don't know if Easton owns this place, knows someone who knows someone, or if he paid the difference, but I'm thankful as fuck to him because with my hands tied, I couldn't do shit, and the thought of her living in some of those places had me considering kidnapping her ass and locking her in my bedroom so I'd know she's safe.

Me: Thank you.

Easton: Don't know what you're talking about ;)

"She said I can move in any time," Kaylee says with a huge smile on her face. "And the price is locked in for the entire year lease." She twirls around, grinning from ear to ear in excitement. "I can't believe this place is all mine."

I should probably feel guilty about whatever strings Easton pulled, but as I watch her face light up in pure happiness and pride, knowing she'll be safe, I don't give a shit. Kaylee is mine to take care of. She can have her independence, but she's still *mine.*

"HE'S CALLING AGAIN?"

"Every day."

"Brax, please answer him. If you don't want to talk to him, fine, but tell him that. Stop ignoring him."

I sigh, staring at the phone, knowing Kaylee is right.

"Dad."

"Braxton, finally. What the hell is going on? You're claiming that kid as your brother, and you won't return my damn calls—"

"He is my brother," I say, getting out of bed and walking away from Kaylee, who's lying there. We were in the middle of searching for furniture for her place since she's moving in this weekend. She wants to be out before Layla gives birth so the Blackwoods have their home to themselves.

"I ran into Denise. She has a husband and three kids."

"I'm well aware." Of course, he knew and never said a word

to me.

"She had some things to say about you, about what happened when you guys split up."

"Braxton, let me explain."

"Explain what, Dad? That you lied to me about how shit went down? That you cheated on her with the fucking nanny and then took me away, filing for divorce and refusing to give her any custody?"

"She didn't want us! She chose her career over us. I gave up everything for that bitch, and I knew she was cheating. That piece of shit she's married to... She was cheating with him. It was all over the gossip rags. She wouldn't admit it, but I knew she was."

"Or maybe you let yourself believe it because you resented the fact that she was making more money than you."

"She didn't even fight for you," he says, switching gears.

"And you put her in that position."

We both go quiet, and I wonder if we'll be able to get past this. If I can forgive him for what he did. I thought I could talk to him about this, but I realize I'm too bitter to have this conversation.

"Look, Dad, I need some time."

"For what?"

"To deal with all this. You're saying one thing, and she's saying another..."

"And who the fuck has been there for you all these years? Who's had your back? Not her!"

"I know, but I just need some time."

"Fine," he says harshly. "I see you're back together with

Kaylee..."

"Dad," I groan, not wanting to do this with him.

"Just remember when she fucks you over the same way your mom did to me that I warned you. Don't do anything stupid, Braxton. I've seen the rumors about the band breaking up. You've worked too hard to—"

"Dad, enough. I said I need time. I'll talk to you soon."

We hang up, and I head back inside the condo, where I find Kaylee right where I left her—lying in bed and searching for furniture.

"How'd it go?" she asks, genuinely concerned. She has every right to hate my dad after what he did when we were younger, but she puts it aside because he's my dad.

"His story doesn't match hers."

"Most breakup stories don't."

"True. I told him I need some time." I shrug, and Kaylee nods in understanding, not needing me to say anything more.

"Wait until you see the couch I picked out," she says, changing the subject. "It's so big, it's practically a bed."

"Good." I pull her into my arms, tossing her phone to the side. "That will make it easier when I'm fucking you on it because you know damn well we'll spend the first week at your place christening every inch of it."

Just as our mouths are connecting, my phone goes off. I quickly check it, seeing a text from Bailey: **You're keeping PR busy LOL**

Attached is a picture of Kaylee and me standing outside an apartment complex with the real estate agent with the caption: **With the lead singer recently married and about to have a baby,**

and the guitarist (see image) settling down, we have to wonder what this means for Raging Chaos's future. What are your thoughts? Comment below...

Kaylee looks over my shoulder and sighs, shaking her head. "They're vultures."

"It's how they make a living," I say, refusing to let that shit get to me. "The bigger you get, the more they feel entitled to know, and the higher you get, the more they want to see you fall."

"Yesterday when I was coming out of work, they practically attacked me with questions."

I whip my head to the side. "What? Why didn't you say anything?" It's one thing to have pictures taken, but for them to go after her. Fuck no.

"I honestly forgot. I got stuck on the train, and then we met Declan for dinner. It slipped my mind."

"What did they do? Say?"

"They were just asking questions about us, but now, seeing that photo, it makes sense. I had to set all my social media stuff to private because women started sending me messages threatening me." She shrugs like it's no big deal when it's a damn big deal. "Apparently, they don't like that the notorious playboy Braxton Lutz is off the market." She rolls her eyes playfully, not taking it seriously.

"From now on, until I hire a guard for you, Justin goes where you go."

"What?" she gasps. "Why? I can handle some nosy-ass paps."

"You don't get it because you haven't seen it, but they can be crazy. Especially the fans. For the most part, when we're in

New York, they leave us alone, but since shit is new, they're out for dirt. I'm not taking any chances." She opens her mouth to argue, but I keep going. "Even Layla has a guard, so I don't want to hear it."

"Only because they're married, and she has a kid."

"Because Camden wants to make sure they're safe, and I'm going to do the same. Shit will calm down, but for now, Justin goes with you when you go out."

"And what about you?"

"I'm fine. I'm here or at the studio for the most part, and I'm usually with one of the other guys who has security with them anyway."

I can tell she's about to continue arguing, but I give her a look that says I'm dead serious about this, and she sighs, knowing I'm not going to bend. She wants to be independent? Great. But I will *not* risk her safety, ever.

Twenty-Eight

Kaylee

"THIS PLACE IS AMAZING!" LAYLA WADDLES HER CUTE BEHIND THROUGH MY NEWLY furnished apartment, checking it out. It's been nearly a month since I signed the lease, and I've used the spare time I'm not working to decorate and furnish it. I love it, and for the first time, it's mine. All freaking mine.

The only downfall is that Braxton isn't living here. Because I was stubborn. I had it in my head that I needed to do it myself, and after giving me a little bit of shit, he respected that. But now I'm regretting it. I've quickly realized a home, a *real* home, is the place filled with the people you love. It's not about the dwelling, but who's inside it.

It hit me last night. Since the day I moved in, Braxton's spent every night with me, having dinner together at the dining room table, watching our nightly show we're currently bingeing while making out, showering in my shower, and sleeping in my bed, wrapped around me. Then last night, he had to fly to California for a business meeting for a couple of days that Camden asked him to handle since Layla is about to pop any day, and my home felt empty. And that's when I realized that I don't care about being independent and proving myself—about saying the place is mine—because without the person I love here, it means nothing.

"I'm going to ask Braxton to move in with me," I blurt out to Layla, who's checking out the gorgeous state-of-the-art kitchen.

"Yeah?" She glances back at me.

"Yeah. It might be too soon—"

"Stop." She walks over and presses her hands to my shoulders. "We only get one life. How we spend it is up to us. It doesn't matter what you choose to do as long as you're doing what makes you happy." Her voice cracks, and I know she's speaking from experience. "You deserve to be happy, Kaylee. Fuck anyone who thinks or says otherwise."

I hug her tightly—albeit a bit awkwardly since her big belly is in the way. "Thank you for being my best friend," I choke out.

"Always." She pulls back. "Now, what do you say we go out tonight? I know Braxton is gone for the night. Camden's at home with Felix, and Bailey, Cynthia, and Kendall are all on board. I can't drink obviously, but with me due soon, I want one night with my besties before things get crazy."

"Before you're a mom of two." I grin because despite her sounding like her life is about to be over, I know she's excited... just nervous.

"I'm a little scared," she admits, just as I thought. "The last time..."

"Camden is not *him*," I say, referring to her ex-husband.

"I know, but what if having a kid changes Camden?"

"That's not going to happen. What that asshole did and how he behaved is not normal. And you know better than to compare them to each other. Camden is amazing with Felix. He treats him like he's his own son. And he loves you more than I've seen any man love someone. You're just super pregnant and even more hormonal. You're right. We need to go out. You need yourself a virgin something and to relax because your life is damn near as perfect as it gets, and you're just having a moment. One that will pass."

"You're right," she says. And then, as if her husband can sense her struggle, her phone goes off. It's a text from Camden, with a video of him and Felix dancing to a new song. They're both laughing while they bust a move. And when it's over, they both look at the screen and tell Layla that they love her.

By the time the video cuts off, Layla is in tears. "God, I love them so much."

"And they love you. Camden is going to be an amazing dad to this little girl, just like he is to Felix, so take a deep breath, stop thinking the worst, and let's go out and have one last drink before you become a family of four."

"LET ME SMELL IT."

"What?" I crack up.

"Just a little sniff..." I pass the lemon drop shot under Layla's nose, and she inhales deeply. "God, I'm not even a drinker, but it smells sooo good."

Kendall laughs. "Just close your eyes and pretend you can drink."

Layla does as she says, taking another whiff. "When I'm back to myself, we're totally having a real girls' night, one I can properly participate in."

Kendall, Bailey, Cynthia, and I down our shots at the same time as our server arrives with another round. Thanks to Kendall's status, we were able to get into Lush and are partying VIP style. We have our own server, a private dance floor, and bottle service. Our bodyguards are standing in the corner, chatting quietly, watching us in case of anything, but it feels good to be somewhere the media can't document our every move. After the pictures came out about Braxton having a half brother and then us apartment hunting, the paparazzi have been relentless, hell-bent on getting the scoop on the status of Raging Chaos.

Around this time is when they usually announce a teaser for their next album and their upcoming tour dates since they go on sale months and sometimes a year ahead of time, but for the first time, they've been quiet. Braxton goes to the studio during the day to hang out with Declan and write, and I know they've been messing around with some possible songs, but Camden's been focused on Layla, and Gage has been MIA. I've seen the woman he's been hanging out with a couple of times, and she seems sweet and very pretty but, like Braxton mentioned, kind of sad looking. Gage won't willingly bring her around to hang out, but she doesn't look to be held against her will, so we're all just giving Gage some space since he doesn't look to be doing any hard drugs for the first time in years. Braxton has said they have no concrete plans to record at this time, and he seems to be completely okay with that.

"Oh, I love this song! Let's dance!" Kendall yells when "I Don't Mind" by Usher comes on.

"You down?" I ask Layla.

"Hell yes! Maybe I'll dance Marianna right out of me."

We all stop in our places, and Layla's eyes go wide. They weren't giving the name until the baby comes, but she totally just gave it away.

"Marianna?" Kendall asks.

"Yeah." Layla nods, giving her a watery smile. "We wanted to include Maria in her name..."

"Oh." Bailey sighs, her hand going to her chest over her heart. "It's so beautiful."

Maria was the Blackwoods' nanny when they were growing up. She was especially close with Camden, and when she passed away last year, he was absolutely devastated.

"It's perfect, Layles. What's her middle name?"

"Hope. It's not after anyone. We just thought it was pretty."

"Marianna Hope Blackwood," I say. "It's beautiful."

"It is," Kendall agrees. "Now, let's get our dancing on."

We spend the next several songs dancing and drinking, only stopping once Layla announces that her feet can't handle another second standing.

"Guess I didn't dance her out." Layla pouts jokingly, rubbing her belly.

"Nope, but she'll be here soon enough." I give her a kiss on the cheek. "Love ya, girlie."

"Love you more."

After saying goodbye to everyone with the promise we'll do brunch soon, I get in the SUV with Justin.

"Here you go, Miss Thomas." Justin reaches back and hands me a bottle of water.

"Thank you." I sigh, grateful. It's nearly one in the morning, and between the dancing and drinking, I'm exhausted and sweaty and dying of thirst.

I twist the cap and down half the bottle in one gulp, take a deep breath, then drink the rest, already feeling slightly more hydrated.

My phone goes off with a text from Braxton asking how it's going. I had sent him a few pictures of us drinking and dancing, and he messaged me back that he wished he were dancing with me.

Me: Heading home. Miss you.

Braxton: Miss you more.

Me: My bed will be lonely without you...

Braxton: I'll be back in it tomorrow night.

Me: I was thinking...

Braxton: About?

Me: You moving in with me...

Braxton: Are you drunk?

I laugh and am about to type back that I'm nowhere near drunk, but as I try to find the right letters, my vision goes a bit fuzzy, and I wonder if maybe I am drunker than I thought.

Regardless, I came to the conclusion that I wanted him to move in with me before I had any drinks. However, now that I'm thinking about it, it's probably for the best if we talk face-to-face and not through text messages after I have been drinking.

"Miss Thomas, we're here," Justin announces, pulling into the garage that's connected to my building.

He opens the door for me, and when I try to grab the handle as support, I stumble forward, almost doing a face-plant into the concrete before Justin catches me.

"Thank you," I say, my words coming out a bit slurred. "My alcohol must be catching up with me."

"It's okay," he says. "I'm going to walk you up to your place."

"Oh, it's okay, I can..." But before I finish my sentence, I trip over my heels, and Justin grabs my arms to stabilize me.

"I've got you," he says.

Since I don't want to die, and I'm clearly drunker than I thought, I let him help me up to my apartment. We're coming in from the garage, so we head straight into the elevator. Justin has a key for emergencies, and he uses it, pressing the correct number for my floor.

As the elevator ascends, my body seems to heat, and my limbs begin to tingle. I find my phone in my clutch, where I dropped it, and send a message to Braxton.

Me: I miss yu

Braxton: You already said that, Crazy.

Me: Yeh but I realllllyyyyy mis yu

Braxton: You okay, baby?

Me: I want u send me a pic

While I wait for him to respond, the elevator doors open, and Justin helps me out and down the hall to my place. As we walk, it feels as though the floor is bouncy, making it hard to take each step.

"Is it hot in here?" I ask when he unlocks the door for me, and we walk inside.

"Not really."

"I'm so... hot." My body is on fire, my heart pounding behind my rib cage. "Maybe I just need to get naked. Thank you for bringing me home." I drop my clutch on the table and then stumble to my room, lifting my dress over my head as I go. Next, my bra and panties come off and finally, my heels. I'm so warm and my body buzzing. I can't decide if I want to take a shower or go to bed.

Needing to cool down, I turn the shower water on. But before I make it in, a masculine voice comes from behind. "I think you should go straight to bed."

I twirl around—at least in my head, I do—but since my body isn't cooperating, it's more like a stumble. I'm not sure why Justin's still here, but my head is too fuzzy to give it much thought.

Justin enters the bathroom and reaches around me to turn off the water. When his arm rubs against my front, the material brushes against my nipple, and it hits me... I'm naked in the bathroom with Justin.

"I think you need to go," I say, glancing around for my robe. As my eyes scan the bathroom, everything goes blurry. My legs feel like Jell-O, and it's hard to focus. I think Justin says something, but I can't concentrate enough to make it out. My skin is scorching hot, and I just want to get cold. It's hard to catch my breath. I need to call Braxton. Something is wrong. Very wrong.

I hear more words being said, but it now sounds like I'm underwater. How is that possible? My apartment is on the eleventh floor.

And then I'm lifted. *Oh, thank God. I didn't want to drown.* Someone is carrying me. I try to open my eyes to see who it is, but the room is spinning. I'm hot and drowning and floating all at the same time.

I'm set on something soft.

More words.

I can't hear anything, though.

And then a warm breath is on me. "It's okay, Kaylee. Just close your eyes, and everything will be okay."

Braxton? Is that Braxton? I don't think it is. He's across the country still... I think. But maybe he came home.

I try to call his name, tell him I'm feeling funny, but the words... they just won't come out.

Twenty-Nine

Braxton

Bailey: Call me ASAP.

Bailey: There's no way this is real.

Camden: Call me.

Declan: As soon as you land, call me. Don't do anything stupid.

Easton: Call me.

Layla: I know Kaylee, and she wouldn't do this. I'm going over to see her now.

I STARE AT THE ONSLAUGHT OF TEXTS THAT HIT MY PHONE THE SECOND I TURNED IT back on. Normally, when we need to go somewhere, we take the Blackwood jet, which means we have cell service, but since the meeting was scheduled at the last minute, the jet was already being used, so I had to fly commercial, and my phone has been off for the past four hours.

When Kaylee never texted me back last night, I assumed she drank a bit too much and passed out. Since Justin was with her, I knew she was safe—which was confirmed when he texted me that she arrived safely at her apartment. But now, as I read the texts in utter confusion, my stomach roils in fear of what could've happened while I was without service. Clearly, something happened with Kaylee, but what? What the fuck could've happened from the time Justin made sure she got home to now? It's only been six damn hours. None of this makes any sense.

Ignoring everyone's texts, I call Kaylee first, but her phone goes straight to voicemail. I try again and again, but each time, it doesn't even ring, telling me it's either turned off or dead.

With my phone blowing up with notifications from social media, I click on one of them, which takes me to Justin's Instagram page—where I've been tagged in one of many comments.

@BraxtonLutz fuck that bitch is the first one I see. Maybe it's the jet lag, but I'm not sure what the hell is going on until my eyes move to the pictures in the post.

And then the comments and texts make sense... *perfect* fucking sense.

Because right there in front of me are several pictures of Kaylee and Justin in her bed.

She's naked.

He's without his damn shirt on.

Kissing her neck.

Grabbing her tit.

Her head is thrown back.

Eyes closed.

I swipe through them until I get to the end, and then I swipe back, refusing to believe what I see. My initial thought is déjà motherfucking vu. But then I remember she never cheated back then. It was all a lie to push me away, to get me to go to LA. So what the fuck is going on now?

I swipe through them again and again, analyzing each picture. His lips on her neck, his hand covering her nipple.

Why the fuck is my bodyguard touching my woman's nipple?

I swear to God when I get ahold of him, I'm going to break his hand, along with every single fucking finger that touched my woman.

My woman. She's mine. She told me so over and over again. We were supposed to be fighting for each other. *And this is how she fights?*

No, fuck that. She wouldn't do this to me. She wouldn't hurt me like this. I know Kaylee. She loves me. And Justin... why the hell would he fuck my woman and then post that shit for all the world to see? It makes no goddamn sense. He's about to lose his job. He'll never work in security again. That's if I don't kill him first.

I try to think back to the past several months. They've never shown a single sign of liking each other like that. Sure, they get along, but Kaylee gets along with everyone. But to jump in bed with each other?

She was drunk last night, but he sure as fuck wasn't. And I don't believe for a second she would ever be drunk enough to cheat on me.

But fuck, the proof is right in front of me. I want to trust her and believe this is all somehow a fucked-up misunderstanding.

But. His. Hand. Is. On her motherfucking tit.

His goddamn mouth is touching her flesh.

His body is pressed up against hers.

And fuck! I can see the fluffy body pillow she sleeps with at night.

Unable to look at the photos any longer, I close out the app and have my driver take me straight to Kaylee's apartment. I considered going to Justin's, but the pictures were taken at her place, so he's either there with her still—in which case that motherfucker is dead—or she's there alone, and I want to hear from her what happened. I want her to look me in the eyes and tell me why the hell she's in photos with another man touching her when she's mine.

I'm using another guard from the security company we have on retainer. If he's heard anything, he doesn't say a word, just drives me to where I need to go. When we arrive, I tell him to stay here, and he simply nods.

I get up to Kaylee's apartment and use the key she gave me to get in—expecting the worst but hoping for the best—although I'm not sure exactly what the best is.

The place is quiet, *too quiet*, and as I walk through the apartment, checking each room—living room, kitchen, bathroom—I'm holding my breath, praying she's alone. That the images were a figment of my imagination. That I'm jet-lagged and seeing shit, and everyone has lost their damn mind.

Like the wuss I am, I save the master bedroom for last. The

door is closed, so I slowly turn the knob and open it. A part of me is expecting Justin to be in here, in her bed, tangled up in her sheets with her. His hand still on her tit, his face nuzzled into the crook of her neck—my favorite position to sleep with her.

But when I finally get the courage to look at the bed, she's sleeping alone. The blanket covers her bottom half and shows her bare body from the waist up.

I check her bathroom just to be sure, but it's empty—no sign of another man having been here. I open the app up again, just in case I was seeing shit, but the pictures are still there. Comments are multiplying, and I'm being tagged left and right. I wasn't seeing shit. They're still there for all the world to see.

I close out of the app again and stop at the edge of the bed, watching her for a few minutes sleeping, her chest rising and falling. She never removed her makeup from last night, and it's created dark circles under her eyes. Her blond tresses are a mess, fanned out across her pillow, and her beautiful plump lips are slightly parted.

My phone is going off in my pocket, but I ignore it, focusing my attention on the woman I love more than life itself. I try to convince myself that the images were a joke even though I know damn well she would never think that's funny. Photos, just like those, tore us apart once before, and there's no way she would pose for those photos, let alone allow someone to post them as a joke.

As I sit and watch her sleep, I wonder why I'm so calm after seeing those photos. I should be freaking the fuck out, yelling and screaming, going after both of them. But I'm not, and I know why. Because deep down, I know, *fucking know*, my woman wouldn't betray me, which means someone else has—Justin being my main suspect—and once I get to the bottom of this shit, once she tells me what happened, I'm going to act accordingly. But I won't freak out yet because the last time I did that and took off for LA, I lost Kaylee—and I'll be damned if I'm going to let history repeat itself.

Maybe this makes me a pussy, or maybe it makes me a dumbass, but I just can't find it in me to believe she cheated on me. I know what the pictures look like, but I also know her, and until I hear her say the words, I'm not going to believe she cheated.

"Brax," she croaks, her voice tiny and rough. Her lids are hooded, and her eyes are bloodshot. "You're..." She glances around, then drags her body up—either not noticing or remembering or caring that she's naked—leaving her soft breasts on display. "I... don't feel good."

She clambers off the bed, and I jump to help her, but before either of us can do anything, she vomits all over the hardwood floor. And when she's done, she does it again and again. I kneel next to her, holding back her hair while she gags and sobs between throwing up. The smell is rancid as fuck, but something is wrong with her, so I block it out.

Once she seems to be done, she tries to stand, but her legs are shaky. She's barely on her feet before she collapses back onto the ground.

"Let's get you to the shower," I offer, picking her up and carrying her to the bathroom—ignoring the fact that she's not just naked from her waist up but completely naked. Like without a single piece of clothing on her body.

In response, she snuggles into my chest, her eyes closing. Not giving a shit about my clothes or phone or anything, I turn the shower on warm and step inside, sitting on the bench with her laid out across my lap and in my arms. I wash her the best I can while she stays where she is, not saying a word, not moving or helping at all. As I wipe her face and wash her hair, her eyes remain closed. I want to demand answers, but I first need to make sure she's cleaned up and is okay.

"Kaylee, can you stand?" I ask, needing her to get on her feet so I can clean the rest of her.

Her eyes flutter open, meeting mine, and her gray orbs appear lifeless. "I think so," she whispers softly.

I gently set her on her feet, not letting go, and she uses the wall to hold herself up. I wash the rest of her body and rinse out her hair while looking for any signs she had sex—hickeys, bruises, I don't fucking know. I'm confused as hell and have no idea what I'm doing, so I turn off the water. Grabbing two towels, I quickly strip out of my wet clothes and secure a towel around my waist, then use the other one to dry her off and wrap her up.

When we get back to her room, it smells like vomit, so I quickly set her on the bed and slip into some clothes I have here, then help her get dressed. She's barely moving, reacting, and in my gut, I know something is very wrong. She either did what those pictures implied or something worse happened—and at this point, I'm not sure what I'm hoping for.

When she's in a T-shirt and sweats, I carry her out to the living room to get away from that smell and lay her on the couch. I grab her blanket and tuck it around her, then prop a pillow up under her head.

Figuring she's in pain and probably dehydrated, I snag a cold water bottle from the fridge and two pain pills from the cabinet. After she's taken them and drunk half the bottle of water, I sit across from her so we can talk.

"I know you're not feeling well, but I need you to tell me what happened last night."

Her brows knit together in confusion, so I pull out my phone—thankfully, it's waterproof—and click on the post, turning it to face her. She stares at each of the photos while I swipe from picture to picture until I get to the last one.

"Can you tell me what happened?"

A single tear wells in her eye, then skates down her cheek, and my stomach tightens in anticipation.

"Kaylee... You didn't sleep with Justin, right? There's a reason you're naked in bed with him and he's touching you."

More tears fall down her face, and then finally, she speaks, and I almost wish she wouldn't have. "I... think..." Her face scrunches up in agony, and she bites her bottom lip hard as if the words hurt too much to come out, and I know whatever she says is going to kill me. "I think I did... sleep with him."

And just like that, my entire world is blown apart for the second time by this woman.

"You had sex with him?" I choke out, needing a verbal confirmation.

"I think so."

"What do you mean, you think so?" I ask, staying calm even though I want to lash out. My blood is boiling beneath my skin, and my heart is racing behind my rib cage. I have so many thoughts running through my head, and the only reason I can think as to why I'm not freaking out is because I'm numb.

"I didn't think I drank a lot, but I must've," she says, making no fucking sense. "I thought I was alone, and then he was there. I... I think I wanted to take a shower. I was naked, and he helped me to my bed." She swallows thickly, and a fresh wave of tears fills her lids and falls over. She drops her chin to her chest and shakes her head. "I don't really remember," she whispers, refusing to look at me. "I think he kissed me... maybe. I'm so sorry. I wish I could tell you more, but I don't remember. I must've drunk more than I thought, but I swear..." She glances up at me, her eyes rimmed red in devastation. "I wouldn't cheat on you, and I wouldn't let someone take my picture. I don't know what happened, but..." She chokes on a sob and covers her face. "I'm so sorry."

We sit in silence—her crying and me trying to figure out what the fuck happened—and finally, after several minutes, I come to a conclusion. She didn't do this. She *wouldn't* do this. I don't care how drunk she was. And since she doesn't remember—and yes, I believe she really doesn't fucking remember—I'm going to need to get my answers from the only other person who would know anything, who has absolutely no reason not to remember.

"I need to go talk to Justin," I tell her gently, making her eyes pop open in shock. "Will you be okay here while I'm gone?" Layla had said she was coming over, but she never showed up. I don't want to leave Kaylee, but I need answers, and I'm not going to get them here. There are pictures all over the goddamn internet that make it look like my girlfriend cheated on me, and I need to know what the hell happened.

Kaylee nods, and I lean forward, kissing her forehead. "I'm going to find out what happened," I promise. Before I go, I find her dead phone and put it to charge near her on the couch, then help her get situated, so she's lying down. She's still crying softly, and I hate that. Fucking hate it. "I'll be back soon," I tell her, then head out, locking up behind me.

Thirty

Braxton

ON MY WAY TO JUSTIN'S APARTMENT, I PULL UP LAYLA'S NAME TO SEE IF SHE'S STILL coming over and find a text from her: **My freaking water broke! Camden is driving me to the hospital. I can't get ahold of Kaylee. Please call me! I know she wouldn't do this.**

I press call, and she picks up on the first ring. "Have you seen her?"

"Yeah, I just left her apartment. She was sleeping, and when she woke up, she threw up everywhere." Speaking of which, I need to call someone to clean that shit up because there's no way I'm touching it.

"Is she okay?" The worry in her tone is evident.

"Yeah, I helped her shower and gave her some pain pills. Layla...did she drink a lot last night?" I ask, flinching when the question comes out sounding accusatory.

"What? Why? She didn't do this, Brax. She loves you so

much! She was just saying she wants to live with you. None of this makes any sense."

"I know, I know, but she said she doesn't remember what happened, so I'm just trying to piece it all together. I'm going to find Justin."

"I mean, yeah, she drank. So did Kendall, Bailey, and Cynthia. But when we said goodbye, she wasn't obliterated. She was walking and talking and laughing. She wouldn't cheat on you. Something is wrong."

"I agree."

"Please call me once you know anything and tell Kaylee to call me. Her phone is off..."

I hear Camden in the background grumbling about her needing to focus on giving birth, so I quickly agree to keep her updated and wish them both luck, promising to come by the hospital as soon as the baby is born.

When I get to Justin's apartment, I knock on his door, half expecting him not to answer. With the images flitting through my head of him kissing her neck and grabbing her tit, the calm I forced myself to have with Kaylee gets thrown out the window the second Justin opens the door, his guilty as fuck eyes meeting mine.

My fist hits his jaw so hard, he flies sideways, his head bouncing against the wall. "What the fuck did you do?" I bark, grabbing him by the front of his shirt and dragging him backward until his ass hits his couch. I don't wait for him to answer, though, instead decking him in the face again. This time, blood spurts from his mouth, and he groans, not even trying to block me.

"What happened?"

He licks the blood on his lip, his gaze meeting mine. "What do you think happened?" he says dryly. "We fucked."

"Wrong fucking answer." I hit him again and again, and when I'm about to hit him a third time, he stumbles off the couch to get away. "Let's try this again. And this time, tell the truth. What the fuck happened last night?"

He stares at me for several seconds, and just when I think I'm going to have to punch him again, he speaks. "I already told you. We fucked. If you don't want to believe me, that's on you."

"So you're telling me that while I was paying you to keep Kaylee safe, you let her get drunk, then you brought her home and fucked her?" I stalk toward him, shoving him up against the wall. "She says she doesn't remember shit! Are you telling me you raped her?" I grab his throat and bang the back of his head against the wall, wanting to kill him but knowing I can't.

When he doesn't answer me right away, I tighten my grip on him, slowly cutting off his airway. "Answer me."

"No, no, fuck, no! I didn't rape her," he chokes out as I tighten my grip.

"You're saying she consented? The woman who woke up this morning throwing up everywhere and swearing she can't remember shit. You're saying she agreed to fuck you?" I don't believe it for a fucking second, but I want to hear it from him. Something is off, and I'm going to get answers. "Because if she didn't consent, it's rape, and I'll use every dollar I have to make sure you're put away."

"Nothing happened!" he yells. "I didn't touch her."

"Bullshit! I saw the pictures." I slam his head back. "And I'll use them to prove you raped her."

"We didn't have sex. Nothing happened, I swear! I just made it look like it did. I drugged her so she would let me, and once she was pliable, I took pictures to make it look like we were together. I swear, I didn't rape her. Nothing happened."

I step back, and he sucks in a sharp breath, thinking I'm letting him go. Just as he releases his breath, I punch him straight in the face. Blood flies from his nostrils, and a cracking sound indicates I broke his nose. He cries out in pain, trying to get away, but I'm not done with him, not even close.

Dragging him to a chair, I throw him into it, so I'm standing over him. "Why the fuck would you want it to look like you and my woman had sex?"

Blood's pouring down his face, and his eye and mouth are both swelling up. He closes his eyes and shakes his head as if trying to decide what to say.

"If you even think about lying, I'm going to add a broken jaw to your nose."

He sighs, his eyes opening back up. "My brother is sick, and his meds are expensive. They were covered by insurance until my mom lost her job and her insurance. He needed them, and they didn't want to tell me. Without them, he got really sick and ended up in the hospital. They would make sure he's comfortable, but in order to treat him, they needed to move him to a different hospital... a private one. You have to pay up front or have insurance.

"I tried to get him insurance, but because he has a preexisting condition, they make you wait six months before covering anything. I didn't know what to do. And then..." He swallows thickly. "Your dad came to me."

Motherfucker.

"What did he do?"

"He said he'd pay me to seduce Kaylee, but the problem was I couldn't do it because she's so in love with you. I told him that, but he wouldn't take no for an answer. So I drugged her and took pictures so it would look like she cheated. But I swear, nothing happened. I sent them to him, and he told me once I posted them, he would wire me the money."

He has the decency to at least look like he feels bad for what he's done, but that doesn't make it all right.

"How much?" I ask. "How much was destroying Kaylee's reputation and our relationship worth?"

"Two million."

I laugh humorlessly. "That's it? If you would've come to me, I would've given you double that just for being honest."

I step back, done with this piece of shit. "I'll speak to Kaylee and find out if she wants to press charges. Hopefully, you have some money left over if she does because I meant what I said before. I'll spend every dime of my money to drag your ass through the mud, and guess what? I have way fucking more than your measly two mil."

Without waiting for him to respond, I turn my back on him and walk out the door. When I get downstairs, Paul is waiting for me.

"Where to, boss?" he asks, opening the back door for me.

"To my dad's office."

Forty minutes later—thanks to the city's fucked traffic—we arrive at Lutz, Burger, and Goldstein, the firm my dad is a partner at. Once again, I have Paul wait in the SUV since this won't take long. Unlike the beating I gave Justin, I would never hit my dad—even if he deserves it.

His secretary isn't at her desk, so I walk straight back to his office, not bothering to knock before entering. Of course, once I open the door, I find his secretary with her face between his legs, sucking his dick.

"Real nice, *Dad*," I say, making him jump. "Next time, try locking the door."

The woman's head pops up, looking like she's young enough to be my sister, and scrambles to her feet, righting her dress and attempting to wipe the smeared lipstick off her lips.

"We need to talk."

Dad tucks his dick back in his pants and zips them up. "Jewel, please hold my calls."

She nods, scurrying out and closing the door behind her. Once we're alone, my dad stands and walks over to me as if to hug me, but before he gets close enough, I raise my hand.

"I'm going to ask you something, and I suggest you not lie about it."

His brow furrows in confusion, and if I didn't already know what I know, I would believe he genuinely has no idea why I'm here.

"Did you have anything to do with the pictures posted of Kaylee and Justin?"

He must realize that I already know because, unlike Justin, who tried to follow through with the lie, he nods. "I did. I asked him to seduce her, but only because I was afraid she wasn't loyal, and based on those pictures, I was right."

"You were right?" I bark out a humorless laugh. "You were right? I guess the man you paid two million to didn't explain what happened?" I cross my arms over my chest and shake my head. "He didn't seduce my girlfriend. He drugged her."

Dad's eyes go wide in shock. "No, I... What are you talking about? Is that what she's saying? That's her excuse for cheating on you? That she was drugged?"

"That's not her excuse." I drop my hands and stalk toward him, shoving him against the wall behind him. "It's what happened. Justin was desperate. He needed the money to pay his brother's medical bills, but I bet you already knew that, didn't you? It's why you targeted him. Why you thought it would be easy. Dangle a couple of million in front of his face, and he'd fuck my girlfriend, proving she's like Denise."

I slam my hand against the wall next to his face, wanting so fucking badly to punch him but knowing it's not worth it. Because if I do, I'm sinking to his level. No, I'm going to say what I need to say and then walk out the door. "He couldn't figure out a way to get in her pants while she was sober because she's fucking loyal, so he drugged her. Then after she was naked, he staged it to look like they fucked, posted the pictures, and collected his money."

Realizing he's been had, he scrunches his face up, and it turns red in anger. "That's not what was supposed to happen!"

"I'm sure." I step back. "I hope it was worth it. Paying two million and in exchange you lost your son."

His brows hit his forehead. "Braxton... Son, I did this for you. I didn't know—"

"You didn't do this for me. You did it for you. Just like you did all those years ago. You're so determined to prove that all women are deceitful like Denise that you're willing to fuck over your own son in the process. I loved Kaylee, I still love her, and by trying to break us up to prove your point both times, you not only hurt her, but you also hurt me."

I slam my fist into my chest. "It sucks you chose Denise over some job, and she let you down. It *sucks* that you guys had different visions of what life should look like, and in the end, it tore you guys apart. It *fucking sucks* that you felt betrayed and were hurt by her actions. Although, now, I know you weren't the completely innocent bystander you led me to believe all these years."

I shrug, done with this shit, done with him. Just. Fucking. Done. "But you are not me, and not every woman is *her*. And if you truly loved me, you wouldn't be trying to manipulate me. You wouldn't be trying to take the one person who makes me happy away. And you sure as hell wouldn't be okay with putting her in danger."

"Braxton, please. I fucked up. You have to understand—"

"I don't have to understand shit," I hiss. "You've lied to me, manipulated me, and fucked with me for the last time while using the excuse of having my best interests at heart. You and me..." I grab the knob and yank open the door. "We're done. And if you ever contact Kaylee or me, I'll run your ass right through the mud. I don't know the legal terms, but I'd bet paying and soliciting someone to seduce and fuck someone else, then paying them to post the pictures online is illegal. And even if I can't sue you, I'll tell everyone what you did until your name is so dirty, nobody will want to touch you or this law firm."

Without waiting for him to respond, because I don't give a fuck what he has to say, I walk out the door, slamming it behind me.

When I arrive at Kaylee's, she's still where I left her, wrapped in a blanket on the couch. She's passed out, and not even me opening the door and walking in wakes her. I want to go to her, pull her into my arms and hold her tight. What my dad did is unforgivable. Had Justin decided to take advantage, she could've been fucking raped. And my dad didn't give a shit. All he cared about was proving his point—that women can't be trusted and you should never put them first.

For years, I felt sorry for him, but now that I know the truth and have witnessed the shit he's pulled, I don't have it in me. He made his bed, and now he has to lie in it.

The longer I sit here, thinking about what he's done, the more worked up I get. I told him I would leave him alone as long as he left us alone, but when I click on Instagram and see all the posts about Kaylee, calling her names and accusing her of cheating, my blood boils, and I know I have to do something. Because if it's between my dad and Kaylee, I'm going to choose her every damn time.

Not wanting to leave her, I take my phone to the other room so I can make a call without waking her up. "Hey," Easton says, answering on the first ring. "How're you doing?"

"Not good, man. I don't want to leave Kaylee, so I'm going to conference the guys and tell everyone what happened at once."

I add Gage, Declan, and Bailey to the call—leaving Camden out since he's at the hospital with Layla—then start talking.

"She didn't do it, what everyone is saying. She was set up."

I explain everything, from the deal my dad made to Justin drugging her and staging the pictures so he could get his money, and once I'm done, the guys are damn near as pissed as I am.

"Are we taking legal action?" Gage growls.

"I want to, but I don't think taking this to court, dragging Kaylee through all that, will be worth it. I told my dad if he didn't leave us alone, I would destroy him, but..."

"But you're not going to let him get away with this, right?" Declan says. "We're going to do something. Kaylee could've been fucking raped! And what the fuck... Justin? His ass is never working in security again."

"I agree," I say. "I thought if he deleted them, it would go away, but it all blew up so fast, and the only way to clear Kaylee of what she's being accused of is to throw them under the bus."

"Then that's what we do," Bailey adds. "We publicly set the facts straight."

We're discussing the details when footsteps sound, and a second later, Kaylee appears in the doorway, looking like the most beautiful hot mess.

"Hey, guys, Kaylee just woke up. Let me call you back."

We hang up, and my eyes lock with Kaylee's. She doesn't move closer, just stands in the doorway. "You're here..."

"Of course I'm here. Where else would I be?"

"I just figured... since I..." She swallows thickly, and tears fill her eyes. "Since I had sex with Justin, you wouldn't want anything to do with me anymore."

"One, you didn't have sex with anyone," I tell her, walking over to the couch. "And two, there's nowhere I'd rather be than here with you." I pull her into my arms and settle her on my lap, needing to hold her.

Thirty-One

Kaylee

I DIDN'T SLEEP WITH HIM.

I was set up.

Drugged.

Framed.

Pictures were staged.

I'm torn between being angry as hell, disgusted, and relieved. I knew Braxton's dad was shitty, but to take it to that level takes some serious balls. When Braxton finishes telling me everything, I settle on relief. The disgust and anger can wait. Right now, I'm just so damn relieved that I didn't cheat on Braxton. He's my entire world, the love of my life, my home. I don't know what I would do if something tore us apart again.

My phone goes off in the distance, and I have every intention of ignoring it until Braxton says, "You better get that. It might be Layla. She's in labor at the hospital."

"What?" I shriek, jumping up and running to my phone. Sure enough, there's a picture of a teary-eyed Layla holding the most beautiful baby in the world—after Felix, of course—in her arms with the caption: Please welcome Marianna Hope Blackwood. 7 lbs, 3 oz. 20 inches.

"She had the baby! We have to go." Instead of texting her back, I call her, hating that I'm not there.

"Hey," she says, sounding exhausted in the best way possible.

"I'm on my way. I'm so sorry—"

"Stop, it's okay. How are you? I was coming to check on you, and my water broke, but Braxton kept us updated, so I knew you were okay."

"Don't worry about me. How are you?"

"Of course I'm going to worry about you. You're my sister from another mister." I can hear her smile through the phone. "She came so fast. My water broke, and when we arrived and got settled, the doctor said she was ready. I was in shock since I was in labor with Felix for damn near two days."

"She was ready to meet her mommy and daddy and big brother. Has Felix met her yet?"

"He's on his way over with my mom."

"Should I wait to come over? I don't want to crowd you guys." With Felix, her ex left to go home and sleep because he said he needed a bed to sleep on, so I stayed with her until her mom arrived. But now she has Camden who, unlike her dumbass ex, is amazing and would never leave her or that baby's side.

"Kaylee, you're family. Get your ass over here."

We hang up, and I let Braxton know I'm going to take a

shower. I took one earlier with him, but I want to take a real one to wash my hair properly and shave.

As I step under the hot water, flashes of last night come back to me—of Justin offering me a bottle of water, me feeling light-headed, then disoriented shortly after. Stumbling out of the SUV, him offering to help me up to my place... Him—

"Hey, what's wrong?" Braxton asks, stepping into the shower, still fully clothed. "Why are you crying?" I have no clue what he's talking about until my hand goes to my chest in shock from him appearing out of nowhere, and I realize I'm sobbing, my chest rising and falling in quick succession.

"Talk to me, baby. Are you hurt?"

"He drugged my water." Braxton tightens his hold on me. "He wasn't anywhere near me all night. But when I got in the SUV, he offered me a bottle of water. He's never done that before, and really, why would he keep bottles of water in there? I drank the entire bottle and that's when I started to feel weird. He helped me to my place, and I thought he was gone, but when I was about to get in the shower, he appeared, telling me I needed to go straight to bed."

I told Braxton some of this earlier this morning, but I was still out of it and unsure what happened. But now that my head is clear, I remember everything until I blacked out in the bed.

"He saw me naked," I cry. "Took pictures of me. What if he took more? What if there's ones of me completely naked?" I feel invaded. I know Braxton said we never had sex, but he still saw me... every part of me.

My eyes meet his, and I find them burning with intensity, his jaw clenched. "I'll handle it. I promise you. By the time I'm done with him and my dad, they'll wish they never fucked with us." He kisses me softly, tenderly. "Let's get you showered, so we can go meet the little Blackwood princess."

Once we're both showered and dressed, we head to the hospital, stopping at the store to pick up a couple of little gifts on the way. When we get up to the room, Declan is there, holding the baby, but everyone else is gone.

"Where is everyone?" I ask, giving Layla a kiss on her cheek.

"You actually just missed them. They went downstairs to get breakfast. My mom and Felix are on their way. He insisted he make a card for the baby first, so she said they'll be a little while."

"Where's Gage?" Braxton asks Declan.

"He must've fallen back asleep after we got off the phone. I knocked, but he wouldn't answer. I'm sure he'll be by later."

"My turn!" I wiggle my fingers, indicating for Declan to hand the baby over. He rolls his eyes and steps toward me as the door swings open and in walks Kendall and—

"Oh, my God! Is that a ring on your finger?" Layla squeals, waking up Marianna, who starts to whimper. I glance at Kendall, who's sporting a massive shimmering diamond on her left hand.

"It is!" Kendall gushes. "We're engaged."

Camden's eyes go wide. Kendall has dated a lot of guys, but none of them, and I mean none of them, have managed to put a ring on her finger. She's been proposed to a handful of times, but every time she's said no, ending their relationship.

"Congratulations," Layla says, giving her a hug.

"Thanks. He literally proposed this morning. I wasn't going to say anything until later. I figured, with you having a baby and all, you wouldn't even notice."

"Not notice that ring?" Layla laughs. "You'd have to be blind not to notice that thing." She takes Kendall's hand and admires the ring. "It's beautiful."

"Thanks."

"Congrats," Camden says, giving his sister a hug. "Congrats, man." He shakes her fiancé's hand.

The baby whimpers again, and I glance over at Declan, who's quiet, staring down at the baby. Everyone—besides Kendall, who has no idea—knows how he feels about her, and now she's engaged.

"Hey, want me to hold the baby?" I ask quietly.

"Yeah." He clears his throat. "I should get going. Congrats, guys," he says to Layla and Camden, kissing her on the cheek and hugging him.

He walks toward the door, and I swear all of us—well, all of us who know how he feels about Kendall—are waiting with bated breath to see what happens next. He stops in front of Kendall, and she smiles, oblivious as hell. "Congratulations," he says, his gaze aimed at her fiancé. "You're a lucky man."

Then without another word, he walks out the door. I notice Kendall frowns slightly, but she doesn't comment on it. Instead, she walks over to see Marianna up close. "She's beautiful," Kendall coos, giving her a kiss on her head. "And she smells so good."

"Right?" I say with a laugh, having just smelled her myself. "Want to hold her?"

"Oh, yes." Kendall beams. "I can't wait to have a cute little bundle of joy."

"You're pregnant?" Camden asks, not even caring about blurting it out in front of everyone.

"What?" We all look over and see Sophia and Easton standing in the doorway. "You're pregnant?"

"What? No." Kendall laughs. "I just meant one day..." She side-eyes Camden, who just shrugs. "But there is something I need to tell you..." She hands the baby back to Layla and shows her mom her ring. "We're engaged!"

Sophia and Easton both blanche but quickly recover, congratulating their daughter and soon-to-be son-in-law.

A few minutes later, Layla's mom and Felix arrive, and I tell her we're going to get going so they can have some time with Felix. "Call me if you need anything," I tell her before we go.

Since neither of us has eaten, we stop at a deli and pick up some food and drinks, then go home. We spend the day lounging around the condo, watching movies, cuddling, and kissing. When it's dinnertime, we order in Thai and eat while we watch my favorite movie, *Save the Last Dance*. Braxton lets me know that Bailey handled the announcement that will destroy Justin's and Michael's reputations, but I stay off social media, not wanting to see anything being said about me.

Around ten o'clock, my eyes start to flutter closed, and Braxton says I need to go to bed, that I've had a long couple of days and need my sleep.

"You're staying, right?" I ask, which is stupid since he's been here every night, aside from when he had to fly to LA for that business meeting. But for some reason, I'm suddenly insecure even though he's given me no reason to be.

"Are you serious?" he asks. "I'm not leaving until you make

me."

"And what if I said I didn't want you to ever leave?"

A small smile quirks at the tips of his lips. "Are you asking me to move in with you, Crazy?"

"I know I said I wanted to live on my own, that I needed to do this on my own, but... I love waking up and falling asleep with you."

He encircles his arms around me and kisses my forehead. "I never planned for you to live here long on your own anyway. You've been here for less than a month, and half my clothes are in the drawers."

I laugh at that because he isn't lying. Every time he comes over, he brings a bag full of his stuff. I knew what he was doing, but I didn't stop him because I love his stuff being here.

"We wasted too much time being apart." I snuggle into his side. "I don't care what's right or wrong, or if this is too fast. I just want to be with you every day." I wrap my arms around his neck and kiss his lips. "I want to love you and be loved by you."

"You have me, baby," he says, pecking my lips. "Forever."

"So is that a yes? Will you move in with me?"

"Damn right, I will," he says with a melodic laugh, tightening his arms around me. "I'm actually glad you asked because I had no intention of ever leaving anyway. At least now, I can say it was your idea."

He presses his mouth to mine again, this time harder. "Now, how about we head to bed? You're tired, and tomorrow, we have plans."

"We do?" Tomorrow is Sunday, and I don't recall making any plans.

"Yep. We're going to spend the day christening every inch of this place and making it ours. We have years to make up for, so you're going to need to be well-rested." He waggles his brows and lifts me into his arms, carrying me to bed... *to our bed.*

Once there, he reaches around my neck. I have no clue what he's doing until the necklace holding the infinity heart promise ring lifts off my chest.

"What are you doing?" I breathe.

"Something long overdue." He takes the ring off the chain and slides it onto my finger. "There," he says, kissing my finger and the ring. "It's back where it belongs."

He pulls me into his arms, where he holds me tight as I drift off to sleep, feeling safe and protected and loved. For the first time in a long time, I feel like I've finally found my home.

Epilogue

Kaylee

THREE MONTHS LATER

"I CAN'T BELIEVE YOU BOUGHT THIS PLACE." I TWIRL IN A CIRCLE IN THE MIDDLE OF THE beach house in The Hamptons, the same beach house where Braxton and I came to reconnect. It's right down the street from the beach house that Camden bought recently, so his family can vacation together since his parents have one nearby as well.

"I know how much you love it here," Braxton says, gripping the curves of my hips and tugging me toward him. "I tried to buy Easton and Sophia's since it's where I took your virginity..." He smirks, and I slap his chest playfully. "But he wasn't having it, so I figured this was the next best thing."

"I love it." I kiss him. "And I love you."

"Good. I'm glad you love me because I have a question for you, and I think you loving me will help tip the odds in my favor."

I bark out a laugh at that. "You already know I love you. What do you want?"

"To marry you." His words are so simple and said so softly that it takes me a second to wrap my head around them, and while I do that, he drops to one knee and pulls a ring box out of his pocket, popping it open.

"I've loved you for the past seven years, and I plan to love you for the rest of our lives. You're not only my girlfriend and my lover, but my best friend, and I would love it if you would become my fiancée, and soon... like, as soon as possible, my wife."

I can't help but laugh through my falling tears at his little declaration. We've spent the past three months falling in love all over again. It hasn't been easy, especially after the posts were made, throwing Justin and his dad to the wolves. People had things to say, not all of it nice, but we got through it together. Justin disappeared, his social media accounts deleted, and from what Braxton told me, his father was forced to resign from the firm where he was partner. His brother's been there and they've been growing their relationship, which is hard for Braxton because while he loves his brother, he still wants nothing to do with their mom. But he's taking it day by day... we both are.

The band has been on an unofficial hiatus since they returned, and no decisions have been made about when they'll be releasing their next album or scheduling their next tour. A lot has happened, but through it all, we've remained strong, united, and I love him more now than I did before. So as he looks at me, waiting for me to speak, there's really only one answer to give him.

"Yes. Yes, I'll marry you."

A beautiful smile splits his face, and he stands, pulling me into his arms and lifting me off the ground, kissing me hard and passionately. When he sets me down, he takes my left hand in his and slides the infinity promise ring off my finger, replacing it with the engagement ring. The platinum band has two encrusted infinity symbols intertwined around one another, framing the circle diamond on top.

Once the ring is safely on my finger, Braxton's mouth descends on mine, kissing me reverently, passionately, silently telling me how much he loves and wants me. He lifts me, my legs encircling his waist, and carries me to our bed—I never get sick of saying that—then he lays me on the center of the mattress.

Our mouths stay connected, kissing, caressing. Our tongues swirl and dance together. We only break apart long enough to shed our clothes, and then we're back to kissing, touching, feeling.

I love how Braxton tastes sweet with a hint of warmth. The way he smells fresh and masculine from the mixture of the cologne I bought him all those years ago and his own scent. I'm obsessed with the way he feels hard and smooth. But what I love the most is the way he fits perfectly with me. The way, as he spreads my legs and enters me, our bodies connect and align as if we were made for each other.

And I truly believe we were. Braxton is my soul mate, my other half. The yin to my yang, one-half of the infinity symbol in our forever. He makes love to me, devouring me, stroking me, working me up, up, up until I'm falling off the ledge and taking him with me.

When we've both come down from our high, he doesn't let me go clean up. He pulls me into his arms and holds me tightly, kissing me, massaging me, loving me. We stay like this for several minutes, reveling in the silence and the peace we bring each other.

"I don't want to wait," he says when he finally speaks. "Do you want a big wedding?" I know if I say yes, Braxton will ensure I have the wedding of my dreams, but the truth is, I have no desire for a huge wedding.

"Nope, I don't even care about a wedding. I just want to be yours as soon as possible."

He nods in agreement, his eyes sparkling in excitement. "Then it's settled. Tomorrow, we're applying for a marriage license, and as soon as we're allowed, we're saying I do."

Butterflies attack my belly at the thought that Braxton could be my husband by the end of the week. "That sounds perfect."

He rolls me onto my back and kisses me softly. "I can't wait to make you mine."

"I'm already yours... I've always been."

He kisses me again, this time harder, deeper, and that's all it takes for us to get lost in each other once again—in the beautiful, silent chaos of our love.

"I'M GOING TO POST A TOTALLY CLICHÉ PICTURE OF MY RING," I WARN BRAXTON AS WE walk to the kitchen, both of us showered and somewhat dressed. Hours of sex have left us starving, so we agreed to eat before continuing our engagement celebration.

"Nothing cliché about telling the world you're going to be *legally* mine," he says with a laugh, playfully smacking my ass.

I grab my phone from the counter and am about to pull up the camera app when I notice several missed calls and texts. Something must've happened.

"Hey, Brax," I say, my heart in my stomach. "Did you get...?"

Before I can finish my question, a voice speaks from his phone. I don't know if it's a voicemail or what, until the woman says, "This is Evelyn from *Hollywood Gossip...*" And then I know he's watching or listening to something. "According to our sources, Gage Sharpe, the drummer for Raging Chaos, was brought in to New York Medical after he was found in his home unconscious. While we don't know the specifics, our—"

Braxton cuts off the video and dials someone, putting it on speakerphone. "Is he okay?" he asks, not giving whoever is on the other end a chance to even say hello.

"I don't know..." It's Declan. "They're not telling me anything, but it's not good, man. I think... I think he tried to kill himself."

The Love & Lyrics Series isn't over!

Want more of Kaylee and Braxton?
Find some sexy and sweet bonus scenes on my website.

Did you know Camden, Declan, and Gage have books?
Check out the whole *Love & Lyrics Series.*

About the Author

Reading is like breathing in, writing is like breathing out.
– Pam Allyn

Nikki Ash resides in South Florida where she is an English teacher by day and a writer by night. When she's not writing, you can find her with a book in her hand. From the Boxcar Children, to Wuthering Heights, to the latest single parent romance, she has lived and breathed every type of book. While reading and writing are her passions, her two children are her entire world. You can probably find them at a Disney park before you would find them at home on the weekends!

Made in United States
North Haven, CT
31 May 2023

37169682R00180